GREASY GRASS

Center Point
Large Print

Also by Johnny D. Boggs and available from
Center Point Large Print:

And There I'll Be a Soldier
Top Soldier
Return to Red River
Wreaths of Glory
The Raven's Honor
Poison Spring
Taos Lightning

**This Large Print Book carries the
Seal of Approval of N.A.V.H.**

GREASY GRASS

A Story of the Little Big Horn

Johnny D. Boggs

CENTER POINT LARGE PRINT
THORNDIKE, MAINE

This Center Point Large Print edition
is published in the year 2018 by arrangement with
Golden West Literary Agency.

The text of this Large Print edition is unabridged.
In other aspects, this book may vary
from the original edition.
Printed in the United States of America
on permanent paper.
Set in 16-point Times New Roman type.

ISBN: 978-1-68324-933-7 (hardcover)
ISBN: 978-1-68324-937-5 (paperback)

Library of Congress Cataloging-in-Publication Data

Names: Boggs, Johnny D., author.
Title: Greasy grass : a story of the Little Big Horn / Johnny D. Boggs.
Description: Center Point Large Print edition. | Thorndike, Maine :
    Center Point Large Print, 2018.
Identifiers: LCCN 2018024558| ISBN 9781683249337
    (hardcover : alk. paper) | ISBN 9781683249375 (pbk. : alk. paper)
Subjects: LCSH: Little Bighorn, Battle of the, Mont., 1876—Fiction. |
    Large type books. | GSAFD: Historical fiction.
Classification: LCC PS3552.O4375 G74 2018 | DDC 813/.54—dc23
LC record available at https://lccn.loc.gov/2018024558

For Errol Flynn and Richard Mulligan;
Otto Becker and Thom Ross;
Evan S. Connell and Joseph M. Marshall III;
Thomas Berger and Quentin Reynolds;
Comanche and Crazy Horse.

"I feel sorry that too many were killed on each side, but when Indians must fight, they must."

Sitting Bull

"Oh what a slaughter how Manny homes Made desolate by the Sad disaster eavery one of them were Scalped and otherwise Mutiliated but the General he lay with a smile on his face the indians eaven respected the great Chief"

Private Thomas Coleman

"What kind of war is it, where if we kill the enemy it is death; if he kills us it is a massacre?"

Wendell Phillips

Preface

At the time of his death, George Custer was a brevet major general, but his actual 7th Cavalry rank was lieutenant colonel. Military etiquette, however, allowed officers to be addressed by their brevet rank. Hence, in this novel, Army officers are often called by their brevet rank (Colonel, instead of Captain, Frederick Benteen; Lieutenant Colonel Myles Keogh; Major Tom Custer). I chose to go with the brevets to be historically accurate.

Likewise, for historical accuracy, I've opted to spell the river Little Big Horn. Some sources often write Bighorn—there's about as much disagreement over the spelling today as there is on all other aspects of the battle—but in 1876, the most common spelling was Little Big Horn.

Finally an Indian in South Dakota once told me and other journalists: "Never call me a Sioux. That is a name given our people by our enemies. I am Lakota." I haven't forgotten that. Sioux comes from the French Canadian *Nadoüessioüak*, or *Nadouessioux*. White characters in this novel might refer to those Indians as Sioux, but when using the Indian point-of-view, I have generally opted for Indian names.

A short glossary is at the end of this book for your reference.

1926

Prologue

Libbie Custer

Fifty years have passed since my darling Autie, my love, my husband, my inspiration, was called to Glory, yet despite the aches (of aging bones and five decades of loneliness), I feel as if it happened only yesterday.

New York City is two thousand miles and twenty million memories away from the Little Big Horn in Montana, but today it feels closer. Too close.

Tears fill my eighty-four-year-old eyes as I sit in the sunroom of the Doral Hotel and listen to the radio. The radio announcer's voice squeaks that he sees an aeroplane flying over the battlefield, but I can't hear the motor. Now, the voice tells me and millions of other listeners that William S. Hart, the great actor of those Western moving-picture shows, is among the tens of thousands of people in attendance. Fourteen thousand automobiles line the road leading to the battlefield where my dashing, gallant Autie—and nigh three hundred other brave Americans—breathed their last. Automobiles and flying machines! I wonder what Autie would think of that had he lived, if he were on the

Little Big Horn this day, watching the festivities.

Watching? Hardly. Not my love. No, George Armstrong Custer would not be *standing* on that hill, scarlet neckerchief flapping in the wind. Not the dashing boy who once, riding a spirited horse during the Grand Review of the Army of the Potomac, bolted down Pennsylvania Avenue and passed General Grant at the head of the parade, right in front of the White House. Autie claimed that his horse had been spooked by a thrown bouquet of flowers, but I, and General Grant, knew better. On the other hand, were it not for Autie, such a parade might have been held in Richmond, Virginia, in 1865, rather than in our nation's capital. No, Autie would not be *watching,* standing still. He would be *flying* that biplane, swooping down from the skies, laughing wildly as he frightened the tourists, dignitaries, and Indians on the ground.

Now, I can hear music as the announcer begs us to listen for a moment. Recognizing the funeral march, I sigh, and dab my eyes with a handkerchief. They should be playing "Garry Owen," Autie's favorite song, the song of the 7th Cavalry.

The announcer now describes the terrain, a land I have never seen except in my mind, my nightmares. Only once did I even come close, begging Captain Marsh of the *Far West* to take me with him just a few days after Autie had marched away, but Captain Marsh would not allow me to steam into harm's way.

Oh, I was invited to this grand fiftieth celebration, and considered traveling the long distance, stopping in Monroe, Michigan, but I could not acquiesce. It was my age, I told them, and how could they argue with a white-haired widow who has nothing but memories and a cherished name?

Yet I did not decline on account of my age. I could not feel my heart break again, and surely it would were I to stand beside the marker where Autie—and Tom, his brave, tortured brother . . . and young Boston, another brother, always the butt of Tom's and Autie's jokes . . . and Jimmi Calhoun, my sister-in-law's husband . . . and Myles Keogh, that gallant Irishman of sad songs and sadder eyes . . . and sweet William Cooke with his flowing Dundrearies . . . and our nephew Harry Reed, just eighteen years old, who carried Autie's nickname—fell.

The dirge has ended. Here in Manhattan, cars crawl and pedestrians hurry about their business, oblivious to this momentous day. Yet inside the sunroom, I feel the heat of the Montana summer. The announcer speaks again, excited. He can see the 7th Cavalry, coming from the southeast, led on this day not by the fabled Boy General, but Colonel Fitzhugh Lee and retired Brigadier General Edward Godfrey. The radio falls silent.

No words are necessary. Wind rustles across the microphone. I close my eyes. I see the 7th, clear as day, but not being led by Colonel Lee and wonderful, kind, courageous General Godfrey.

I see Autie.

I see myself.

We are not at the place the savages call the Greasy Grass, but rather at Fort Abraham Lincoln along the Missouri River in Dakota Territory.

The morning of May 17, 1876, dawned gloomy at the fort. A thick, foreboding mist hugged the water-logged quagmire that once had been a parade ground. In all my twelve married years, I had seen Autie prepare to march to battle, yet never had I felt like this. I cried, and even he could not comfort me. "I just can't help it," I told him again and again, sobbing my final words: "I wish Grant hadn't let you go."

President Grant had, however, and Autie, ever the child, could not contain his excitement about this campaign. A great present for our country, he thought, on our Centennial celebration. He acted like a boy eagerly awaiting Christmas or his birthday. Happy as I'd ever seen him, while my heart failed me.

"You must be brave," he told me. "Come." He kissed the tears off my cheeks, and led me outside into the gloom, which matched my mood.

16

We joined Maggie, Autie's sister, wife of Lieutenant James Calhoun—Jimmi to us—and were assisted onto our horses, for we had been allowed the privilege—or perhaps it was a curse—to accompany the soldiers on that first day's march.

"Garry Owen" played as we slogged through the mud and muck. Then "The Girl I Left Behind Me." Through tear-filled eyes, I looked at the other wives watching from the shadows of the buildings. I felt their pain, for it must be the same as mine. Some held their little children in outstretched arms, letting them watch their fathers ride off. The wives knew, but their children did not, that this might be the last time they were to see those brave young soldiers.

Soon, we passed the Indians, the peaceful ones, the families of the scouts who rode with the 7th. Some of the old ones, men and women, sang that awful wail—so unlike "Garry Owen"—while the women, the wives, busied themselves with their work. Or maybe, as I think back on it now, they did not want to watch their husbands ride to their deaths.

At the point, I rode with Autie, and as we crested the first true hillside, I turned to watch horses, men, wagons—twelve hundred soldiers, seventeen hundred animals in all—stretching two miles long. Then . . . I saw it.

The sun rose higher now, hotter, the last

remnants of the fog burning off but still some mist hanging in the air overhead. Off this mist reflected a mirage, a premonition, an omen. I could see the soldiers of the 7th marching.

Marching on the earth. Marching in the sky.

Toward heaven.

Lips trembling, tears streaming again, I turned my horse, and caught up with Autie. The band's music had been replaced by the sounds of a campaign. Sabers rattling. Leather squeaking. Traces jingling. Wagons rattling. Hoofs slurping through muck. No one spoke.

That evening, we camped along the Heart River. The paymaster paid the soldiers. The soldiers paid the sutler, who wanted all debts settled before our boys rode off on one of the biggest Indian campaigns in our nation's history. Autie and I retired to our tent for our last evening together. The next morning, I clutched Autie as tightly as I could, and cried again. He practically pried my arms off his neck and told me that all would be well, that Custer's luck had never failed him, that if he died a soldier's death, so be it.

Thusly the 7th marched to destiny, and Maggie and I returned to Fort Abraham Lincoln with the paymaster . . . to wait, the most unholy, inhumane task for a soldier's wife.

Daily I wrote Autie letters, to be mailed on the steamers. Nightly I cried.

The radio voice is talking again, almost in a church-like whisper, but I cannot hear.

I am thinking to that Sunday exactly fifty years ago.

Fort Abraham Lincoln fell quiet after a startling "Reveille." Twenty-five mounted Indians were spotted, but, as it turned out, this was not a raiding party, for all of those savages had reservation passes. So the day transpired without fanfare. The troopers left behind were likely still condemning themselves at the hog ranches like My Lady's Bowery or the Dew Drop Inn on the banks of the Missouri. There was no baseball game to be played, for the first nine and the muffins of The Benteen Baseball Club were somewhere in Montana Territory with their back-stabbing coach and commander, Captain Frederick Benteen, a lout and wastrel.

After church, the ladies of the 7th met in my home. We sang hymns, but "Nearer My God to Thee" could not comfort us. In fact, when I suggested that we sing it, Emma Reed choked: "Not that one, dear."

Eventually, Katie Gibson could no longer strike a chord on the piano, so she simply sat there, head bowed, staring at the ebonies and ivories in profound silence. Poor Maggie lay on the carpet, sobbing into the pillowed lap of Annie Yates.

The lemon cookies Katie had baked for us were tasteless; the tea I brewed, bitter. The Bible passages Annie tried to read offered no solace.

I closed my eyes, and thought of Autie. I forgave him of his transgressions. I pleaded for God to absolve me of mine. Just let me see Autie again; let his beard scratch my face as he kisses me. Let me give him a son to continue his name.

Forcing a smile, I hugged my guests before they departed to the doleful and solitude of their homes. I listened to "Taps" and prepared myself for another sleepless night.

That evening, I went to bed a widow.

But did not know it.

1876

Chapter One

Boston Custer

Almost twenty-eight years old, yet Tom and Autie still treat me like a kid. If you go by their immature actions, however, they are the children.

God blessed Tom and Autie with good health and glory. On the other hand, like big brother Nevin, I was cursed and saddled with asthma. No West Point. No wars. No medals. Unlike Nevin, however, I refused to become a farmer, and Autie allowed me to accompany the 7th Cavalry as a forage master when we explored the Black Hills two years ago. Now I ride with my brothers, and nephew Harry Reed, against the red heathens. I am assigned as a packer and forager, though I prefer the assignments as guide and scout.

I do not shirk my duties. I do my work. I do not complain. Often, since I am also a "guide" and "scout," I leave the pack train and ride at the head of the command with Autie. Better still, I even accompany my brothers on their "scouts." Yet this is what happens when you are the youngest brother, when you do not have two Medals of Honor (as brother Tom earned during the late Rebellion) or the legend of George Armstrong Custer.

On May 31, two weeks after our departure from Fort Abraham Lincoln, Tom, Autie, and I rode out on what Autie called a scout, but in actuality was nothing more than a lark as we explored these badlands near the Little Missouri River. Alas, my horse picked up a pebble, forcing me to dismount, unfold my pocket knife, and begin freeing the stone embedded in its left forehoof. Would my brothers wait for me in hostile Indian country? No. Of course not. Abandoning me to my chore, they disappeared over the hill.

Finally I found myself back in the saddle. The air had turned cold, yet I sweated. Not even a breath of wind found its way between the rough ridges through which I rode. I knew better than to cry out for Tom or Autie, fearing some red devil would hear my voice and disembowel me, for we had already pushed to the edge of Dakota Territory and neared Montana Territory and its hostile Sioux and Cheyennes.

Visions of such savages had just entered my mind when a gunshot rang out. Another. Another. One bullet whined off a rock several rods to my left.

Heart pounding, I wheeled my horse, raking Army-issue spurs over its flanks, feeling the horse's power as it exploded into a gallop, for this beast of burden was as terrified as I.

Leaning low in the saddle, I topped the ridge, turned more northwestward, thinking that might bring me to the safety of our column sooner. The biting wind now blasted my face. My straw hat flew off. I wanted to reach for my revolver, but could not loosen my grip on the reins. Then the most fearful sounds reached my ears.

Hoofbeats. Right behind me.

"Come on!" I cried out to my mount. "Run, confound you, run!"

The horse stumbled, almost flung me over its neck, but both of us righted our balance. Somehow, I managed to release my grip on the reins with one hand, and pounded the horse's side.

"Faster! Faster!"

We reached a hill, and I leaned forward, urging the mare up. I wanted to look behind me, but could not summon the courage, fearful of those fiendish painted faces. As the horse picked its path up the hill, the wind stopped again, and I heard a new sound.

Laughter.

Immediately my face flushed red, and I turned the gelding to spot my big, brave brothers sitting in their saddles, laughing, pointing. Tom, having dropped his reins across his mount's neck, carried my hat in his left hand. Autie swung down, almost doubling over with laughter as he tried three times to thrust the reins into Tom's free hand before he managed. As I eased down the ridge, Tom extended my hat toward me. By that time, Autie had dropped to one knee, laughing that belly laugh of his, wiping his eyes with the end of his scarlet neckwear.

"Bos," Tom said as I eased my mare toward him, "I don't know what Autie and I would do if we did not have you to tease so."

I snatched the hat, and jerked it on my head. "Why not pull your pranks on Harry Reed?" I demanded.

"He's . . . too . . . young." Lieutenant Colonel George Armstrong Custer, brevet major general, hero of Gettysburg, Trevilian Station, Winchester, and the Washita, my big brother, snorted.

"He is standing this trip first-rate," I said.

"But he's not our brother," Tom said.

Autie managed to stand and take the reins from Tom. He patted my thigh, then sniffed, and turned to Tom again. "Do you smell something?" Autie asked.

"Do you mean . . . like a . . . latrine?" Tom queried.

They both stared at me.

"Check your pants, Mister Custer," Autie said in his most commanding voice.

I replied with a most indelicate suggestion, turned my mount, and loped away from my two brothers, whose howls tormented me as I rode up the hill.

I concede feeling my own taste of victory—or perhaps revenge—that afternoon, when, upon our return to the column, Colonel Custer himself met with a severe rebuking from our commanding officer, General Alfred Terry.

For while my brother was off scouting with Tom and myself, General Terry had managed to have lost his entire command.

Lost!

Well, it is quite easy in this harsh wasteland.

"Without any authority," the general scolded, "you left the column. This is not a game, Custer. It is a military operation, the most important of your, and my, career."

"I thought I could be more service to you, General, and the column, acting with the advance," Autie replied, rather humbly for him, like a punished child. A lie, of course. I doubt if either Tom or Autie even looked for Indian sign.

"Stop acting recklessly, Custer," General Terry snapped. "Don't make me sorry, sir, that I helped the President change his mind and let you join this expedition. Without my intervention, you wouldn't be here at all."

Tears filled my brother's eyes, and suddenly I no longer felt the joy of vengeance. I felt bile. Shame. Anger for this pencil-pushing commander with the audacity to chastise my brother. General Terry had no business leading this campaign. Autie was the Indian fighter. Autie was the hero. Autie was the bravest man I ever knew.

"General Terry," Custer said mildly, "with

your permission, I will remain with, and exercise command of, the main portion of the regiment. For the rest of the campaign."

"Don't forget that, Custer." The general saluted, and returned to his tent.

Tom and I followed Autie to his.

"That Terry," I said, quietly defending my brother, "has a highly exalted opinion of himself."

This campaign had three prongs. The Wyoming Column, commanded by General George Crook, marched north from Fort Fetterman in Wyoming Territory. The Montana Column, led by Colonel John Gibbon, came east from Fort Ellis near Bozeman. Heading westward came us, the Dakota Column, commanded by General Terry when it should have been led by Autie.

Tom opened a flask, and drank. Autie sat on his bunk, scratching the ears of one of his hounds, while, outside, Autie's striker, quiet, dumb but loyal Private John Burkman, prepared our supper.

"Don't be hard on Terry," Autie said.

"But you should be leading this campaign," I countered. "Not him. If you were in command, this campaign would be a success. Of that I am certain."

"If not for the general," Autie said, "I would be at Fort Lincoln, writing orders of the day, sitting at a desk, bored beyond my senses."

I knew what he meant. President Grant, who

despised my brother, had relieved Autie of his command, citing this lame excuse that Autie had left Washington, D.C., without permission of the President or General Sherman. In reality, our President was smarting over the fact that Autie had the courage and integrity to testify before the Senate and condemn Secretary of War William Belknap and those rascals and cheats who call themselves Indian and Army traders. Autie, as honest as George Washington, had joined the myriad voices attacking the President and his corrupt regime.

So Grant, a bitter, vindictive man, knew how to hurt my brother the most. He would not allow him to accompany his command on its greatest campaign.

On the way back to Dakota Territory, Autie stopped in St. Paul, to plead, with tear-filled eyes, with General Terry. Knowing Autie to be the best—the only, I dare say—man to lead this expedition, General Terry gladly helped Custer write a note of contrition to our steaming President. The last words of that letter, however, came directly and solely from Autie:

> I appeal to you as a soldier to spare me the humiliation of seeing my regiment march to meet the enemy and I not share in its dangers.

Chapter Two
Sitting Bull

Before I came into this world, I knew my destiny: To be a *wicasa wakan*, a holy man, to guide the Lakota people. While still in my mother's insides, I saw what was happening. I saw the spotted death that killed my people. I saw our sacred hills, *Paha Sapa*, saw the eagle sitting on the rocks high above the blue lake. I heard the eagle sing to me:

> My father has given me this nation;
> In protecting them I have a hard time.

I saw the *tatanka* and the *pte*, the great shaggy beasts that give us life, that covered the land like grass. I saw them slowly disappear.

I saw The People of the Buffalo Nation dying.

And I saw the *wasicus*, those strange pale eyes. I saw *Mila Hanska*, the bluecoats who slash and kill with their long knives.

I saw many of my own people leaving the freedom of the Buffalo Nation, to live among the *wasicus*, to do as the *wasicus* tell them to do. To abandon *Wakan Tanka*.

More than forty-five summers have passed

since, and I have traveled far. I have seen these things I saw before I was born come true. Now I have been asked to see again.

To other Lakota bands, and our *Sahiyela* allies, I have sent word. We must talk about the *wasicus*, those white eyes who keep coming into Lakota land. This spring, the Lakotas and our friends have come, first to the Chalk Buttes, then to Ash Creek. A few in number in the beginning, but like grasshoppers and rabbits, those numbers grew. Two hundred. Five hundred. One thousand. Five thousand. Now six thousand. More arrive each day.

It is good.

Even in dark days, it is good to see friends. It is good to be part of the Buffalo Nation. It is good to sing songs.

They have asked for the *Wiwanyang Wacipi*. The Sun Dance.

This Sun Dance is held maybe during the Thunder Moon, or the Moon of Black Cherries, but in these days of uncertainty, the People have asked me to do it now, during the Moon of Green Leaves.

It is right.

It is good.

I sit on a buffalo robe and lean against the sacred tree. To *Wakan Tanka* I have promised a scarlet blanket, so Jumping Bull comes to my side, awl in hand. Above my left wrist, he begins to cut and slice and carve, up to my shoulder. Fifty times he does this, and now my arm flows red. I raise my head, and pray to *Wakan Tanka*.

I pray for peace. Not just peace for The People, but peace for all, even the Long Knives, even our enemy the Crows.

I sing out for food, so our babies do not grow hungry, so that our old women and old men have full bellies.

I cry out that all we want is to live undisturbed.

Jumping Bull has moved to my right arm, and his awl cuts away my flesh, my gift to *Wakan Tanka*. I feel nothing but the blood flowing down to my fingers, dripping onto the hide. A sage wreath has been placed over my head.

When my prayer is finished, I stand.

As I stare into the sky, the sun blinds me. I begin to dance.

Day becomes dark.

I dance.

I hear the song of the whistle.

I dance.

Night brings cold.

I dance.

Dawn arrives.

Still I dance.

The sun becomes blistering.

I dance. Then . . . then . . . I see . . .

The sky has been clear blue, but now comes this white cloud, large, fluffy, like the tail of a doe. In this cloud, I see the lodges of the Lakotas. No, no, the cloud is made of many Lakota lodges. It is a village. A large village. Mountains, with snow still on their peaks, guard one side of this encampment to the west.

Now, I see something else, coming from the rising sun, a brown stain on the sky. The dust of a storm of stinging sand borne by the wind. It moves at great speed, and I find myself caught in the middle, covering my eyes from the blinding sand, tasting the grit, and hearing . . . hearing . . .

The whinnies of horses . . . the pounding of hoofs . . . the rattling of the armaments of *Mila Hanska*.

This is no dust storm. It is the dust from hundreds of charging horses.

I hear The People singing: "The Long Knives are coming! The Long Knives are coming!"

The dust cloud roars past me, and, turning, I watch as it charges for the white cloud, charges for the village of the Lakotas.

With a deafening crash, the brown cloud smashes into the large white one. Lightning flashes, blinding me. Thunder rumbles. Rain blasts my face. I open my eyes to see.

The white cloud stands as it has, but the brown cloud has vanished, washed away everything, cloud, dust, soldiers, horses, all gone.

My eyes close. I hear the sounds of hoofs again.

Again, I open my eyes to see.

This is clearer. The sun is high, bright, burning. Long Knives, but armed with firearms and not their silver knives, gallop on their horses. There are many, many bluecoats. Some Indians ride with them, not Lakotas or *Sahiyelas*, but wolves for bluecoats.

They are not on the ground. They ride in the air. Then they fall, dropping like locusts, falling upside down into the village.

A voice whispers to me: "These soldiers have no ears."

My eyes close.

When they open, I feel the pain in my arms at last.

The scene now before me is blurry. Water trickles onto my face, onto my parched tongue. I blink. I see a face. Another. Jumping Bull asks if I am all right. Someone rubs grease onto my arm wounds. Black Moon bends his ears close to my mouth.

"I have had a vision," I tell him.

After I drink water, after my wounds have been treated, after we have all smoked a pipe, I tell Black Moon, Jumping Bull, Crazy Horse, and the others what I have seen. I tell them what it means.

"The Long Knives will come from the east. They will not listen, for their ears have been cut off, so we must teach them a lesson. The People of the Buffalo Nation will be victorious."

Excitedly they shout out to all what I have seen, what it means. Yet another voice reaches me, something I heard in my vision but until now have forgotten.

"Wait!" I yell. "There is more. It is a warning. The People will defeat the Long Knives, but we must not take anything from the dead. Anything belonging to a dead *wasicu* must stay. It is wrong for The People to take the things the *wasicus* use. We must not claim the spoils. We must not claim any spoils."

I yell this again. I rise, hurry to Black Moon, I tell him this is a warning from *Wakan Tanka*. Nodding, he walks away, but soon stops, slapping a jubilant *Sahiyela* warrior on the back, smiling, joking, already preparing victory songs. Others dance.

I yell for them to hear me, but they dance and sing, joyous to learn of the great victory that is to come.

My head drops. My heart feels heavy.

Sometimes, the brave warriors of The People of the Buffalo Nation have no ears, either.

Chapter Three
Red Cloud

I am Lakota.

My eyes do not see as once they did, for I have grown old. I would like to see more clearly into the eyes of the bluecoat *wasicu* who sits in this dark cabin with the government man. I would like to be able to look into his eyes, to see if he speaks the truth. It does not matter. I do not need to see his eyes.

"As I have told the man in your great city to the east," I say, "I have been wronged. This I know. The words of the Great Father never reach me, however, and my words never reach the Great Father. So why do we persist in talking? There are too many streams to cross before my words reach the Great Father."

The man who smells, scratches, and spits speaks my words to the Long Knife and the agent. I wonder if he tells them what I have said, or what he thinks the *wasicus* want to hear me say. Once, *wasicus* and I spoke with our hands, but my eyes no longer read the signs very well.

It is difficult to be an old man. By the measures of the *wasicus*, I am not even that old, but living as a Lakota . . . well . . . I have lived a long time.

36

I have fought in eighty battles. I have led my people. I have tried to live the Lakota way.

The bluecoat starts to say something, but I raise my right hand, and he does not speak. "Have you looked around this a-gen-cy?" I speak the *wasicu* word a-gen-cy. It is one of the few *wasicu* words that I know.

My words are again spoken in the *wasicu* tongue. The bluecoat nods. He is younger than the last bluecoat to visit me only one moon ago. That *wasicu* I gave the name, Gray Fox. Others call him Three Stars. To the *wasicus*, he is Crook. A funny name for that *wasicu*, for he seems to me to be one of the few Long Knives who I can trust, who speaks plainly, who speaks words of truth, and wisdom. Yet even Gray Fox had foolish ideas. He came to this a-gen-cy, this place where I have lived at peace with the *wasicus* for many summers, to ask Lakotas to serve as wolves for *Mila Hanska*. To help track down the Lakotas who do not live in the a-gen-cy, who do not want peace with the *wasicus*, who merely want to be left alone.

Gray Fox left without any Lakotas. The only person—other than the treacherous Arikarees and Crows—who joined *Mila Hanska* was the *wasicun sapa* who took a Hunkpapa woman for his wife. This black white man, with hair like a buffalo in summer, lived at the Standing Rock A-gen-cy far to the north of my a-gen-cy. It was thought, with his darker skin, that he would remain one of us. But *Mila Hanska* lured him away with money, this man we call Teat. He did not go with Gray Fox, however. He went with *Pehin Hanska*. Long Hair.

Long Hair does not understand our people. Even Gray Fox does not understand the Lakotas. And this bluecoat who speaks to me now? Even though I cannot see his eyes with clearness, I think not.

He is different than Gray Fox, this bluecoat called Mer-ritt. Gray Fox wore a funny hat and did not dress like a soldier. This one not only wears the blue, and carries a long knife, but sits erect, speaks firmly. He even rides a horse well. Were I a younger man, I would have liked to have raced a horse against him.

"I do not believe in the ways of Sitting Bull," I tell the bluecoat, and the agent, Mr. Hastings. "I do not think Crazy Horse is good for our people. But we are all Lakotas. In the end, we desire the same thing."

"Sitting Bull and Crazy Horse," Mr. Hastings says, "are the biggest Sioux problem we have today. They are the worst Indians on these Northern Plains."

When the words are translated again into the Lakota tongue, I laugh. "Once," I tell them, "you called me 'the biggest Sioux problem.' Once, I was 'the worst Indian on the Plains.'"

These words silence the *wasicus* for a moment. These words bring back long-forgotten memories to me.

Six winters ago—no, much longer than that—*wasicus* built a road through the land of the Lakotas, the land of the *Sahiyelas*. They put up soldier forts to protect all these strange people heading through Lakota country, wanting to dig up the yellow rocks that make *wasicus* crazy. This was not right. This was our land. We made marks on papers at Horse Creek, but the *wasicus* never kept their word. The *wasicus* have never kept their word. So we fought the *wasicus*. We defeated *Mila Hanska*, who were fools. We wiped them out in the Battle of the Hundred in the Hand. The blood of *Mila Hanska* froze in the snow. All of the *wasicus* were killed. A dog that had followed the Long Knives was alive for a moment. A Lakota brave, I do not remember who it was, said—"Let the dog take back the story to the Long Knives at the soldier fort."—but the *Sahiyela* known as Big Rascal yelled: "No, kill the dog. Not even a dog shall be left alive!" So, the dog was shot dead.

Crazy Horse . . . that was the fight that earned him much honor among our people. He proved his bravery. He helped lead *Mila Hanska* to their deaths.

Yet now, Crazy Horse, and Sitting Bull, they do not see what the future holds. Their eyes may remain stronger than mine, they may not walk slowly for fear of falling, but they are blind in many ways. We Lakotas must learn to live with the *wasicus*. To resist them, to fight them, will result in death.

That is a hard thing for me to admit. It is hard for my people to understand. But these are hard times for the Lakotas.

"You have seen this a-gen-cy?" I ask again.

Again, they nod.

"My people starve here," I tell them. "I cannot keep my people here. To starve? To rot? We were promised many things to stay at this a-gen-cy. What has happened to those promises?"

"And what of yours?" the bluecoat Mer-ritt asks. "We believe many of your young warriors have gone to join the hostiles. I have heard reports that powder and percussion caps have been found here on the agency. That means that some of your people are working in conjunction with the hostiles. This is not proper. This is not what I would expect from those who follow the great Sioux chief, Red Cloud."

It takes a while for the man who stinks, scratches, and spits to say those words to me.

"I am told that my braves leave the a-gen-cy," I answer after a moment's thought, "to hunt buffalo. So they might have meat to feed their wives, their children. Besides, we are Lakotas. We are hunters. Young men do not want to accept . . ."—I pause, trying to remember the *wasicu* word—". . . cha-ri-ty."

It is not a lie. That is what I am told. Of course, as I think of something else, I cannot help but smile. That is what I have been asked to be told.

Before Hastings can say something, my hand raises. Hastings talks—he is not as respectful as the bluecoat—but my voice is louder, and soon he must be quiet and let me finish.

"*Paha Sapa!*" I shout. "*Paha Sapa!*"

Let them think of that. The Black Hills belong to us, yet the *wasicus* have invaded our sacred country to search for the yellow rocks, the yellow dust. Now, *Mila Hanska* let the *wasicu* invaders stay.

"You ask me to send word to those free Lakotas. You say that they must come in or you will fight them. You give them a"—again, I speak the *wasicu* word—"dead-line." Now, it is my turn to spit into the shiny bowl that the man who stinks, scratches, and spits keeps missing, staining the floor with his nasty brown juice. "Dead-line. Long Hair, Gray Fox, even this young Long Knife who sits before me now . . . even the Great Father . . . you all knew this could not be done. In the dead of winter? When it would be hard for even a Lakota to find a winter camp? Bring my people in? So they might starve like the rest of us?"

I have to stop to catch my breath. My heart pounds against my chest. I wish I were not old.

"You wanted war," I say after a long while. "Now . . . soon you will have it."

"Gray Fox," the bluecoat Mer-ritt says, "does not want war. I do not want war."

"And Long Hair?" I ask.

He starts to answer, stops, and shakes his head. "Custer wants what's good for Custer."

The words are translated to me, and I cannot help but think: *Sitting Bull wants what's good for Sitting Bull.*

Sitting Bull wants to be like Red Cloud. Or like Red Cloud was ten or twelve winters ago.

"How many of your young warriors have left the reservation to join the hostiles?" the bluecoat asks.

"My people are ready," I answer. "I tell you what I told Gray Fox. The Lakotas are not afraid of *Mila Hanska.* They are not afraid of your chiefs. Every lodge will send its young men, and they all will say of the Great Father's dogs . . . 'Let them come!' "

My throat hurts. In this stinking square room, I sweat. Hastings looks scared. Rarely has he heard me speak this way. He thinks of me as the diplomat, the peacekeeper. He was not around at the time of the Battle of the Hundred in the Hand. He was not here when we fought what the *wasicus* came to call "Red Cloud's War."

He does not know how I feel. He thinks I am—how do the *wasicus* say it—a "tame Indian"?

No *wasicu* can understand the heart of a Lakota, or of any Indian. War is our way. When I was born, I was poor. Those eighty battles—most of them not fought against *wasicus*, but our Indian enemies—the Pawnees, the Omahas, the Crows—won me honors, prestige, ponies, and riches, and the respect I have today as an old man whose eyes don't see well, and who has trouble even walking, let alone riding.

The bluecoat takes in a deep breath, and slowly lets it out. "Can you keep any more braves from joining the hostiles?" he asks.

"I am told," I tell him again, "that my young men have left the a-gen-cy to hunt buffalo."

At this, I have no more to say to these *wasicus*. I rise, even as the man who stinks, scratches, and spits is still making Lakota words into *wasicu* ones. I walk out into the sun. I walk to my lodge.

It is a lonely lodge.

My son, Jack—a *wasicu* name, to please the black robes and the a-gen-cy men, but a name whose sound pleases me, too—is no longer there. Jack Red Cloud rode away. To join Crazy Horse and Sitting Bull. I gave him my fast-shooting *wasicu* long gun. I gave him my fastest pony. I gave him my blessing.

I wish I were not an old man. I wish I were with the free Lakotas. I wish they could wipe out all

Chapter Four

Lieutenant Colonel Wesley Merritt

When agent James Hastings, the interpreter, and I left the log cabin and watched Red Cloud feebly make his way back to two of his caretakers, I let out a long sigh, and fished a cigar from my tunic.

Hastings struck a match, holding it close as I tried to get the stogie to fire.

"I don't understand Red Cloud," Hastings said. "I think Crazy Horse, Sitting Bull, all those red devils, have gotten that old codger into thinking the damned Indians might win this war. I've never seen him so fiery." He grinned, shook out the match, and said: "Hell, Custer could ride through the entire Sioux nation with the Seventh." His grin turned into a chuckle, but, seeing me, he stopped. "I mean . . . well . . ." A terrible laugh. "What I meant to say, Colonel, was that you and the entire . . ."

"I seem to recall Fetterman saying the same thing a few years ago." I pointed my cigar at Red Cloud. "Before he ran into that very same fellow."

On December 21, 1866, William J. Fetterman led his command out of Fort Phil Kearny in

Wyoming Territory and was wiped out by a force of Cheyenne and Sioux hostiles. Fetterman had boasted that with eighty men, he could "ride through the Sioux nation." He died alongside exactly eighty soldiers.

Now, almost ten years later, everybody from Washington to here in Nebraska seemed to think that a great Army victory had been preordained. Why, we had George Armstrong Custer, self-proclaimed Indian fighter after he killed a bunch of peaceable Cheyennes at the Washita in '68, and George Crook leading our boys against a bunch of undisciplined savages who scatter and never attack. Indian agents, soldiers, and politicians should have a better grasp of history. This Indian campaign was not yet won, and damned well could be lost.

"Well . . ." Hastings couldn't find anything to counter my argument.

This was my second trip to Fort Robinson and the Red Cloud Agency. In March, General Sheridan had sent me to investigate reports of malfeasance. Mark my words: I was no fan of George "Glory-Hunting" Custer, but every charge he fired at President Grant's corrupt staff regarding Indian affairs proved true. Still, I couldn't find any proof of fraud at Red Cloud, though what I saw of the agency left me sickened.

Now I looked around. A Sioux woman, still in her teens, nursed an infant without shame. She looked wretched. An old Indian man sat beneath a brush arbor. His eyes appeared dead. The place stank of dung.

The place made me sick. I tossed away my cigar.

"Don't you wish you were part of this campaign?" Hastings asked.

Custer—well, Terry was said to be in command—had left Fort Lincoln in Dakota Territory, heading west into Montana. Crook was pushing north from Fort Fetterman in Wyoming. Gibbon was coming east. They would catch the hostiles between them. Then they would fight amongst themselves for the glory. Such were the spoils of war.

And Lieutenant Colonel Wesley Merritt? Well, I was on special assignment. At least eight companies of the 5th Cavalry had arrived near the Red Cloud Agency. Considering the mood of Indians here—Red Cloud's malevolency seemed a pretty good indication—the Army got here none too soon. The war might break out here instead of on the Powder River in Montana, I thought, and smiled.

Wouldn't that gall Custer?

Over the next few days, I continued to tour the Red Cloud Agency.

"The Indians got a way of communicating with 'emselves," my interpreter told me. "They knows what's goin' on at Standing Rock or, I'll be jiggered, all the way over in Montana Territory with their hostile pards. They knows that long before we ever knows it."

"How do they do that?" I didn't believe the poor lout.

"Hell's fire, Colonel, if any white man can ever figure that out. Smoke signals. Carrier pigeons. Specters or talking to coyot's. Your guess's as good as mine. Though I hears . . ."—his voice dropped into a whisper—"I hears that Sittin' Bull's actually a renegade white boy, got kicked out of West Point, soldiered with Napoleon." He winked.

To let me know he was joking.

Imbecile.

We reined up at a flat spot of earth, and the interpreter dismounted, wrapping his reins around a clump of sage, and wandered about the place, kicking through flattened grass, poking around the ashes of a fire pit, breaking open dung.

"Here's another lodge gone," he said, "to join up with ol' Sittin' Bull."

"Louis-Nicolas Savout no doubt," I said, remembering the cad's joke about Napoleon.

"How's that, Col'nel?"

"Nothing. How long?"

"Have they been gone?" He shrugged. "Two days. No more'n that."

On we rode, talking to Sioux men and boys—

48

those who would converse with us—coming across more abandoned lodge sites.

A day later, Mr. Hastings sent word to me that Yellow Robe had arrived at the agency. With due haste, I proceeded from Fort Robinson to the agency, where I met the Sioux chief. Yellow Robe was not as recalcitrant as Red Cloud. He talked. He did not hold back.

What he said, however, unnerved me.

Reports from Standing Rock and Red Cloud were one thing, but, coming across a dozen or so abandoned lodges, I had not been able to comprehend the magnitude of what was happening in Indian country. After hearing Yellow Robe, I galloped back to Fort Robinson, wrote out a message, which I sent by our fastest courier to Fort Laramie. From there, my dispatch would be telegraphed to General Sheridan's headquarters in Chicago, and Sheridan would relay the important information to General Terry, who was already in the field with the 7th Cavalry.

> Yellow Robe, a Sioux chieftain, arrived at Red Cloud Agency today. He says that when he left the hostile camp on the Rosebud six days ago, eighteen hundred lodges were there, about to depart for the Powder River. Yellow Robe says the Indians will fight. He says that they have about three thousand warriors.

• • •

I did not hate Custer. I cannot say that I liked him, although I begrudgingly concede that his pluck and daring made him a fine leader in combat, though I don't think he cared one whit about how many men were killed under his command. Yet I knew that Custer, Terry, *et al.*, should have this information.

Here, however, was where I wished that the United States Army could relay messages like the Indians, be it by smoke signals, pigeons, ghosts, or talking coyotes.

From Fort Laramie, Wyoming Territory, my dispatch was wired to Chicago on June 6. It was then telegraphed to Fort Lincoln, Dakota Territory. Sheridan's staff directed that the message be sent to General Terry by boat or any other means. From Fort Lincoln, the message was forwarded to the steamboats *Yellowstone*, *Key West*, and *Josephine*. On June 24, the *Josephine* reached the military depot established on the Powder River by General Terry's forces. From there, the commander sent the message west by Arikaree scouts on horseback. They reached the general's camp two days later—a punishing ride by anyone's standards—but, alas, the general was already marching south.

The note was finally placed in General Terry's hands on June 30, five days *after* the Battle at the Little Big Horn River.

Chapter Five

Lieutenant Edward Godfrey

My God. Never did I think that I would live to see white men act this way.

Commanding K Troop on the 15th of June, I accompanied General Custer with the 7th Cavalry's left wing. Pursuant to General Terry's orders, Major Marcus Reno's right wing had departed the supply camp we established on the Powder River, following that river south. With General Custer, we rode southeast along the Yellowstone River to rendezvous with Reno, as well as Gibbon's Montana Column at the Tongue River. General Terry had boarded the *Far West* at our supply camp and traveled west to meet up with the Montana Column.

We rode with five days' rations and forage, one wagon for each troop, fifty rounds of ammunition in our belts, another fifty in our saddlebags, and, as always, General Custer's staghounds.

We traveled without the regimental band, thank God, for if I ever hear "Garry Owen" again it will be far too soon. We traveled without our sabers, crating them up to leave at the depot— sabers being practically useless, too heavy, and too cumbersome in the field. Many of us, I now understand, left our dignity and humanity back at the supply camp, as well.

I still have trouble accepting what I witnessed.

The unpredictable weather had changed to dry and hot as we trotted over sagebrush and dust, coming into an old Indian encampment, due east of the Tongue. A Sioux camp, our Indian scouts told us, and our hearts sank at the size.

"How old?" General Custer signed to Red Star.

The Arikaree scout signed back: "Last winter."

With a curt nod, the general walked about camp, pulling his horse, Vic, behind him.

Two other Indians came to Red Star, muttering excitedly in their guttural language. The Arikaree scolded them, pointed harshly, and they mounted their painted ponies, and rode in opposite directions.

I stared at Red Star, and signed: "How many lodges?"

His lips flattened. He picked up a handful of sand, and let the grains slip through his fingers. Later, we would estimate that this camp stretched some two miles, and numbered between twelve hundred to fifteen hundred teepees.

I followed General Custer, catching up with him in front of an old fire pit with his brother, brevet Major Tom Custer, the newspaper reporter Mark Kellogg, and Lieutenant William Cooke. The general was leaning down, and I quickly saw what held his attention.

A human skull, charred.

Major Custer had to keep one of his brother's hounds from digging through the pit, which, we now understood, was also a grave of sorts.

No one spoke until the general removed the gauntlet from his right hand, and fingered through the ash, pulling out a blackened button, which he wiped on his trousers, studied, sighed, and held up for the rest of us to examine.

The button came from a cavalry overcoat. I looked at the fire, at the blackened clubs surrounding the pit, saw the skull again, and pictured the terrible torture this poor soul, a soldier such as myself, had endured, beaten and burned by the godless heathens of the cursed Sioux.

Rising slowly, the general spoke quietly, ordering Lieutenant Cooke to form a burial detail for this unfortunate, unknown soldier. Then General Custer stood, and merely stared at the pit and skull for the longest while.

Such a tragic scene knotted our insides, but, even so, I could not have steeled myself for what next I was to witness. And having enlisted in the 21st Ohio during the late Rebellion, I had seen much horror at Stones River and Snodgrass Hill before entering West Point and earning my commission in 1867.

Before we reached our rendezvous point at the

Tongue River, the command rode into a Sioux burial ground, a forest of trees along the banks of the Yellowstone, and Indian-constructed scaffolds. Dusk was descending, darkening the skies and the mood of my commanding officer.

Reining up in front of a scaffold painted red and black, Custer asked Red Star the meaning of the colors. When the scout answered that it was the sign of a brave warrior, the general ordered three troopers to tear it down.

My mouth fell open. Even Red Star seemed aghast as the troopers, following orders, toppled the body into the dust. The general wasn't finished. Next, he ordered the Negro interpreter, Isaiah Dorman, to unwrap the corpse, take any plunder he so desired, and heave the carcass into the Yellowstone.

A binge of destruction followed.

Lieutenant Donald McIntosh ordered G Troop to tear down all the scaffolds, and his soldiers went about it with such merriment and raucous-ness, my horse turned skittish. Gas and wretched smells escaped several corpses as they crashed to the ground. Soldiers climbed the trees, pushing bodies to the ground, stealing eagle feathers, leather bags, headdresses.

"Boston! Look!" I had managed to calm my horse, and saw young Harry Reed, the general's nephew, holding a quiver of arrows and pair of moccasins to General Custer's younger brother for inspection. Boston grinned, and brandished a bone breastplate.

My eyes closed.

Understand this. I have no love for Indians, but I must respect the dead, red or white. Oh, not all acted like fiends from Hades. I could hear a trooper begging his lieutenant not to let this happen, that they would be sorry. I heard another interpreter, Fred Gerard, tell a Crow scout, that, yes, our white God might call for vengeance for this desecration. I heard Indians singing, praying. Horses squealed in panic. Even two of General Custer's hounds howled over the unholy carnage. One of the new recruits in my troop, who had joined us in St. Paul, prayed in his native, foreign tongue. Mostly, however, what I heard was frivolous, excited banter.

Our soldiers went through the corpses like children hunting Easter eggs.

Instead of joining this barbaric act, General Custer rode off down the river, followed by some of his immediate command and his dogs. But his men . . . *our* men . . . Like grave robbers, officers, enlisted men, and civilians plundered with relish, waving trophies as if they had captured them as trophies of battle.

Neck-reining my horse, I motioned K Troop to follow me, and I rode after Custer. More corpses splashed into the Yellowstone. Isaiah Dorman chastised the troopers, telling them to take those bodies downstream, that they were spoiling his fishing. Yes, the Negro was fishing in the Yellowstone. I have no desire to learn what he was using for bait.

Chapter Six
Buffalo Calf Road Woman

Little Hawk found them, although he was not searching for them. He simply wanted to steal horses from the white people. He rode with four other Human Beings. That is how we call ourselves. The *Hotóhkesos*—Lakotas as they call themselves—call us *Sahiyela*, and the *veho*, the pale eyes, call us Cheyennes. Well, Little Hawk and his friends killed a buffalo cow near the red buttes. They were cooking this meat when Crooked Nose saw two riders who did not notice the Human Beings, and disappeared beyond a bluff. Thinking they were our *Hotóhkeso* friends, Little Hawk said: "Let us have some fun with them."

Such is the way of Little Hawk. Two days earlier, after I had filled a water bag from the river, he sent an arrow through the bag, and yipped like a coyote as the water soaked my deerskin dress.

They rode up a gulch, and Little Hawk crept up the hill. He was going to pretend to attack our *Hotóhkeso* friends, but as soon as he looked over the ridge, his heart leaped, and he quickly backed down. *"Notaxé-ve'hó'e!"* he said urgently.

They were not *Hotóhkesos*, but warrior white men.

"Good." Little Shield smiled. "We can steal ponies from warrior white men."

"How many?" Crooked Nose asked.

"The land is black with them."

Little Shield no longer smiled. Little Hawk mounted his pony, as did the others, and they raced into the timber. They did not stop until they had reached our village at the Deer Medicine Rocks.

Seven suns earlier, the *Hotóhkeso* holy man, Sitting Bull, had finished the Sun Dance, yet everyone still talked about his vision. Yes, we were talking about it as we prepared food when Little Hawk loped into camp. He spoke excitedly about all the warrior white men nearing the Rosebud River. My brother, Comes-In-Sight, turned to Sitting Bull, and asked: "Is this what your vision saw?"

The holy man's head shook. "They will attack the village from the east," he said. "Not the south."

"Let us attack them!" came a cry from another *Hotóhkeso*. "It is a good day to die!"

"Young men," Sitting Bull said, "leave the soldiers alone unless they provoke us."

"As they attacked our mothers and sisters at Sand Creek?" someone sang out. "As they attacked our mothers and sisters at the Washita, where the icy river flowed red with the blood of our loved ones?"

"More of our people join us every day," another said. "We become stronger each morning. Listen to Sitting Bull. Let us wait for the soldiers, for we will be stronger by the time they reach us."

"Let us smoke on this," my brother suggested, and the warriors nodded at Comes-In-Sight's wisdom.

Someone tugged my arm. Other women were already preparing to move. I should help them, but I looked at Little Hawk, I looked at my brother. No matter how many pipes were passed, no matter what the elders like Sitting Bull said, the minds of our young men had already been made up. I knew what they would do. I knew what I must do.

They began slipping out of camp that night, only a few young men at first, then many more. Outside, drums beat, and men and women, *Hotóhkesos*, Human Beings, and others, sang. I threw off my buffalo robe, dressed, grabbed one of my brother's quivers and bows.

My mother sat up, demanding: "*Tosa'a ne-ho-ohtse?*"

"I go with my brother," I answered, and, before she could say any more, I had ducked out of our lodge, and was running to the pony herd.

All night, for fifty miles we rode, stopping only to rest our ponies, to tie up their tails, and paint our faces for war. I dipped my fingers in vermillion and drew a lightning bolt across my forehead. Then Little Hawk roughly grabbed my wrist, twisted, turned, and dumped me on the grass.

"What are you doing here, woman?"

Anger blacked my face, my heart. Suddenly I was aware my right hand gripped the bone handle of my knife.

"Go back!" My brother stood over me, pointing north. "Go back to our village!"

No longer did I feel hatred and anger, for my brother and Little Hawk looked handsome, strong, dressed in their finest clothes, their faces painted for war.

Yet I had no intention of leaving this place. "I came to fight!" I yelled.

"Ha!" a *Hotóhkeso* cried, and others joined him in laughing.

Comes-In-Sight did not laugh. Nor did Little Hawk.

"Only warriors fight," my brother said. "Not women. All the men have come to fight."

"That is not true," a tired voice said, and I stood to see Sitting Bull, standing, buffalo headdress on his weary head. His arms remained ugly and swollen from the wounds he gave to the Great Spirit during the Sun Dance. "I do not believe we should fight these Long Knives, but I come to support you, to encourage you. It is the way."

"It is the way for a man," Little Hawk said. "Not a woman."

"Buffalo Calf Road Woman," Sitting Bull said, "may stay with me, although we Lakotas let our women ride with us into battle. It is good."

"*Hoka hey!*" the *Hotóhkeso* warriors cried out, brandishing their war axes, their rifles, their fists as they mounted their war ponies. Others continued that cry.

"It is a good day to die!"

They rode, whooping, singing, ready for battle. A giant cloud of dust followed, stretching high into the morning sky. Old Sitting Bull took my hand, but I had to gather the bridle of my pony before she took off after the running ponies.

I could not see, only could hear the thunder of hoofs.

"Come," Sitting Bull said, and through the choking dust I followed him as he led his black mare up the ridge. More and more ponies rode by, carrying Human Beings and other Indians. When we reached the top of the ridge with other young boys, and, yes, a few women, I turned to watch.

"There are so many," I whispered.

"Yes," said Sitting Bull. "But there are many Long Knives, too."

Never had we Human Beings attacked a party of warrior white men. Only in defense of our villages, our people. The warrior white men always brought the war to us. This time, we would strike them first. This was different. It was not like stealing ponies or counting coup among the Crows or Snakes.

In the early morning, shots rang out. Sitting Bull mounted his mare, as I did mine, and we followed our warriors, seven hundred or maybe even ten hundred, to watch the fight.

It was a good fight. Many coups were taken.

The warrior white men and their Snakes and Crow scouts were very brave, too. Many died well.

Behind us, the women began to sing death songs. One was already in mourning, for her husband had fallen, his body retrieved by two *Hotóhkeso* braves, who carried him up the hill, dropped him beside his wife, and loped back down to rejoin the fight.

The air smelled of rotten eggs. The warrior white men's big guns on wheels roared. Our men retreated, but they did not continue to run. Wheeling their mounts, they charged back into the thick smoke and dust.

"The white eyes," Sitting Bull said, "did not expect us to fight like this." He turned to me, and smiled. "I did not expect this, either."

My face brightened. I spoke the *Hotóhkeso* words: "*Hoka hey.*"

Sitting Bull answered in my own tongue. "It is a good day to die."

All morning, and into the afternoon, the fight went on. The smell of death became stronger. Sitting Bull had begun to sing, his eyes closed, his scabbed, bloody arms folded over his breastplate.

The warrior white men and their scouts would charge, and be driven back. Our warriors would charge, and be driven back.

A young *Hotóhkeso* rode toward me, dangling in his hand a spotted war bonnet, one he must have taken off a Snake he had killed. He shouted something I could not understand, then a hole appeared in his chest, blood spraying, and his eyes no longer saw me as he slipped from the saddle. The pony ran away. The boy did not move.

Sitting Bull sang. The women behind him wailed.

When I looked away from the dead boy, I saw my brother, leading four other Human Beings against the *vehos*. Many times he had done this. Then his pony fell dead, crashing head over heels, sending Comes-In-Sight slamming into the hard ground. White Elk galloped past him, so focused on the battle that he did not notice my brother, who slowly pulled himself off the ground, and staggered, dizzily, toward the wall of blue-coated white men. Dust from the bullets kicked up around my brother.

"*Hokay hey!*" shouted a *Hotóhkeso* boy behind me.

Another screamed: "Today is a good day to die!"

I kicked my mare's sides, and rode, tears streaming down my face. It may be a good day to die, I thought, but I shall not let my brother die.

My mare, stolen from the Snakes by Comes-In-Sight four summers ago, leaped over the body of a dead Crow, his scalp taken. Shouting my brother's name, I could not even hear my own voice. A bullet tugged my left braid. Another tore off a shell on the side of my dress.

"Comes-In-Sight!" I yelled. This time, he heard me, for he stopped, and turned. Blood smeared his face, which was caked with sand and grass. I jerked hard on the hackamore, and the mare slid to a stop. I reached down and felt the wind pierced by an arrow that sliced over my back. Comes-In-Sight's hand gripped mine, and he swung up behind me. His arms wrapped around my waist, and the mare galloped away, through the dust.

A *Hotóhkeso* jerked his spotted pony to a stop, and shouted at me, raising his bow in honor. I did not stop until I was back on the ridge with Sitting Bull. My brother dropped from my pony. He spit out blood and bits of teeth and grass, and took my hand.

"Step down," he said.

Sitting Bull had stopped singing. He smiled

as Comes-In-Sight helped me down. Then my brother mounted my mare.

"You ride back into battle?" I asked him.

"The day is not done," he said. He started back toward the warrior white men, but pulled the hackamore, and looked back at me. "Buffalo Calf Road Woman," he said, "I am glad I brought you here." Laughing, he kicked my mare into a lope, and the dust swallowed him.

Only long afterward, after the fight that was to come on the Greasy Grass, did we learn that we had beaten the warrior white men led by their great chief, the ones known to us Indian peoples as Gray Wolf or Three Stars, and to the *vehos* as George Crook.

That afternoon, after long, hard fighting, we gathered our dead, and rode away from the Rosebud. The warrior white men did not follow us. They had had enough of battle. Days later, our scouts returned to our camp and told us that those *notaxé-ve'hó'e* had gone back to the south. They would not trouble us any more during that summer.

As darkness fell, my bones felt weary. I rode my mare again, for Comes-In-Sight had captured a fine red stallion belonging to a Crow. We would mourn the dead, but we would celebrate a great victory. Those that were no more had died with honor.

My eyes jerked awake. I had fallen asleep from the clopping of the hoofs. Ahead of me, I heard my fellow Human Beings singing.

They sang my name.

This much remembered fight, they said, will be known among our people as "Where the Girl Saved Her Brother."

Chapter Seven
General Alfred H. Terry

21 June 1876
Aboard the Far West
Yellowstone River at Rosebud Creek, Montana Ty.

To General Philip H. Sheridan
Regimental Headquarters, Chicago
Sir:
I have the honor to report to you the plan of action I have outlined for campaign against the hostiles:

At 2 o'clock this afternoon, I convened with Lieutenant Colonel George A. Custer of the Dakota Column, Colonel John Gibbon, and Major James Brisbin, 2nd Cavalry, of the Montana Column, in the conference room of the steamer that serves as my headquarters. Major Marcus A. Reno, who had commanded the wing of the 7th Cavalry on a scout down the Powder River, was not invited to take part in this meeting.

Major Reno disobeyed my orders in a most flagrant fashion during his "scout" of the Powder and Tongue Rivers to the south and east of our present location. The major, who has little experience in fighting Indians and has been suffering from a state of melancholy since his wife's passing two years ago, was ordered not to go beyond the Rosebud. Yesterday afternoon, I received a note from an Indian courier that he was eight miles above my present location and was following some "hot Indian trails." He had not supplies to warrant such disobedience, and returned to our camp with wearied horses and broken-down mules.

Colonel Custer chastised his junior officer for failing to obtain more information on the location of the hostiles. Major Reno's "scout" produced little information and no results, and he had been on this assignment for ten days. Colonel Custer threatened a court-martial, but I intervened, saying that my rebuke was punishment enough. Also, Reno may have disregarded written orders, but we now know where the hostiles are not.

"They are not on the lower Rosebud," Colonel Gibbon said as we unrolled our Raynolds-Maynadier map.

"Too bad," Major Brisbin quipped. "General Crook might have whipped them by now."

"I hope not," Custer cheerily stated.

Having reports from the Crow scouts of seeing smoke in the valley of the Little Big Horn River, we now believe that the hostiles must be on the headwaters of the Rosebud, Big Horn, or Little Big Horn.

"Probably it is at the latter where we shall find

them." Major Brisbin's suggestion was met with affirmations from Custer and Gibbon.

Thus, I outlined my plan:

Colonel Custer would lead the 7th up the Rosebud toward the supposed hostile encampment. I would join the Montana Column and approach with Colonel Gibbon's command from the west, and thus we would catch the Indians in a pincer. Since Colonel Custer would have less country to maneuver across and would be unencumbered by the infantry with Colonel Gibbon's forces, I outlined his path with stick pins, then asked Major Brisbin to trace this route with a blue pencil. Custer would march almost to the Wyoming border before turning north toward the Indians' supposed location.

"Should you find a trail leading to the Little Big Horn," I told Custer, "do not follow it with due haste. Proceed up the Rosebud, get closer to the mountains, then strike west, feeling to your left. But do as you deem best."

"The hostiles would, in all likelihood, retreat south," Colonel Gibbon suggested. "If they reach the Big Horn Mountains, they will be able to live on game and wild berries."

"If they run south," Major Brisbin said, "they will meet up with General Crook's command."

"If they get that far," Colonel Custer said with a devilish grin.

That remark chilled me briefly, and I reminded

Custer of his orders. The colonel merely nodded, and I suggested to him: "The Gatling guns and twelve-pounders are at your disposal."

He shook his head, and, upon Colonel Gibbon's suggestion, we sent for a scout named George Herendeen, who has been employed by Colonel Gibbon.

Herendeen is a rough sort of Irish heritage, but knows this area. We queried him on a place on the map named Tullock's Creek, and for possible locations of hostiles. This man had impressed Colonel Gibbon much during the campaign, and his knowledge of the area gained him favor with Colonel Custer.

"Do you know this place?" Custer jabbed at the map.

"Like this." Herendeen held out the back of his hand.

"Then you are the man I want." Custer looked at Colonel Gibbon, who nodded his approval at the transfer of the scout to Custer's command.

"After you have scouted the head of Tullock's Creek," I told the scout, "you will take a dispatch from Colonel Custer immediately to me. At which point, we should be . . ."

Major Brisbin finished my sentence. "Near the mouth of the Little Big Horn."

"How much?" Herendeen asked.

"Excuse me?" I inquired.

"How much money?"

Colonel Gibbon could not hold in his snigger.

Realizing the scout was serious, and understanding the deadly nature of such an assignment, I told him: "Would two hundred dollars satisfy you?"

"Indeed, sir, it would."

So it was agreed, and the scout departed.

"There are a lot of Indians, General Custer," Major Brisbin told him. "With General Terry's and Colonel Gibbon's permission, I would gladly lend my four troops to join you, sir."

"The Seventh is all I need, Major," Colonel Custer said.

"Now, Custer," Colonel Gibbon said—and I am not certain if this was meant in jest or in all seriousness—"don't be greedy, but wait for us."

Ever so joyous, Custer waved off Colonel Gibbon's suggestion, and left the steamer to prepare his command for the expedition.

Colonel Gibbon eyed me, pursed his lips as if thinking of something to say, but, instead, saluted, and disembarked the Far West to see to his troops.

Alone with Major Brisbin, an old, dear colleague, the cavalry commander said to me: "Permission to speak plainly, General?"

"You may always speak plainly to me," I answered.

"Colonel Custer is brash, sir. I understand, after Major Reno's disobedience, you not putting the major in command, but I believe you should command the 7th, sir, and not Colonel Custer."

I shook my head. "Colonel Custer needs a chance at redemption after incurring the wrath of President Grant."

"You should command, General," Major Brisbin repeated.

With a tired smile, I thanked the major for his confidence in me, but told him that I had no experience fighting Indians.

"You have more sense in your little finger than Custer has in his whole body," Brisbin said. "You underrate your ability and overrate Custer's. I say this, sir, not only out of my affection and respect for you, General, but for the care of the lives of my men and officers during such perilous times."

"I thank you, Major," I told Brisbin, "but I must let Custer do what he does best. Lead."

Detecting Brisbin's frown, I said: "You do not seem to have confidence in Custer, Major."

"None in the world," he said.

Slowly I removed the pins, and rolled up the map, watching the blue line Major Brisbin had traced disappear.

"If Colonel Custer finds a trail, he will follow it," Brisbin said softly. "He will attack regardless of your orders."

"If he is successful, unlike Major Reno . . ." My words trailed off.

"I fear, General," Major Brisbin said, "that you have turned this wild man loose."

This evening, I found Custer in his tent, telling him: "I do not know what to say for the last."

"Say whatever you want to say," he told me.

"Use your own judgment," I said, "and do what you think best if you strike the trail." I took a deep breath, exhaled, and cautioned him. "And whatever you do, Custer, hold on to your wounded."

At noon tomorrow, Colonel Custer will lead the 7th. Colonel Gibbon's command, the Far West, and I will proceed west along the Yellowstone River, then south on the Big Horn River and to the Little Big Horn. We expect to find the Indians somewhere between Rotten Grass Creek and the Wolf Mountains. It is my fervent wish that the next report you hear from me will detail a great victory and the defeat of the hostiles.

Your obt. servant,
Alfred H. Terry,
Brigadier General, Commanding

Chapter Eight

Mark Kellogg

Special to the Bismarck *Tribune*

WITH THE DAKOTA COLUMN, YELLOW-STONE RIVER, MOUTH OF ROSEBUD, Montana Territory (June 22)—To go with Custer, or remain with the Montana Column?

Having met with Major James Brisbin—"Grasshopper Jim" to those who know of his entomological interest in those insects prevalent on these summer Montana plains—and General Alfred H. Terry on the deck of Captain Marsh's Far West for our nightly cigars the previous evening, I asked myself that very question.

Accompanying Major Brisbin and General Terry would be easier, yet I felt as if I might miss something if I did not accompany Lieutenant Colonel George Armstrong Custer, brevet major general. The look on General Terry's face when I informed him of my decision, pending his approval, told me that he feared I was making a mistake, but Terry's words earlier that week had convinced me of the path a journalist should take.

"There is to be no child's play in regard to the Indians," the general told me. "They must be taught that the government is not to be trifled with, and measures shall be taken to teach them to feel and recognize that there exists in this land an arm and power which they must obey."

Custer is one to teach the Indians this.

I am not alone in my opinion. Many desire to follow Custer, and not only his civilian relations who have joined this campaign. A rugged but educated scout called Lonesome Charley Reynolds was aboard the riverboat steamer to allow Dr. Henry Porter to treat a serious hand infection. Captain Grant Marsh, able skipper of the Far West, and Dr. Porter recommended that Reynolds stay aboard the ship, but Reynolds would not be deprived of this once-in-a-lifetime opportunity.

"I've been waiting and getting ready for this expedition for two years," the scout said, "and I would sooner be dead than miss it."

Since my last dispatch, much has happened. We have traveled from the abandoned Indian village, following the Yellowstone River upstream to the mouth of the Rosebud. The weather has turned blistering hot, and the air is choking with dust. To many soldiers, the land is uninspiring, monotonous, yet I feel alive as we traverse this rugged, wind-swept region. More importantly, never have I seen a sky so big. Oftentimes, it seems as if it might swallow the entire earth.

Custer has displayed superior marksmanship, bringing down an antelope no fewer than four hundred yards in distance, and practically shooting the heads off several sage hens. The hostile Indians we seek are in grave danger should they find themselves in Custer's gunsights.

I have dubbed Custer "Iron Britches," by which I do not refer to the light-colored buckskin attire he prefers. He rides hard, leaving many of his soldiers, and one tired newspaper reporter, perspiring and panting just trying to keep pace with our fearless leader.

Allow me to paint his portrait in words, which I base not only from actual observation, but experience.

George Custer's courage is undaunted, his temperament is one of quickness but also of nervousness. A leader of quick impulse, he does what he feels is right. He is a man of honest integrity and wit, devoted to his family—which includes his brother, Tom Custer, captain and aide-de-camp; another brother, Boston, serving as a guide and with the pack train; and a nephew, a civilian employee—and writes to his charming wife, Libbie, every evening after retiring to his tent.

Some of those letters were almost lost during a tragic incident a few days back in which a sergeant was drowned while carrying the mail and dispatches to the Far West. Later, after I retrieved the mailbag from the Yellowstone, and, finding Custer's soaked letters to his wife, I attempted to dry them so that his words might reach Fort Lincoln. I did not do this to win the confidence of Custer; I would have done likewise for any leader of this campaign.

Custer has earned the bitter wrath of some men, including one who sits in the White House in Washington, D.C., and perhaps two junior officers whose names will go unmentioned in this report. Most of the soldiers of the 7th, however, would surely follow Custer into the jaws of hell.

Last night, I left the Far West, where Captain Marsh was handily taking script and coin from Tom Custer and Lieutenant James Calhoun in one stiff poker game during which time many stiff drinks were consumed. Major Marcus Reno, having purchased and consumed much of a half-gallon jug of whiskey, sang sad songs on the deck of the steamboat. His vocals haunted me as I wandered around camp, finding many soldiers excited for the fight certain to come.

Some troopers stuffed their greatcoats into the forks of trees, preferring not to be encumbered with extra weight. Each trooper has been ordered to carry fifteen days of rations and twelve pounds of oats for their mounts.

I overheard Custer telling two officers: "You had better carry along an extra supply of salt. We may have to live on horse meat before we get through."

On the other hand, Custer was jubilant when he talked to the younger officers, and they shared his excitement.

After one lieutenant exclaimed: "Won't we step high if we do get those fellows?," Custer responded: "Won't we? It all depends on you young officers. We can't get Indians without hard riding and plenty of it."

There will be much riding, beginning today, which has dawned clear and beautiful, an omen, perhaps, of the great victory to come.

Everything moves like clockwork. That has not changed since I joined the campaign in Dakota Territory on May 14. Yet after more than a month in the saddle, all seem to sense that our hard work shall soon pay massive dividends. In the days to come, surely this campaign will have met and defeated the enemy. For the Indians are soon to be a thing of the past on these Western lands. They go with the buffalo, they go with the bees, they become weaker and cannot stand against the massive force of the white men. When I file my next report, it is likely to include details of the defeat of the red devils. With the noon hour and our departure approaching, I must close and hand this to Captain Marsh for delivery. Major Brisbin has outfitted me with a mule, thus I am ready to ride.

Everyone is confident of victory.

To go with Custer, or stay with General Terry and join the Montana Column? For me, the answer is obvious.

I go with Custer, and will be there at the death.

Chapter Nine

Lieutenant Francis Gibson

22 June 1876
My Darling Katherine:
I take pencil in hand to express my everlasting love for you as soon I ride with Colonel Benteen, joining General Custer as we head south down the Rosebud in search of hostile Indians.

Last night, Benteen and General Custer quarreled again. They hate each other, a hatred that dates all the way back to the Battle of the Washita of 1868 in the Indian Territory. General Custer accused Benteen of killing an Indian child during that affair, to which the colonel replied that he had no choice, and that at least he did not abandon his men to be slaughtered by the Cheyennes.

In all likelihood, we are about to engage in a great battle, one for the history books, yet the captain of my troop and the leader of this campaign still fight over events that transpired eight years earlier. I pray that their disposition toward one another will play no part in the outcome of a fight between our soldiers and the Sioux.

I have been told that the general slept not at all last night. Nor did I.

My insomnia came not because of the argument

between Benteen and Custer. I dare say I have seen far too much bickering between those two men to keep me from slumber.

No, last night, Lieutenant William Cooke, our regimental adjutant, approached me with an unnerving request.

"This is my last will and testament," he said as he handed me a piece of paper. "I would like you to witness it for me."

I tried to make light of this. "What? Getting cold feet, Cookie? After all those years amongst the savages?"

For the longest while, he stared at me, his lips trembling, before he said in a ghostly whisper, "No. But I have a feeling that the next fight will be my last."

I signed his paper.

We are about to depart into uncertainty. Most of the command seems confident of victory, and, indeed, I feel no sense of dread or doom, yet Cookie's comments of last night, and that resigned look on his face, stay with me. I have no last will and testament, and fear that, should I die, I leave you nothing other than my name, my devotion, my love.

Don't fear the worst for me, my love. I will survive this campaign for no other reason than to feel your lips once more.

Your loving husband,
Francis

Chapter Ten

Black Elk

It was said that the first *wasicus* came from the place of water all over. Perhaps, after our great victory over the *wasicus* on the Rosebud, we have driven them back to the water, and now they shall let us live in peace.

I will speak of our camp. We had moved from the rugged hills of Ash Creek because our ponies had eaten most of the grass there, and so we put up our lodges across the Greasy Grass. It was *Wipazuke Waste Wi*, the Moon When Berries Are Good, and the grass here was good, high, feeding the thousands of ponies of our camp.

The Hunkpapas set up their lodges before the ford at the Dry Creek. At the far side of the camp, across from the ridge, were our friends, the *Sahiyelas*. Between the *Sahiyelas* and the Hunkpapa came the villages of the Sicangus, we Oglalas, the Minneconjous, and the Itazipacolas. Of the other Lakotas, the Oohenunpas and Sihasapas were so few in number, they joined other camps, as did some Gros Ventres, and maybe five warriors of *Mahpiya To*, the Arapahoes, who came looking for some Shoshones to fight.

It was funny. I must tell you of this. When the

Arapahoes arrived, we did not know them, and thought they were wolves of the *wasicus*, come to find us, to tell the *wasicus* where we were, so that they might attack and kill our women and ponies and dogs. Our warriors took their weapons, and were about to turn the strangers over to our women to be killed, when a *Sahiyela* called Two Moon stepped forward. He told us that, yes, these men were *Mahpiya To*, and meant no harm to us. So we did not kill them. We gave them back their weapons. We let them stay with us. We did not let them leave, just in case Two Moon was wrong, and that these men were wolves for the bluecoats.

In my twelve summers, never had I seen so many of The People of the Buffalo Nation and our friends together. It was good. More joined our village every day. Tired of living with the *wasicus* at the reservation called Standing Rock, Gall arrived. So did Crow King. Another one hundred and twenty lodges went up. Then Rain-In-The-Face came to join us. More lodges. More warriors. More friends. I could not count them all.

"Remember this," my father said to me. "It is unlikely that you or I or your sons or the sons of your sons shall ever see such a gathering."

The Greasy Grass was a good place. There were deer. There were antelope. There were cotton-woods, some ash, some willows. There were ravines, some very deep, and coulées, in which a boy like me could play, and hunt, and hide from my friends, or practice shooting grasshoppers with bow and arrow. The bluffs protected our village, and the Greasy Grass flowed wide and deep from much snow melt, much rain. The water tasted good, and cool. Here, we felt safe from the *wasicus*. It was a good place to be.

One of the wives of Sitting Bull, the Hunkpapa holy man, gave birth to twin boys, and there was much to celebrate. Yet not all could celebrate. Not all could be happy. Many remained in mourning, their hair shorn, their arms cut, some fingers chopped off for their loved ones lost in the big fight against the *wasicus* south along the Rosebud.

It was strange, moving across this great village, where singing and laughter came from the inside of one lodge to another where the wails of women and children filled me with much sadness.

Sitting Bull kept praying for peace, but some of the older warriors sang their strong-heart songs and did the Dying Dancing. If more *wasicus* come, they said, they were ready to fight. Many weapons, including the fast-shooting holy irons that could kill many without reloading, were in camp, although we had not many bullets for those weapons. I had only bow, arrows, and a knife. That was enough.

On the evening before the remembered Greasy Grass Fight, Sitting Bull stopped where I played with a dog's puppies. He spoke to me, a great honor, and said that he had seen me around the Oglalas, that he saw something deep in me, that he saw me becoming a holy man for The People of the Buffalo Nation. I was humbled, but proud. I stopped playing with the puppies. He handed me his pipe, and asked me to follow him.

I did.

We climbed a hill. The sun was setting. The wind blew warm, and the smell of the sweet grass mingled with the smoke from our cook fires, the smell of good food. It was good.

Sitting Bull had carried a robe with him, which he laid on the ground. To *Wakan Tanka*, he made offerings, and, standing on the robe, prayed.

This is what he said:

> "Great Spirit, pity me.
> In the name of the tribe I offer this pipe.
> Wherever the sun, the moon, the earth,
>   the four points of the winds, there you
>   are always.
> Father, save the tribe, I beg you.
> Pity me, we wish to live.
> Guard us against all misfortunes or
>   calamities.
> Pity me."

After he had smoked, letting me partake, too, we gathered his robe, and descended into camp.

"Will the *wasicus* come?" I asked him.

"If they do, they will die."

I had heard of his vision. Everyone had heard of his vision.

"Why do they fight us?" I asked.

He stopped, shook his head, and told me that years ago, perhaps even before I came to be with The People of the Buffalo Nation, the *wasicus* had attacked a village at *Takahokuty*, The Place Where They Killed the Deer, far to the east. During that fight, Sitting Bull said, he cried out to the enemy: "The Indians here have no fight with the *wasicus*. Why is it the *wasicus* come to fight with the Indians?"

I thought of that, and wondered how a *wasicu* might answer should I ask him those words.

Soon, however, I forgot all about that, what Sitting Bull had said, how I had felt, for we were back in camp. Sitting Bull retired to the circle of Hunkpapa lodges, and I stayed with my Oglalas. I found my friends. I was twelve years old. I was hungry. I was excited.

I was a boy.

The next morning, other boys and I went to the Greasy Grass. We wanted to swim, to play in the cool water, to cleanse ourselves.

Before I left the lodge, my father told me to take our stallions to graze. Then I could go swimming. "If anything happens," my father said, "you must bring the horses back as fast as you can, and keep your eyes on the camp."

So we took the stallions by the grass near the river, and then we went in to swim.

It was there, in that water, where I first would see the bluecoats, the people who came from the place of water all over. It was there that the Greasy Grass Fight was to begin.

Chapter Eleven

Lieutenant George Wallace

The bad feeling struck me after our first day's ride south along the Rosebud. Our pace had been unhurried, perhaps due to the slow, worn-out pack train, and we had covered twelve miles before General Custer called a halt, and we set up camp at the base of a towering bluff where the water tasted of alkali, but at least it was drinkable. On a hot day such as June 22, that was enough.

At sunset, "Officers' Call" sounded, and we gathered outside of the general's tent. General Custer said we would hear no more trumpets, except in an emergency, and that our troops should be prepared to march at five hundred hours each morning. "Reveille" would be silent. Rest halts would be at the discretion of troop commanders, but all troops should stay within supporting distance in case of a surprise attack.

"Husband your rations, gentlemen, and the strength of your livestock, for we might be out for a great deal longer than for which we have been rationed." He let those words sink in. "For I intend to follow this trail until we find the Indians, even if it takes us to the agencies on the Missouri River or all the way into Nebraska."

I glanced at Lieutenant Ed Godfrey, but said nothing. Those were not our orders.

"Any questions?"

"Why did we not bring the Gatling guns, sir?" someone behind me asked.

"For the same reason I declined Major Brisbin's offer of his troops. The Seventh, mister, can handle any Indians, and, believe me, when we meet those hostiles, there will be plenty to go around."

"I, for one, am very sorry you didn't take them," Colonel Benteen said, and Custer frowned. "Not so much the Gatlings, but I fear we might have need of those extra troops of cavalry."

"How many Indians do you anticipate, sir?" Lieutenant Godfrey asked.

"One thousand," he said cheerfully. "Mayhap fifteen hundred, but no more. As I say, plenty for all of us."

That was brash, confident, typical George Armstrong Custer, but what he said next troubled me.

"I will be glad to listen to suggestions from any officer of this command," he said, and I straightened, my mouth slackening. The general never asked to hear anything, especially a suggestion, from a junior officer. He told us what he was doing, and we knew what he expected from us. Always.

"Just make such a suggestion in the proper manner." He raised his hand, almost wagging his gauntleted finger. "But I want it distinctly understood that I shall allow no grumbling, and shall exact the strictest compliance with orders from everybody. I don't want it said of this regiment that it would be a good one if he could get rid of the old captains and let the lieutenants command the company."

Benteen stepped forward. I sucked in a breath.

"And who do you mean when you say 'grumbling'?"

"I want the saddle to go just where it fits," Custer shot back.

"Lieutenant Colonel Custer, do you know of any criticisms or grumblings from me?"

That was like Benteen, not only challenging the general, but refusing to bow to common military courtesy and refer to him by his brevet rank. Benteen would always remind the general that, according to his pay, he was a lieutenant colonel.

"No," Custer said, and that caused a thought to race through my mind: *Then, General, you must be deaf, for the captain would criticize you to anyone from a muleskinner to that newspaper reporter tagging along with us.*

"None of my remarks has been directed toward you, *Captain* Benteen." Not *colonel,* our white-haired malcontent's brevet rank. Custer could play that game, for whether a general or lieutenant colonel, he still outranked the captain.

"Does anyone else have anything to say?"

No one spoke, so Custer pulled out his pocket watch and suggested that we all synchronize our watches to Chicago time. As stems were wound, Lieutenant Calhoun said that his wife had sent him a cake, which now traveled with the pack train. "After we meet and defeat the savages," he said, "every officer in the regiment shall have a slice."

Custer laughed, said he hoped it was a chocolate cake, and dismissed our assembly.

As I walked with Lieutenant Donald McIntosh and Lieutenant Godfrey toward our bivouac, I glanced over my shoulder and saw the general sitting on a box in front of his tent as his striker, Burkman, pulled off his boots.

"Godfrey," I said softly, "I believe General Custer is going to be killed. At least, I think he believes that."

Godfrey stopped, his face paling. "What makes you think so, Wallace?"

"Asking *us* for *our* opinions, our suggestions? I've never heard Custer talk in that way before."

The next morning, after crossing the meandering Rosebud several times, we finally came across the lodge-pole trail Major Reno had found and followed during his "scout." A few miles later, we came into the abandoned campsite of the

Indians, and this was a most numbing experience. Again, I shot a nervous glance at Godfrey, and found him sucking in a deep breath.

We thought the great campsite we had found along the Yellowstone River had been enormous. The grass here had been almost eaten down to the sand, meaning this village had a great many horses.

General Custer saw things differently. "Here's where Reno made the mistake of his life," I overheard him telling Lieutenant Charles Varnum, who commanded our Indian scouts. "He had six troops of cavalry and rations enough for a number of days." He laughed, sounding more like the boy general we knew and less like that somber one from last night. "He'd have made a name for himself if he'd pushed on after them."

We made thirty-three grueling miles that day. Yet I could not sleep that night.

On the 24th of June, on another hot, sun-baked morning, we came to yet another old campsite. This one proved even more unnerving, not because of its size, but because of the scalp found hanging from what a Ree scout said was a dance lodge. The scalp, which the general passed around, was grotesque, but the Indians seemed troubled by something different.

Having no interest in fondling what had once belonged to a living white man, a soldier, in all likelihood, I turned my attention to the Arikarees, who pointed at odd drawings. Lieutenant Varnum signed with one of the scouts, and looked toward Custer. The general was busy talking to the newspaper reporter and Major Reno. That was rare, I thought—not meaning his conversing with Mr. Kellogg, but with Major Reno. The Crow scouts arrived, and Custer hurried toward them.

Our guidon flapped in the wind. Troopers wandered about the site, some looking for plunder, some trying to guess the size of the village we now pursued.

I stepped toward Varnum. "What is it that excites them so?"

Varnum spit. We had both been graduated from West Point in '72, so he knew he could trust me. Pointing at the symbols, he said: "Those are drawings of dead men. White men."

"Yes."

"All of their heads face east, toward the Dakotas, toward the Black Hills."

"And that means?"

"To the Arikarees, it means the Sioux medicine is strong. Too strong."

Varnum's face looked pale, sad, and I started to joke with him that he wasn't the superstitious sort, but then I remembered my own feelings after hearing General Custer talk at camp two nights earlier.

"God." Varnum straightened.

I whirled to see Lieutenant Godfrey bending to pick up the staff of the guidon. The wind had blown it down. He stuck it back into the sod, but almost immediately another gust of wind knocked it to the ground.

Another omen? I shut my eyes against such a thought.

General Custer signaled for us to join him, and my heavy boots carried me to our officers' conference.

"The Crows have found fresh tracks. Four ponies, one man afoot."

"Have they spotted us?" Lieutenant McIntosh asked.

"I don't think so," Custer said. "Not yet. And to keep it that way, we will march on separate trails. That should reduce the dust. Captains, you will go slowly. I do not wish any troop to overtake the scouts."

"It's a big camp," someone said.

"Yes, it is. And I don't want it to be a smaller one. If any of you find trails leading away from the main trail, I desire to know of it immediately. We don't want these boys to scatter."

"No trails are leading out, sir," Varnum said.

"Let's hope that stays true, Mister Varnum. It's a big village, gentlemen, but don't worry. What the Seventh can't lick, the entire U.S. Army can't lick." He smiled again. "I believe we shall find the village tomorrow. We will attack on Monday.

And mayhap we'll be back in Philadelphia to celebrate at the Centennial. Wouldn't that be crackerjack?" Before anyone could answer, he asked: "Where the devil is Colonel Benteen with the pack train?"

"He's having a devil of a time, General," Colonel Keogh said. "Or was the last time I saw him."

"It's the mules, sir . . . ," someone said.

Custer waved off the excuse. "He'll catch up. He'll have to. Let's ride, gentlemen. Ride into the valley. You have your orders. Dismissed."

So onward we rode. Deeper into the valley. And as I rode, watching the ridges, the skies, words I long thought I had forgotten escaped from the darkest recesses of my mind. My lips mouthed them silently at first, but soon, as we approached the place where we would camp on the night of June 24th, 1876, I heard myself saying them.

"Yea, though I walk through the valley of the shadow of death, I will fear no evil: for thou art with me; thy rod and thy staff they comfort me.

Thou preparest a table before me in the presence of mine enemies: thou anointest my head with oil; my cup runneth over.

Surely goodness and mercy shall follow me all the days of my life: and I will dwell in the house of the Lord forever."

Chapter Twelve

Captain Tom Custer

"What I'd hate," Bos says as he picks at his breakfast, "is to get killed by a tomahawk."

"Me, too," little Harry Reed says.

"You're a Custer, Bos!" Autie comes over, slapping our brother Boston's back. "You'll live forever."

"I'm not a Custer!" Harry fires back, smiling, but he isn't happy. He's nervous as hell.

"The blazes you aren't!" Autie argues. "We call you by my nickname sometimes, don't we?" Brevet Major General George Armstrong Custer lifts his mug of coffee. "We're all blessed with Custer's luck!"

Which reminds me of a joke, so I tell my older brother: "I do hope you live forever, Autie, and mine is the last voice you hear."

We laugh. Jimmi Calhoun steps inside to ask what's so funny, and we start laughing again.

I even laugh.

But the laughter dies, and I find my flask, to sweeten my coffee. Then I decide: *Who the hell needs coffee?*

Two Medals of Honor. Brevetted to first lieutenant after Waynesboro, to captain after

Namozine Church, to major after Sayler's Creek. Part of my right cheek is still blacked from a powder burn, another medal I reckon I won during the Rebellion. I arrested that man-killing savage, Rain-In-The-Face, at the Standing Rock Agency, and thought for sure my sun would set before I ever got him to the Fort Lincoln stockade, where, damn it all to hell, some friendlies helped that sumbitch escape. Hell, I even chased after that gunman—assassin is a better word—Wild Bill Hickok down in Kansas after he shot down two of our troopers.

Live forever? Hell, I have lived forever.

Autie comes over, takes my flask, begins screwing on the cap.

"Really, Tom," he says in stern rebuke. Libbie has turned him into a teetotaler. "It's three a.m."

Three in the morn. Dawn comes early in this country.

Something flashes through my mind. *Wouldn't it have been nice to have watched the sun rise this morn? Might have been your last.*

With a shrug, I reach for my tin cup. Autie paces nervously—I don't think he's even touched his coffee, and his breakfast is already cold— while Bos and Harry chatter quietly. Outside, I hear and smell the second helping of salt pork Autie's striker is frying up for breakfast.

And I laugh.

"What's so funny?" Bos asks.

Another shrug, and I say: "Nothing."

What I was thinking was: *Salt pork, lousy coffee, and three sips of rye. Is that fitting for a man's last breakfast?*

Yet that is something I shall not let my relations know.

This feeling I have been unable to shake. In all my years in this man's army, never have I been overcome by such dread. And, despite Autie's cocksureness, I fear he is of a similar vein. But, being Custers, we sha'n't let anyone see those pessimistic outlooks.

Sergeant Hughes sticks his head inside the tent. "Beggin' the general's pardon, sir, but that Ree scout, Red Star, just rode in. Says they've found a big village."

"Bully!" Autie tries to put his coffee on the table Private Burkman has set up, but misses it completely, and coffee spills onto the ground.

"Excellent!" Jimmi Calhoun pumps his fist in the air.

"Yeah," Harry Reed and Bos chime in, but their voices betray their true emotions.

Wetting my lips, I follow my brother, as his aide-de-camp, into the morning.

Live forever, eh? Forever ends today.

Chapter Thirteen

Private John Burkman

This ain't for no damned newspaper. I'm just tellin' you it, is all. Ain't for no newspaper. Ain't for nobody, 'less you want to tell Mrs. Libbie some of it.

Mrs. Libbie, oncet she told me that she didn't know how the gen'ral and herself could get along without me.

She said that. Ask her. She'll tell you it's so.

They call me Old Neutriment. 'Cause back at Fort Lincoln, I'm always raidin' the kitchen. But that grub ain't for me. Usually, it ain't. It's for Gen'ral Custer's dogs. Hell's fire, he must own pract'ly a hundred of 'em. Or the gen'ral hisself. Or Mrs. Libbie. Sometimes, I admit, it's for me, 'cause I gets hungry.

Old Neutriment. Don't care for that handle. Prefer what Mrs. Libbie calls me. Old Standby. 'Cause that what I was to 'em fine people.

Now, the gen'ral. He sure loved them hounds of his'n. That's how come he asked me to serve as his striker. Most troopers, they frown upon that job. Say it ain't fit. Say it's for cowards. Or for coloreds or Chinamen. But I don't mind. And I ain't no damned coward. Was one of the first from Allegheny County, Pennsylvania, to join

98

the fight against the Rebs. Seen the elephant at Bull Run. Seen it many a time. Ain't no damned coward. I'm a soldier. Been soldierin' longer than most of the boys in this here regiment.

Back to 'em hounds. I loved 'em dogs. All dogs. Some, their mamas died, so I had to raise 'em from pups. That'll bond you to 'em. Love hosses, too. So that's how come the gen'ral chose me. And how I come to love him so.

Oh, we had our share of disagreements. He had a mean temper, but so did I. But I'd learnt to control mine. Least, 'round Gen'ral Custer, and Mrs. Libbie. You couldn't get angry at Mrs. Libbie, but the gen'ral, well . . .

Anyhows, the gen'ral, he taken some of his hounds with him. Like he's goin' huntin'. On this campaign, he taken with him Bleuch, Tuck, and Lady. They's good huntin' dogs. Good hounds. Full of energy, full of spunk. Like Gen'ral Custer hisself.

And Gen'ral Custer, he's a good man. A great man.

Loved to talk. Fact is, when I'd go to sleep whilst he was still conversin', he'd toss dirt clods at me till I waken up, and I'd roll over, cussin', and see him just sittin' there, grinnin', and I'd take to grinnin' my ownself, and the gen'ral would start talkin' ag'in. Hard to get any sleep around him, yes, sir. Mighty hard.

So oncet that Injun scout rode in, we finally

knowed where the hostiles was. Breakfast ended real quick-like, and ever'body was in a commotion. I seen little Harry Reed, just bustin' his gut, gettin' ready, and I hurried over to him, and I tell him . . . "Harry, don't go with the gen'ral today. 'Pears like they's goin' to be considerable fightin'. You stay and guard camp."

Harry whirled. That kid could be as hot-headed as his uncle. "Me stay!" he shouted. "When there will be a fight? Why, John, you're crazy. That's what I came out West for, to see an Indian fight."

Couldn't argue none with him, and I knowed I couldn't argue with the gen'ral, but I tried. Not for young Harry Reed. For me.

The gen'ral was runnin' like a chicken with his head cut off, yellin' orders at officers and sergeants, wavin' me over. "Saddle Vic," he says to me. I knowed why he wanted Vic. His other horse, Dandy, he's a good one, too, but Vic is short for Victory, and the gen'ral, he can be a touch superstitious. So I got Vic ready, and handed him the reins, and says I to him, I says . . . " 'Pears like I ought to be goin' along, Gen'ral."

He leaped in his saddle like he hadn't heard. But his ears was always sharp, and he knowed what I said, and he turned to me, frownin' at first, but then his face started relaxin', and he smiled. "No, John," says he. "You've been doing guard duty three nights in succession. You're tired out. Your place is with Captain McDougall and the pack train. But if we should have to send for more ammunition, you can come in on the home-stretch."

Wouldn't let me argue none with him. Turned Vic around, and loped over to one of his trumpeters. By then, all the soldiers was ready. One of 'em turned to me and shouted . . . "Hey, Old Neutriment! Shall we bring you a scalp, or do you want a live squaw?"

Then the dogs, the gen'ral's hounds, they's up in a roar, barkin' and pullin' at their chains. And I knowed Bleuch, knowed that if he gotten loose, wouldn't be no stoppin' him. He'd be racin' ahead of the gen'ral's entire command. Likely to warn the Injuns that the wrath of God was comin'. So I run over to the dogs, and I grabbed chains and collars, and they's tuggin' on me so bad, and my heart's just breakin' as the gen'ral rode off.

Couldn't hardly see 'em no more, 'cause tears was blindin' me so.

And I recollected after we'd just left the fort, how Mrs. Libbie, her eyes red from all her own cryin', she had come to me, and she had said . . . "Good bye, John. You'll look after the gen'ral, won't you?"

I just leaned down, and whispered in Bleuch's ears. I told him . . . "Damn it all to hell. Gen'ral Custer's gone and left me. Wouldn't let me come with him. How can I keep my promise to Missus Libbie? How can I look after the gen'ral now?"

Chapter Fourteen

Half Yellow Face

The trail we follow is big. Many big. Many warriors. We know this. Even some white men in blue coats know this.

The one called Godfrey once asked the white-eye scout, Charley Reynolds, how many Indians he think we follow. Godfrey say one thousand five hundred.

Reynolds say: "You think you can whip that many?"

Godfrey say: "I guess so."

I laugh. Reynolds laughs. Reynolds tells soldier . . . "Well, we are going to have a damned big fight."

Big damned fight. Reynolds, who signed me what was said, knows. I know.

Long Hair thinks he shall have easy fight. He read no signs. Lakota medicine is strong. Big strong. Long Hair medicine is weak. Long Hair even cut own hair before leaving the soldier fort. No long hair. Short. Remind me of story a black robe told us at soldier fort, about a big, strong man who let white woman cut his hair. When hair was gone, he lost power. Was weak. Got eyes burned out. Made into slave.

Finally he die. Maybe so same with Long Hair.

Me, other Arikarees, and Crows join Peaked Face, the white bluecoat leader of us Indian scouts, and pick our way at night into Mountains of the Wolf. As sun rises, we look down to where all hills seem to go flat.

There, for first time, we see how many Lakotas and other bad Indians we are about to fight. It is the pony herd, and there are more horses than stars at night.

Peaked Face looks through his see-far glasses, lowers them, rubs his eyes with the rag around his neck. "Too much dust," he says. "Not enough sleep. I can't see a damned thing."

I do not know what those white man words mean, but I can tell that he not see pony herd.

A Crow scout speaks to Mitch Boyer. I sign to Boyer, who can see that herd. He turns to Peaked Face, and says . . . "Varnum, look for worms on the grass. They say that's what horses will look like from this distance."

Peaked Face tries again, but, frustrated, cusses white man words, and lowers see-far glasses. "I just can't see them."

Boyer now is as frustrated as Crows and me. "Well, they are there, damn it."

"I believe you, Mitch," Peaked Face says. "I just can't see them."

Peaked Face can't see, but he knows we speak truth. That much I can see.

I can see something else, though, and it is not Lakota ponies. It is smoke from the fires of the bluecoats. Cooking breakfast.

I scream. Crow scouts scream. We point.

"What are they saying now?" Peaked Face asks.

Boyer can see, too. He spits, wipes his mouth, cusses more white man words, and says . . . "They are angry, Varnum, that the soldiers are cooking breakfast. They want to know if you want to let all of the Sioux know we're this close to them. They want to know if you want to get killed."

Boyer signs to me what he has told Peaked Face, who looks at the smoke where his warriors cook their breakfast and make their coffee. He cusses white man words.

Peaked Face writes on paper, hands the paper to Red Star, a good Arikaree scout, tells him to take this to Long Hair. So Red Star and our friend, Bull, mount their ponies, and ride away.

So now we wait for Long Hair, but then I see dust. Not far. A couple of Crows and I mount our horses, ride. Now it is my turn to cuss white man words, for there are two Lakotas, an older man riding a pony and leading another with a rope, and a young boy trailing, whipping the roped pony along. They ride toward the bluecoats.

We hurry back to Peaked Face, tell him. He cusses. "If they spot the column, they'll warn the village, and the Indians will scatter to the winds. We have to kill them before they can send out a warning."

Boyer signs again to me. I nod. So we ride, hiding our presence in trees and coulées, but the Lakotas turn another way. Then we see more dust.

Peaked Face shouts. He is saying that this dust comes from Long Hair and all his warriors.

Seven Indians are on another ridge, watching the bluecoats come. When I point, Peaked Face cusses again, and the Indians disappear.

Instead of riding after those Indians, Peaked Face decides to go to Long Hair. There is no reason to ride after any Lakotas. By now, whole village must know the bluecoats are coming.

We meet Long Hair, who seems happy. "Well, you've had a time of it," Long Hair says, and Peaked Face nods.

We ride back to the spot from where we saw the pony herd.

Long Hair is just like Peaked Face. Blind when it comes to seeing plenty of ponies.

"I've been on the prairie for many years," Long Hair says. "I've got mighty good eyes, and I can't see anything that looks like Indian ponies."

Boyer screams. "If you do not find more Indians in that valley than you ever saw together before, you can hang me!"

Boyer never scout for Long Hair till this time. Many time, we hear what good Indian fighter Long Hair is. Now we know. Long Hair blind. Long Hair damned fool.

Long Hair jumps up. Laughs, but mood not good. "It would do a damned sight of good to hang you now, wouldn't it?"

Don't know what words mean, but know that Long Hair cannot see the ponies, either. Are all white men so blind?

Reynolds pulls out see-far glasses from a leather case, offers them to Long Hair. Boyer and Peaked Face point in the direction of the herd, of the massive village. This time, Long Hair whistles.

At last, he can see.

While Long Hair and Peaked Face talk with the other white men, I walk over to Red Star and Bull.

Bull has started his death song.

I speak to Red Star.

Red Star shakes head. "I tell Long Hair that we will find enough Lakotas to keep us fighting two or three days. He says . . . 'I guess we will get through them in one day.' "

"They have seen us," I tell him.

"I know," Red Star says.

"It has been good riding with you all these years."

"Yes."

Behind me, Long Hair make orders. Other bluecoats laugh. A Crow signs to me what they are saying.

One says that Long Hair will take them all to some big white man party in some big white man city many days' travel from here.

"And we will take Sitting Bull with us," another says.

They laugh.

I look toward pony herd, toward more dust from the village.

"It will be all over soon!" a bluecoat shouts. A Crow signs to me what this fool white man has said.

Yes, I think, it will be all over soon.

Long Hair has decided to hide all bluecoats until the next day. The Crow scouts and Peaked Face try to change his mind. Long Hair does not want to believe that the Lakotas and Cheyennes have seen us. Only when Long Hair's bluecoat brother rides to the hill and tells him of Indian sign does he change his mind.

A bluecoat blows on horn. It has been days since we have heard this noise. The bluecoats meet, but only Long Hair talks until one bluecoat points off in another direction. I know what he means, even if I do not know the words and there is no one to sign to me what he says. But I know. He knows that the other bluecoats are in that direction.

And I know what Long Hair says. He jabs his finger toward the Indian camp. He is telling the bluecoats that there are no Indians that way, only his way. That is where we go. No get help from other bluecoats. Long Hair will do this by himself, with men he has.

Reynolds and Boyer speak up now, and I know what they say. They warn Long Hair that this is largest bunch of Indians any of them ever see. I know what Long Hair is saying. He say he no care how many Indians, long as they no scatter.

Reynolds and Boyer turn away. Both angry.

After more talk from Long Hair, bluecoats head to horses. Some excited. Some pale. One wets britches.

We mount our horses, and ride downhill.

We ride toward village.

Then, Long Hair does foolish thing. He orders bluecoats to divide. One will go with long-face soldier in straw hat named Reno. Others will go with mules and wagons and white-haired one named Benteen. Long Hair lead others.

A foolish, foolish thing. I ride to Boyer. I beg him to tell Long Hair not to divide men.

"There are too many of the enemy for us," I say. "Even if we stay together. If you must fight, keep us all together."

Long Hair has no ears. He will not listen. He tells Boyer, who tells me . . . "You do the scouting, and I will attend to the fighting."

So this is where journey ends.

I slip off my pony, and take off clothes. I join Arikaree and Crow brothers in singing our death songs. I paint face.

Through Boyer, Long Hair angrily asks what I am doing.

I look up at Long Hair, whose hair is short now like the man who got blinded and was made a slave and died many winters ago.

"Because you and I going home today," I tell Long Hair, "by trail that is strange to us both."

Chapter Fifteen

Major Marcus Reno

To be delivered to:
Ross Reno
C/O J.W. & Bertie Orth
Pittsburgh, Penn.
In the event of my death
Son:

I write you from a hole dug on a hill in Montana Ty. all around me is Death. The smudge on the torn corner of this paper comes from the Brains & Blood of an indian scout. God! It splattered across my face, blinded me. Yes it More of that I will tell you, tell the world, later. I write you because, I fear, in the months to come my name, my reputation, my career, my honor, & your last name will be dragged through the mud. I fear I will not survive to spare you the ordeal other 12-year-olds might subject you to.

Please know this. Believe this.

I was not Drunk.

I am not a coward.

I did the best any soldier could. I am no indian fighter. I did not want to be here. I asked for a leave to be with you after your mother's untimely passing. Damn this man's army.

It's Custer's fault. where the hell is he?

I am not drunk.

I am scared. I admit that. Most of my command is. I hear praying. Begging. Crying. God. Has Someone else has just been Shot? I did the best . . . I am NOT DRUNK!

Where is Custer? he said he would support me.

This might be the only record to survive this butchery. I pray no savage will burn this. Or tear it in shreds & let the winds scatter it.

Here is my account of what happened:

I am not drunk. I was not drunk when it all went to hell.

The command left the place where Lt. Varnum saw the indian village, the place he said reminded him of the old Crow's Nest at West Point, we were in column of 4s. Custer sent Capt. Benteen's men toward the bluffs. He told him to "pitch into anything." Custer took 5 companies down one side of a creek. I led my 3 companies down the other.

God, it was hot. Dry. dusty. miserable. We rode on, mouths parched, horses already lathered with a salty foam of sweat. My lips were cracked. I wet them, slaked my thirst, from my canteen.

Then rode up the scout, Fred Gerard, like he was in a race. "We've found our indians!" he shouted. "Runnin' like devils! The damned Rees won't go after them."

"Let us at them!" said some damned young fool in my command.

I drank again. Just to calm my nerves. It wasn't just whiskey in the canteen. It had been cut with water. I was thirsty. I wasn't drunk.

Wm. Cooke was suddenly there. Don't know where he came from. Well, from Custer, of course, on a horse.

"Major," he said, "I have orders from Gen. Custer. The indians are about 2½ miles ahead. On the jump they are. Go forward as fast as you think proper. Charge them wherever you find them. Gen. Custer will support you."

Read THAT AGAIN! Custer said he would support me, Ross. He said that. There were witnesses. If any of them's still alive now.

Well, I was about to pitch into the savages. They'd accused me of butchering my chance at a brevet, at glory, at maybe even rivaling Custer when I hadn't attacked or tried to attack those indians when I'd led my command down the Powder. Now I'd get a chance. I'd show Custer. I'd show Gen. Terry. I'd show everyone.

I waved my straw hat, damned near dropped my canteen. Rode on toward the village. As I crossed the creek, I saw Gen. Custer, waving his big hat. "Take your battalion & try & overtake & bring them to battle!" Custer cried. "I will support you." See. He said it, too. The general.

where the hell is he?

"& take the scouts along with you."

That's all the orders I had. That's all the plan was. I was to find the village. Attack. Custer would come in to help. to reap all the glory. Some Crows stuck with the general. The Arikarees, practically all of them, followed me. Even Bloody Knife. He was half-Arikaree, half-Sioux. Varnum & Wallace left Custer. They wanted to be in on the fight. I had a 100, 150, I don't know. Not enough. Not even with three dozen indian scouts.

Most of the recruits riding with me were just that. Recruits. Green as spring. Could barely stay in the saddles. We rode a hard trot maybe three miles. I had to keep barking over my shoulder, "Keep your horses well in hand, boys. Stay in formation."

I noticed dr. porter, my lone surgeon, a contract surgeon, not a career Army man. Asked him if he were armed. he said, "No, Major." Therefore, I offered him my Remington Rolling Block rifle.

He declined. "I'm a doctor, Major," he said, trying to smile.

he's a damned fool. too young, too inexperienced. I bet now he wished he'd taken up my generous offer.

Contract surgeons. College boys. We need military men in the Army.

Then we reached where the creek flowed into a

river. We rode into the Little Big Horn River. I let my horse drink.

Lt. DeRudio—Count No Account, as we call the pompous ass—rode past me, drenching me with water. I cussed him, returned my flask. Told him not to drown me before a bullet could kill me.

Yes, I thought I would die. I might yet still.

Then here came Gerard, the interpreter. It is said that he had once married a Ree. Custer loved that old boy. I cared not a whit for him. He yelled at me, "Major, the indians are coming up the valley to meet us."

Meet us? Fight us? Surely, the indians must be running. Scattering. Like they always do. I stared, said, "Forward," & led my canteen command.

Gerard rode away. I guess to tell Custer what he figured the indians were doing. I led my men out of the water, over the hills, out of the timber. Let the recruits dismount, tighten their cinches. we reassembled into columns of 4s.

after climbing the bank, I could see indians. Teepees. Scores of them. Women & children running around like chickens with their heads chopped off. The Arikarees rode across. Downstream, I saw a bunch of indian ponies. Some of my scouts rode after them. I reached inside my tunic, brought out my flask. It wasn't cut with water. I wasn't drunk, Ross. I was not drunk. There's nothing wrong with taking a bracer, a good, strong bracer, before mixing into a fight like this. I drank. Just a sip. For my parched tongue, my throat caked with dust. Checked my watch. It was almost 3 o'clock on the nose. Damned not.

"There goes Custer!" somebody yelled.

Across the river, Sure enough, I saw the general, riding old Vic, his white-legged sorrel. riding hard. Away from us. I guess to circle the village. Prevent them from scattering.

We rode at a trot. Then a gallop. The land was flatter here. I could see indians. Some of the boys saw Custer leading his men. They cheered. Waved their hats. One of them even began singing some foreign ditty.

I tossed my flask to Benny Hodgson. He looked like he needed a bracer worse than me.

"Stop that damned noise!" I shouted. Then I yelled something else.

"Charge!"

Spurring my mount, I bit my lip, leaned forward, & rode into battle.

"There's only 50 of them, boys!" one of my lieutenants called out. He stupidly fired a pistol.

50. We could handle that. I could see a bunch of indians, 50 I guess, working their horses, running those mounts not toward us, just back & forth. A dust cloud must have stretched a mile into the sky. I barked out for G Troop to take the right flank, along the timber. M Troop rode on the left, next A. I glanced over my shoulder. Saw Custer's

men riding. But not toward us. Going elsewhere still. some of his boys seemed to be raising their hats.

Hell.

There was a ditch ravine. Looked as if it led to the depths of Hades, & out of this hole came those red devils.

The indians were supposed to be running. These weren't. They were, God, standing to fight. by this time I could see beyond that thick dust, see the hostile village maybe a half mile away. 50 lodges my ass. God. 400. 500. Mayhap 1,000.

I was not drunk.

I was not about to lead my command to be slaughtered.

"Battalion halt!" I yelled. "Prepare to fight on foot. Dismount!"

Hodgson rode off to relay my orders.

Jesus. Green horses. Untrained mounts. Not all of the boys could stop their horses. Some of them kept on riding. Riding straight to all those damned indians. disappeared in the dust. Still now, I can hear their screams, hear the bullets, hear the savages wail out. Thank God I could not see what happened to those damned young white men.

We approached in skirmish line, shooting, marching, shooting. Sweat blinded me. I admit that I wished I hadn't given Hodgson my flask. With our boys, I marched. The indians put up furious resistance. I wanted to look back, for once, to see Custer coming. But couldn't.

Maybe we'd gone 100 yards. I called out to halt. The boys dropped to the ground, firing prone. Some turned mounds from prairie dog holes into breastworks. Our officers marched behind them, yelling out for them to make their shots count, to steady their nerves.

"My rifle's jammed!" some soldier cried out.

"Use your knife to pry out the cartridge!" Capt. French ordered. I glanced down at the skirmishers. Hell, half the boys' Springfields had become overheated. They were pulling those hot copper cartridges out of the chambers.

We were doing all right. Few casualties. Some of the boys sang out that we'd have them on the run soon. a few recruits even laughed. But, God, those indians . . . More & more seemed to pour from that village, out of the ravines, into the woods.

Everything will be fine, I told myself. Custer's coming. We're all right. We're all right. I'm all right. I'm not drunk.

Some trooper with his face blacked by powder tugged my sleeve. I spun, almost shot the dumb bastard.

"What is it, you damned fool?"

"I been screamin' your name, Major," he says back at me. "Capt. Moylan wants to speak to you, sir. It's urgent."

Hell. I fumbled with cartridges to reload my revolver as I followed the trooper to Capt. Myles Moylan.

Moylan looked steady enough. I wiped my brow as he told me, "Major, about 200 hostiles have flanked us to the left. Indians are behind us now, sir."

"Custer?" I demanded.

"I asked Billy Jackson if he could ride to the general, Major," Moylan says. "He says there are too many to ride through."

What the hell else could I do? I spun around, yelling, "Retreat to your horses, men." Then I began walking—no, son, I was not running, not abandoning my men—I just had to get to the trees. But there was Hodgson, so I took back my flask, emptied it, kept going.

A few troopers, bloody cowards, shot past me. Running.

Good old Capt. French, though, he was strong. I heard him yell: "I'll shoot the first man that turns his back on the enemy! We're falling back, slowly. Slowly, do you hear me? In order. Keep up a continual fire, you damned fools!"

We reached the timbers. I thought it would be better there, but, God. The din surrounded us. Bullets. Indian yells. The horrible noise from bone whistles. Men—white men—begging, crying, screaming from wounds. Horses bolting. Dust & gunsmoke blinded us.

I found Varnum. No, I guess, he found me.

"How are things on the line?" I asked him.

"I don't know."

"Well, hell, find out. And let me know."

He ran. I figured I'd never see him again.

Cowards. Surrounded by cowards. Surrounded by indians. Damn, there were 1,000s of them. Arrows whistled overhead. I smelled the odors of Hell. Like Satan had opened the door.

Where was Custer? & Benteen? Had they both forsaken ~~me~~ us?

Some Rees rode into the trees. Dismounted. One ran to me, signed that they had reached the village, killed some Sioux.

Angrily, I snapped at him, "Why didn't you stay & kill more?"

I didn't sign this, but my tone must have been enough. He signed back: "Too many."

Some damned Sgt. ran up to me. "Sir, the indians have killed about a dozen horses in the rear."

I just stared. At the arrow shaft sticking through his left shoulder.

In control. I remained in control. Was not panicked. But I knew this. This was clear. If we stayed in these damned woods, we'd all be BUTCHERED. "Tell Capt. Moylan to mount up. Column of 4s." He ran, the sergeant, & I could see the bloody trail he was leaving from that arrow. That arrow. In his arm. God.

"Hodgson!" I hurried over to Benny. "Benny, find French. Tell him we're retreating. Column of 4s. Be ready."

"Retreating?" Hodgson asked. "Where?"

"How the hell do I know? Just find French."

A bullet clipped a branch over his head, & Hodgson needed no other inspiration to skedaddle. I found McIntosh, gave him those orders, mounted my own horse, rode over to Moylan.

I could hear, above those damned indian whistles, above the screams of my soldiers, my boys. They were yelling out names, the names of their horse holders. Varnum was shouting at them. "For God's sake, don't leave the line. Don't leave the line. Boys, boys, boys, we have enough here to whip the whole Sioux nation!"

Who was he kidding?

I found Moylan, but the fool wasn't in his saddle. He held the reins to his nervous horse in one hand, a revolver in his right. Saw me. Aimed. Fired at some indian.

"Where should we go?" I asked him.

He didn't answer. kept shooting that revolver. I pointed. To the ridge. "There," I said. "That's where Custer was."

Yes. We might make it there. Get there. Regroup. Maybe Custer & Benteen would find us.

Moylan swung into the saddle. A bullet tore off

his hat. His horse side-stepped, but Moylan got the gelding under control. Fired again.

"Major!" I turned. It was Varnum. He yelled, "Where are you going?"

Where did he think we were going? We were getting out of this death trap.

the noise. The damned noise. Eagle whistles & bullets. Men screaming. indians yipping. I'd barely heard Varnum.

Bloody Knife came to me. I had to sign to him. Was trying to find out where the indians would go once we left these woods. Bloody Knife was trying to figure out what I'd asked him.

His mouth opened. And . . . And . . .

God.

Jesus.

Son-of-a-bitch.

His face exploded. Blood. Brains. My face was drenched. The front of my tunic. I spit out the carnage. Wiped my face. Bloody Knife was dead. Dead. Dead.

I dismounted. I had to. Had to wipe the gore away. I don't know. I guess I ordered, "Dismount," because a lot of the boys were doing just that.

"Mount!" I yelled. "Mount." I climbed back into the saddle.

Some boys didn't obey. I yelled again, but they didn't move. Then I understood.

They were dead.

Dead.

God.

One poor guy was on the ground, gut shot. A dead man, for sure. But his pards wouldn't leave him, even though he kept telling them to go on, that he was dead, to save themselves.

Yes. Save themselves. Save us. That's what we had to do.

"Any of you men who wish to make your escape," I said, "draw your revolvers & follow me!"

I gouged my horse's flanks with spurs. & bolted out of those woods.

I pray I shall be able to finish this letter later.

Chapter Sixteen

Pretty White Buffalo Woman

It was said that we Lakota tricked the *wasicus*. That we led them into a trap. Hear me. We did not know the *wasicus* were coming. At least, we did not expect them to come so soon. To attack us. We were not ready. The *wasicus* surprised us that afternoon. They could have captured us. They could have killed us all.

They were fools.

That is why we drove them away.

Oh, we saw *Mila Hanska*, the Long Knives. Saw them on the hills, across the Greasy Grass. We could see the sun, low in the afternoon, reflecting light off their weapons. "*Wasicus*! *Mila Hanska*!" The cry spread across our circle of lodges.

These Long Knives were more than a long-gun shot from the river, so our warriors knew we had time. Time for our brave young men to run to their horses. We had time. Time to get ready to fight before the *wasicus* attacked our Hunkpapa circle.

What we did not see were the other *wasicus*. Those are the ones who surprised us. We planned to move. We busied ourselves. I was taking down my teepee. And then. Like that. The Long Knives were upon us.

I dropped the pole, and turned to look. Dust. Long Knives. Yes, they were far away, but not so far that their long guns could not do damage. Teepee poles were splintered. Bullets tore through our homes.

Sitting Bull came out of his lodge, yelling that we should talk to those *wasicus*, that we should see what they wanted.

We did not listen to our great holy man. Perhaps we were too frightened, or confused. Maybe, however, we knew what Sitting Bull did not.

That these *wasicus* came not to make peace, not bearing gifts. They came to kill. To butcher. To destroy us.

With my own eyes, even I, just a plain Lakota woman, could see what the Long Knives wanted. I did not have to ask some *wasicu*. They were not here to talk to us. They wanted to break our spirit.

I saw one warrior—for most of our men were away gathering the ponies—run toward his painted pony. But he never made it. He stumbled. He fell dead in front of his teepee.

Women screamed in terror. Our little ones cried for their mothers. The mothers called out the names of their children.

It was a time of crying. Of fear. Of death.

Others, brave men, many of them old, rode back

and forth. To hide the village from the *wasicus*. Those devil *Palani* came into the village. They killed our women. They killed our children. But by then, some of our men had come back, and they drove these bad Indians back toward the timber.

Still, I figured we would be dead soon. I heard death songs being sung all around me.

I turned around. How could this be? How could those soldiers, riding on the other side of the river, be attacking we Hunkpapa now. But, no, there they were, those *wasicus* on the ridge, the sunlight still bouncing off their weapons. Some of them I could see were waving their hats toward the other *wasicus*, the ones near our village, the ones killing my friends. Then I knew. I knew that this *wasicu* leader was one of cleverness. His warriors were attacking us from this side while other *wasicus* rode toward the other side of our great Indian village.

Little ones, boys and girls, ran naked from the Greasy Grass, where they had been swimming. Through all this noise, all the smoke and dust, the children somehow could recognize the voices of their mothers, who cried out their names.

This I knew: We would soon be dead.

Wakan Tanka, however, came to save us. He stopped the Long Knives. I could not believe my eyes, but the *wasicus* halted. They could have ridden into our village. They could have destroyed the spirit of the Lakota. They could have—would have—killed me.

Yet they stopped their horses. Some of those in blue coats held three or four horses. Or tried to. For many horses pulled away and fled from our village. Some horses carried their riders right into our camp.

These men, our warriors killed. They were fools.

But more foolish were those who stopped.

That is when I heard Sitting Bull say: "I don't want my children fighting until I tell them to. The *wasicus* may be here to make peace. They may be bringing rations to us." I turned away from the *wasicus*, saw Sitting Bull take a long holy iron from one of his nephews and give his nephew his shield.

Since the Long Knives no longer charged into our village, but still fired their guns, Sitting Bull prayed. Afterward, he told his two nephews, One Bull, to whom he had given his shield, and Good Bear Boy: "Go make peace with the *wasicus*."

So One Bull and Good Bear Boy mounted their ponies and rode. But the fool *wasicus* would not let them make peace. They almost killed Good Bear Boy. One Bull saved him. They rode back to our circle.

By that time, Sitting Bull had mounted his pony, but a *wasicu* bullet killed his pony. This angered Sitting Bull. He yelled: "Now my best horse is shot! It is like they have shot me."

He pointed the holy iron he had taken away from One Bull. He shouted: "Attack them!"

"*Hoka hey!*" our warriors cried out. They rode or ran. They fired holy irons. They fired arrows.

Sitting Bull found another pony. He mounted it. He yelled to our warriors: "We have everything to fight for. And if we are defeated, we shall have nothing to live for. Therefore let us fight like brave men."

I could hear more death songs. So I began to sing a strong-heart song.

Most of the *wasicus* fled into the trees. Our warriors attacked. More warriors came. From the pony herds. From the other circles. Oglalas and Minneconjous, even *Sahiyelas* and other tribes, other Lakota bands. We would fight *Mila Hanska* together.

We numbered many. Far more than those *wasicus* who had tried to surprise us.

I turned around, still singing, but wondering about those other *wasicus*. Yes, they had disappeared from the ridge. They would be attacking other circles soon, but many of our warriors were running off in that direction. We would be waiting.

Yes. It was a good day to die.

Louder I sang my strong-heart song.

As I sang, a young *Sicangu* ran past me. He stopped. He turned and came to me. I stopped singing. He kissed me. He stepped back. He

Chapter Seventeen

George Herendeen

Ah, ain't it grand to be Irish!

How else could I be alive?

Up until three days ago, I was scouting for John Gibbon, but he assigned me to Custer's boys, and Custer sent me off with Major Reno. Let me put it down for the record that I don't truly blame the major for this bloody fiasco. You get warm blood and gore splashed across your face and see how much nerve you still have. Nay, the lad did all he could, and I am not one to begrudge a man for taking a nip or two. But, Mary, Jesus, and Joseph, never should he have ordered us out of those woods.

Granted, things were getting ticklish, but Custer and Benteen would be coming soon, and the trees offered shelter, and Indians didn't care much to go charging into woods. Only then I heard Reno's booming voice: "Any of you men who wish to make your escape, draw your revolvers and follow me!"

Some of those green recruits must have been jumping the gun a mite, or they were raring to go, for they didn't follow the major, they bolted out of those woods even before Reno charged out.

Theirs not to reason why,
Theirs but to do and die.
Into the valley of Death
Rode the six hundred.

Well, maybe not six hundred, but Lord Tennyson, English dung though he may be but one grand poet, could bloody well have been writing about the Little Big Horn and not Balaclava.

I swung onto me blue roan, and joined the horde of white men, scared witless.

We hit the flats, and like madmen rode for the Little Big Horn. At first, the Indians did not give chase, likely because they could not figure out what we were doing. Indians aren't ones to leave their women and children, so I believe they thought we might plan on swinging around and hitting their camp. Yet when they understood that attack wasn't our prevailing sentiment, but saving our arses was, they came charging.

Cannon *(Indians)* to right of them,
Cannon *(Indians)* to left of them,
Cannon *(Indians)* in front of them
Volley'd and thunder'd;
Storm'd at with shot and shell,
Boldly they rode and well,
Into the jaws of Death,
Into the mouth of hell . . .

Ah, but then we hit the prairie dog villages. Holes. Deadly holes. Horses went down, sending blue-clad troopers into the dirt. Down fell me roan, snapping her leg, and over her neck I flew, figuring: *Well, 'tis the end of me. Farewell, old friends from Parkman Township, Ohio. To all the lasses I never had a chance to kiss . . .*

Up I came, if only to me knees, revolver in hand. Horses thundered past me. Some fell. Many made it through. I heard screams of terror. I tried to call out for one of the troopers to stop, but they couldn't have heard me if I had a voice as strong as Major Reno's, and nobody in his right mind would have stopped.

Through the dust, I saw Lieutenant McIntosh shot off his horse. Near him, down went a fellow scout, the black man who once lived with the Indians, Isaiah Dorman. I'd join them soon.

With cocked revolver, I turned to face me death, maybe take a few braves with me, to prove me bravery to these wild bucks, only to freeze at the sight of twenty, nay, thirty Sioux braves, yipping and yelling, brandishing coup sticks or rifles with beaded stocks and forearms. Me breath I held. 'Twas no need to fire. Just watch them ride over me—grand, they looked; no shame in being killed by the likes of warriors as handsome, as bold, as these.

But, by the saints, those Indians rode right by me, as if I were invisible. Maybe it was the dust.

Maybe it was because I was low to the ground, maybe because me hair was dark and long and greasy from sweat. Or maybe it was because those Indians were bound and determined to kill anyone wearing blue, and donned I was in duck trousers and a dark brown shirt.

They rode past me, firing at the soldiers, and I rose like Phoenix and sprinted for the timbers, before the next wave of Indians galloped by.

Dived, I did. Flew what seemed like thirty rods, but in reality no more than a few feet, into the woods. A branch almost scalped me.

Scalped me. Wouldn't that have been something! Surrounded by three thousand five hundred warriors, and get me topknot lifted by a tree branch!

Hearing shouts, twigs snapping, I came up, leveled me revolver, and almost put a bullet in Sergeant Charles White's gut.

"Good God!" I came to me feet, glanced over my shoulder as more Indians galloped after those fleeing soldiers, then turned back to the sergeant, whose right arm was a bloody mess. "What the devil are you still doing here?"

"Where is everybody, George?" he asked. "Where's Reno?"

Damnation. "Retreating." He and other lads from M Troop hadn't heard the order.

"Retreating?" White was a short man, fair-skinned with gray eyes and light hair. A Hun by birth, but a man, as the cowboys often put it, to ride the river with.

"Back across the Little Big Horn." I pointed the Colt's barrel in the general direction. "To find Benteen or Custer. To regroup."

White spun. "Men," he yelled to the handful of troopers still in these woods, "we're mounting . . . !"

Shoving the Colt into my waistband, I barked out something, stepped over a dead body, waving my hands. "No, no, no, no, no."

The sergeant stopped.

"You ride out now," I pleaded with the boys, "you'll all be killed."

I had to catch me breath. Lonesome Charley Reynolds was mounting his horse, and a lot of the soldiers stared at him. Without begging the sergeant's pardon, I hurried over to the scout. "Charley," I cried, "don't ride out! We can't get away from this timber."

Maybe he didn't hear me. Maybe he was too scared. I don't know. He swung into that saddle, spurred his horse, almost ran me over. Now that I think of it, now that I again picture the last time I stared into Charley's face, I don't think he even saw me.

His horse plunged from the woods. I chased after him, stopping at the timber's edge.

"Sergeant!" I turned back to White, but by then most of his men had mounted, some of them riding double, though Sergeant White didn't have the strength to climb up behind a trooper. Figured to walk, he did.

I looked back, saw Charley's horse go down in the prairie dog village, just a rod from where me roan now lay dead. Charley came up, brave he was, firing at a mass of Indians. I heard the yippings, the cries, saw the war clubs raising in the air, saw the Indians and the dust surround Charley. And I never saw him again.

Sergeant White witnessed all of this, too. Which might have saved all of our lives.

Those boys in blue no longer appeared so eager to get out of these woods.

"Listen," I said, now that I had their attention. "We'll go back deeper into this thicket. Sioux and Cheyennes, they don't like charging into woods. Lie down. Don't move. Don't talk."

"Hide?" a corporal said with arrogance and contempt.

"Damn right. We *hide!*" I moved deeper into the woods, wondering what would happen now.

God bless Sergeant White. He might have been born a miserable Hun, but he wasn't a fool, and showed himself to be a damned fine soldier with common sense in his noggin. "Follow Herendeen," he ordered.

So we burrowed ourselves under leaves and grass, hid behind rotting logs, trees, brush. Outside the woods, the screams of our dying comrades, the pops of pistols, the guttural war cries and songs of Indians pricked our nerves. Some of the lads stuffed grass into their horses' mouths, blindfolded them, did anything and everything humanly possible to keep them quiet. Damn. Those horses could mean the death of us, but nary a thing could I do about it now.

Indians were all around the woods. A handful even dared enter the timber and poke around.

I held me breath, bit me bottom lip, felt the Colt revolver in me clammy hand.

An Irishman from Ohio, sweating next to a professional soldier from Germany, next to an Irishman practically just off the boat from Dublin, next to some Southern boy of dubious ancestry, next to another Hun who knew only two English words: fart and charge. Luckily he did neither.

Then, those Indians in the woods left, and I saw a bunch of the devils riding back toward the village.

"George?" White's voice was just a whisper, but I knew he was turning over the command to me.

I rolled over on me back. These boys were scared. Some of them pale as cotton. They looked at me with panic in their eyes, and damned if I'd let them know that I was just as petrified.

"Listen," I told them, me voice quiet, likely quavering but maybe not enough so they could detect me fear. "I'm an old hand at this sort of thing. Been in scrapes worse than this, believe me." Now, there was a bald-faced lie! "Do what I say, and you'll be able to buy me a glass of Irish whiskey at the sutler's store in a few weeks."

I counted twelve men. Plus me. Thirteen.

Thirteen. Shit. What a piece of luck.

"How many horses do we have?"

About seven hands went up. More than I'd expected.

"Let them go," I said.

"Are you kid—?"

"Let them go." I had to cut off any protest. "Warriors will be looking for horses. They find those mounts, they find us, and we're all dead. Let them go, but get those saddlebags. We'll need the ammunition. And grab any saddlebags, any extra revolvers, any Springfields you find lying around."

"Do we make a break for it?" a kid almost cried.

"Not yet. Right now, we keep on waiting. Hiding."

Damn, I could have used a drink right about then. Even an English beer.

The firing had become more sporadic, more distant. The Hun next to Sergeant White handed me his canteen, and I drank good, cold water. I thanked the Hun, who grunted, wiped the lip, drank some himself. As he was putting away his canteen, we heard it. All of it.

Firing. Heavy firing. Volley after volley, but not in the direction of where Reno had been riding. This came to the north. The firing grew more desperate, no longer volleys, but individual shots.

More Indians rode around the woods, bound north, to the fighting.

"What do ye make of that?" the Irishman from Dublin asked.

I shrugged.

"Custer?"

I was wrong. The Hun knew three English words.

Benteen? Had Reno mustered up enough resolve? Who knew? In a few minutes the roaring of guns had faded.

"Boys, stay here." Already I was crawling to the edge of the timber. Bodies lay across those flats. Bodies of horses and of men. White men. If any Indians had been killed or wounded, they'd been carried off. I looked over toward the village, but, by thunder, it looked vacant.

I didn't crawl back. Didn't want to waste any time. I ran, stopped meself at a tree.

"All right," I said, panting. "Walk. Don't run." Even though I'd just been sprinting. "Take it cool, and we'll get out."

Sergeant White, arm still bleeding and his face a ghastly white, spoke through gritted teeth: "I will shoot the first man who starts to run or disobeys orders."

Well, we must have been a sorry-looking lot, limping out of those woods.

"Look straight ahead," I said. "Don't even glance at any of the bodies. Just keep going. Keep going."

Keep going we did, and then we reached the river. A couple of Indians rode over the bank, and I figured, St. Peter, here I am. I fired, missed, but those two braves galloped away.

As the dust from their horses faded, I heard the Dublin boy say: "Criminy, Herendeen, we scared them off."

At that, we all had to laugh, and cackled like ducks we did as we crossed the Little Big Horn.

When we had climbed the bank, Sergeant White called out, pointing up the ridge. Glory, there she waved—well, maybe not waved, maybe she just hung there, limp—but, to us, it was like a beacon, an angel, our mothers waving us home.

'Twas the guidon. We'd found Major Reno.

"Let's go, boys!" Me voice cracked as we scrambled up that hill.

> They that had fought so well
> Came thro' the jaws of Death
> Back from the mouth of Hell,
> All that was left of them,
> Left of six hundred.

Ah, it's grand to be Irish. It's great to be alive.

Chapter Eighteen

Moving Robe Woman

My heart was bad.

When I saw the dust of *Mila Hanska*—the Long Knives—across the Greasy Grass, I had been digging *tinspila*. So I turned, leaving the wild turnips I had harvested, and ran back to the Hunkpapa circle. Before I reached there, I heard the bullets of the *wasicus* and their bad Indian friends. I saw the dust kicked up in front of me by one of their bullets. Still I ran. I ran to my mother's lodge, and there I found my mother wailing, cutting off her braids, slashing her arms with her knife.

She turned to me, tears rolling down her eyes, and told me that Deeds was dead.

I told her that this could not be, and looked around for his body, but saw only screaming women and children, and angry braves.

Deeds was riding with my father, my mother told me. This I knew. They rode out that morning.

They ran into *Mila Hanska*, and the Crow scouts.

I hate the Crows. All Lakotas hate the Crows.

My father and my brother ran from the Crows. Hard they rode their horses, to warn us about the

Long Knives, about the Crows, the other wolves for the bluecoats. But when my father and brother reached the woods on the far side of the Greasy Grass, the Crows caught my brother. They killed him.

Deeds. My brother. Was dead.

He had lived only ten summers.

I placed my palms against my eyes. I dried my tears. I walked into my lodge, and I braided my hair, and painted my face red. It was a good day to die, and I would look my best. I grabbed the *wasicu* holy iron my father had given me. I made sure all six holes were loaded, the nipples covered with the caps that make the holy iron work. My heart cried out for revenge.

Outside, I walked, and saw my father Crawler. He held my black horse. He saw me. He nodded.

I am a woman. But I did not know fear.

My father often said that it is good for a woman to ride into battle for it fills the hearts of the Lakota men with courage.

That day, I would ride with the warriors.

Sitting Bull's horse had been shot. Now he was screaming: "Attack them!"

There were many *Mila Hanska*, although they did not carry their long knives with them, but there were more Lakotas. I rode toward our enemies, the *wasicus* and the bad Indians who had killed my brother. I rode with revenge in my heart. I rode with many braves.

Rain-In-The-Face pulled his horse even with my black. He shouted: *"Hoka hey!"* Then, smiling, he said: "Moving Robe Woman, you are as pretty as a bird."

I did not feel pretty. I felt nothing. Only hatred.

The soldiers had not charged into our village. For some reason, they stopped, and fled into the woods. Then, suddenly, out of the woods they came.

We stopped. We did not understand. Then we knew that they were running. Cowards. Worse than our enemy the Crows. So we chased after them.

Many we killed.

One man, a *wasicun sapa*, a black white man, was shot off his horse. His horse died. This black white man shouted and waved at a rider who thundered past him, saying good bye. He killed one of our horses, spilling a Hunkpapa. He shot another one of our braves. Then Rain-In-The-Face put a bullet in his chest as he galloped by.

There was something about this *wasicun sapa* that made me curious. I stopped my black horse, and swung down. Other Lakotas had gathered around him. Women came charging to him, surrounding him. Pushing my way through my people, I found this black white man leaning against his dead horse. His knees were bloody from where bullets had struck him, and killed his horse. His chest was bloody and bubbling from the bullet Rain-In-The-Face had sent into him.

Soon, this man would be dead.

I knew this man. The *wasicus* called him Isaiah Dorman. We knew him as Teat, for his skin was as black as a buffalo cow's nipple. At Standing Rock, he had married a Hunkpapa woman called Visible.

"My friends," he said. Death rattled in his voice. He spoke not the *wasicu* tongue, but Lakota. "You have already killed me. . . . Don't . . . count coup . . . on me." Blood trickled down his chin.

Every time he breathed, bubbles appeared on his chest, and the hole made an ugly sucking sound.

A boy started to touch Teat with his lance, but Sitting Bull had ridden up and he said: "Do not kill that man. He is a friend of mine." Then Sitting Bull climbed off the horse he rode. He brought a gourd to the dying Teat. He let him drink. Teat thanked him. Then Sitting Bull mounted his horse, and rode after the cowardly *Mila Hanska* fleeing toward the Greasy Grass.

When Sitting Bull had gone, I stepped over to Teat. I cocked my holy iron.

"Don't kill me," Teat said, his voice a fading whisper. "I will . . . be dead . . . in a short . . . while . . . anyway."

"If you did not want to be killed," I told him,

"why did you not stay home where you belong and not come to attack us?"

He could not answer. I pulled the trigger, but the fool *wasicu* weapon only clicked. Teat jumped slightly at the sound, and his eyes showed fear. He started to say something, but, before he could get the words out, I had thumbed back the hammer and squeezed the trigger. This time, the holy iron worked, and my bullet blew out Teat's brains.

This excited the other Lakota women who had gathered around the black white man. One found the metal pin the Long Knives use to tie their horses to. She drove this through Teat's balls. Another slashed his body with a knife. One cut off his manhood and stuck it inside his mouth.

None of this did I witness—others would tell me of it that evening—for as soon as I had killed Teat, I mounted my black horse, and pursued our enemy.

More *wasicus* I would kill on this day, but no matter how many I killed, it would not make my heart any less bad.

That evening, I would mourn my brother. I would cut off my own braids, and slice flesh from my forearms.

Again, I would cry for Deeds.

Chapter Nineteen

Lieutenant Edward Gustave Mathey

Mon Dieu! Never have I seen such a collapse of discipline. Soldiers, even officers, crying. Captain McDougall and B Troop, our escort, raced up the hill, and I made sure all the mules, everyone in my pack train, made it up there, too.

We were supposed to be delivering our packs full of ammunition to General Custer. Instead, Major Reno had intercepted us, directed us up to this hilltop, saying he had lost half his command.

I did not believe it, till I reached the hilltop. There, I got my first look at the disaster. Men lay on buffalo grass, some merely sat there, faces blank, staring into oblivion. Captain Weir raced by, ordering a skirmish line formed.

"Where's Custer?" someone yelled.

"Likely he has abandoned us," I heard Colonel Benteen say.

"Colonel!" I called out. "What am I to do with the pack mules?"

"Ask Major Reno," Benteen said. "He is the ranking officer here."

Mules brayed. Horses kicked up dust. Many

animals simply fell over, dead, their bodies bleeding from bullet holes, arrows.

Quickly I looked around. "Sergeant!" I had to think quickly, but, honestly, that is not my strongest trait. Until, that is, I saw Dr. Porter. Many wounded soldiers lay in this shallow depression on the center of the hill. My mouth hung open. My heart ached.

Mon Dieu! I wanted to grab my Bible, run to the sides of those bloodied, battered, boys. I wanted to pray for them, pray with them. Behind my back, I know the soldiers, especially the sergeants, call me Bible Thumper, but that is fine with me. I love the 7th Cavalry, but I love God and Jesus Christ more.

God's wisdom flashed before me. It was His doing, not mine.

"Sergeant, picket the mules in a circle, around Doctor Porter and the wounded men." I whirled. "You men . . . I want you to picket your animals, all of your animals, in a circle. We must protect the wounded with our mules and horses. Move it, boys. Move it!"

Gunfire sounded, but not near this hill. Off to the north.

I whipped off my hat. Captain Weir was storming away from a man wearing a bandanna instead of a hat. It took several moments before I recognized that person as Major Reno.

"Move!" I snapped at the men. "Damn your

145

lazy asses, I say, move!" That shocked them. Later, when I realized what I had said, it shocked me, as well.

With speed, I stumbled across the terrain toward Reno. Out of the corner of my eye, I spied Captain Weir riding his black horse down the ridge. Was he crazy? Was he deserting? Some of his troopers seemed to be following. Were we moving out, off to join up with General Custer?

God have mercy. Tell me what I should do!

You could add me to the list of dazed soldiers. I had not a clue what our orders were.

"Major!" I shouted a few rods away from Reno. "I am . . ."

Major Marcus A. Reno, the officer in charge of this rag-tag army of beaten, weary, bloodied, confused soldiers, turned to me. He grinned, and saluted, but not formally. He held a flask toward his forehead.

"Hello, Lieutenant," he said, smiling drunkenly. "Look here, I got half a bottle yet."

For the second time in two minutes, I cursed, only, this time, I cursed my commanding officer to his face.

Chapter Twenty

Trumpeter Giovanni Martini

Affidavit of Private John Martin
Given this Thirteenth Day of January, 1879
For Court of Inquiry
Chicago, Illinois
Translated from Italian by H.C. Hollister

My name is Giovanni Martini, but, here in America, I am called John Martin. On the Twenty-Fifth of June in the year 1876, I was a trumpeter in the 7th Cavalry assigned to General George Custer's immediate command.

I came to America from Sola Conzalina. I beat the drums for the army in Italy, so I played the trumpet for the cavalry in America. I love music. I am a musician. I am not really a soldier, at least, I am not what you would call a fighter.

On the afternoon of the Twenty-Fifth, after General Custer had ordered Major Reno to charge the Indian village, the troops commanded by the general proceeded through the rugged country, searching for a good river crossing. We had topped a ridge and could see and hear the battle our fellow soldiers were fighting across the river. At this point, the captain with the long whiskers *[First Lieutenant (Brevet Captain) W. W. Cooke]* waved me out of my column, and I trotted my horse . . . I am not good at riding horses, either . . . to join General Custer and the officers.

The general seemed excited. Very excited.

"Orderly," General Custer said. He said more, but I could not understand. He spoke very rapidly, and my understanding of English is very limited. The general always spoke fast when he was excited. I understood the words "fast," and "Benteen," so I understood that General Custer was telling me to ride fast and bring Colonel Benteen.

There were too many Indians. Too many, even for the general.

After locating the village and seeing the size of it, the general had previously sent a messenger, Sergeant K— I forget his name. *[Sergeant Daniel A. Kanipe, who had been ordered by Custer to bring the pack train forward.]* The sergeant had not returned, and now the general decided he not only needed the pack train for bullets, but he needed more men.

There were many, many Indians. We had expected a lot, but not this many.

I started to ride away, but the captain *[Cooke]* yelled at me in Italian. He said: "Cessare!" So I stopped my horse. The captain said he would write down my orders, and I knew that was because my English is not very good. From his pocket, the captain brought out a pencil and notebook and began to write very quickly.

As the captain wrote, I looked down below and across the river. Major Reno and his soldiers had stopped. They no longer were mounted on their horses. They were no longer charging, but fighting the Indians on foot. Many Indians. Many, many Indians.

The captain ripped the paper from his notebook, and handed it to me.

Speaking in Italian, he told me: "Ride as fast as you can to Colonel Benteen. Take the same trail we came down. If you have time, and there is no danger, come back. But otherwise, stay with your company."

I put the note in my pocket, and spurred my horse. I rode very fast, but glanced back. I saw General Custer riding with all his men. The gray horses were in front. The horses were moving very fast, faster than I usually could ride.

Up and down I rode. Soon, some Indians saw me. They shot at me, so I rode faster. I prayed that I would not fall off my horse, and after a while the Indians no longer shot at me. I do not know where they went, maybe to fight Major Reno, maybe to follow General Custer. I was just happy they no longer shot at me.

A few minutes later, I saw another rider. At first I feared it was an Indian, but I soon saw it was the brother of the general, the one whose name is like that big city in the East *[civilian forage master Boston Custer]*.

"Where's the general?" the general's brother asked.

I pointed to the ridge behind me, and the general's brother whipped his horse hard. He rode to General Custer. I went to find Colonel Benteen.

As I reached the next bluff, I saw Major Reno still fighting Indians. There was much smoke, and much dust. I tried to make my horse go faster.

Finally I found Colonel Benteen. He was riding far ahead of the pack train with his trumpeter. We were between two ridges. It was very hot.

I stopped, saluted, and found the note the captain had given me, and gave it to the colonel. He read the note aloud.

[The Court asked for the note to be read aloud. It said: "Benteen. Come on. Big village. Be quick. Bring packs. W. W. Cooke. P.S.: Bring pacs."]

Colonel Benteen laughed after he read the note. He said something about the captain being in such a hurry, that he had spelled packs wrong. I think he said something like that. He did not laugh for long, however, and soon turned to me. His face looked determined.

"Where is the general now?" the colonel asked. He spoke very slowly. I could understand what he said.

I told him that the Indians were running and that the general, the last I saw him, was charging.

The colonel did not ask me about Major Reno. I did not tell him. I meant to, but the colonel gave me no time, and then he was looking at my horse, and asking what was wrong with the animal.

I answered that it must be tired, but the colonel shook his head, and pointed and told me to look at the horse's hip.

After I dismounted, I saw blood, and put my hand on the horse's hip. The horse moved away, and I glanced at the blood covering my hand.

Colonel Benteen said that I was lucky, that it could have been me and not my horse.

I felt weak. I wiped the blood on my pants, and I reached for my crucifix and Saint Christopher. As I prayed, the other trumpeter dismounted his horse, and came to my injured horse. The trumpeter poured water from his canteen into the dirt and grass, and made some sort of mixture, which he picked up and put on my horse's bullet wound.

I thanked him, and we both mounted our horses. By that time, more soldiers had arrived. One was Captain *[Thomas]* Weir. The other was a lieutenant whose name I do not know *[Winfield Edgerly]*.

The colonel handed the note to the lieutenant, and raised his hands up in the air. He said something about how the general wanted him to come quickly, but he could not do that and bring the packs. He said more, but I could not understand much about what was being said.

Even more officers arrived.

The colonel told them that the Indians were

running. I believed the Indians were running. The general had been so worried that the Indians would run away before we could beat them.

One of the officers said that we would miss out on the glory again. Another said something about congratulating the general one more time, then he cursed. They did not appear to be happy. They seemed . . . jealous?

I do know that Captain Weir reminded Colonel Benteen that his orders were to come quickly.

The colonel said angrily: "We are going."

Then, the colonel told the lieutenants to return to the column. We were to move out at a trot.

Over the hills, we could hear the sounds of gunfire. The colonel told me to rejoin my troop, and that is what I did. I rode to find H Troop.

The soldiers in my troop asked me all about what was going on. I told them about the big village, and we started trotting. I hoped my horse would be able to keep up.

The soldiers in H Troop were very excited. They wanted to fight.

They had not seen the size of the village. They did not know how many Indians were out there.

One of the men in my troop asked me what General Custer was doing when I left.

That made me smile. I never saw the general again, but that is how I will always remember him. The way I saw him that last time.

Charging.

Chapter Twenty-One

Captain Myles Keogh

Notes for Memoir

'76-June 25, afternoon:

Just time for quick thoughts. Reno is engaging hostiles. Wish I had the privilege of leading I Troop with him, but, alas. Riding back with Cooke to rejoin Custer. Not sure of Custer's plan.

Back with Custer. Fred Gerard caught up with us, told us Indians fighting. NOT RUNNING! A Crow scout just told Custer we should assist, but Custer said: "No, let them fight." He's waiting on the packs. Sent Sergeant Kanipe to bring them back. Kanipe hasn't returned. Nor have we seen Benteen after Custer ordered that little Guinea to fetch him.

Much excitement. Custer yells: "If Reno can keep them occupied down below, we'll hit them hard. We can capture the entire village, get the women and kids. Force them to surrender."

"Hurray!" Custer waves hat. "We'll finish them up and then go home to our station!"

Don't think Custer thought there really was an Indian village till now.

Weather hot. Unbearable. Custer has taken off his buckskin coat. So have I, but still sweating like a pig. Still no Benteen. Letting our horses drink, but not too much. Much fighting to come.

Huge village. Two times more than what we thought. Maybe even larger.

Below, all we see are women and children, running around, excited. No warriors.

"Maybe they are off hunting," Tom Custer suggests.

"That must be it," Lieutenant Calhoun says.

Hunting? Who do they think is fighting Reno now?

Enough time to pull out my *Agnus Dei*, a gift from Pope Pius IX back in the Old World, hang it over my neck.

May it bring me luck.

Custer wants to hit rear. Hoping Benteen can hold center, when he gets here. Still hear shooting where Reno has engaged. Glory, what a commotion, what a fight that must be.

Cannot wait on Benteen. Must strike camp. Before Indians scatter.

Crow scouts are dismissed, after a fine job. They located the biggest Indian village ever seen.

Some Rees joined us, only to be dismissed, too. Can see the dust they're raising as they light a shuck for the Powder River depot.

Damn the red heathens. They want no part of our big fight.

Custer divides us. I have honor of commanding three troops in the right wing, with Yates commanding the left wing. Flank attack is planned. Captains Yates and Smith heading over hills toward river. Custer watches with field glasses.

My first sergeant rode over, asked me if I could see the dust, and pointed toward the river.

"Hell, Varden," I replied, "dust is all I see."

It rises like smoke. Little wind to carry it away.

Comanche fights the bit, ready for battle. As am I.

There are our Indians! Not running. Hitting Yates in coulée. Big fight—

Yates pinned down. Heavy fire. Have issued orders to double amount of horses each holder will be in charge of. To give us a few extra shots. Awaiting—Here comes Cus—

Have orders. Victory near.

More later.

Chapter Twenty-Two

Crazy Horse

When the shots first reached us, I was swimming in the Greasy Grass with Long Nose. We knew what those shots meant, for, at that time, both of us said: "*Mila Hanska*!"

Then we heard cries from the Oglala circle, and, just next to our circle, the Hunkpapa, which is where the bullets were near.

"The Long Knives are coming. The Long Knives are coming."

Carrying our breechclouts, we ran. I met Red Feather as he bridled a pony. "Take any horse!" he yelled at me, but that was no good. I decided that I would wait to find my own pony. Long Nose, however, caught the first pony he saw.

The boy named Black Elk, naked and dripping wet, ran past us, bringing two stallions behind him. He had been swimming in the river just below Long Nose and me. Now as he hurried to find his father, Black Elk sang, though his voice cracked with nervousness, a strong-heart song.

Next, I heard singing from inside the lodge of a *wicasa wakan*. I asked to enter, and he stopped singing long enough to tell me to come. Inside, I donned my breechclout, and asked the holy man

156

to pray for all Lakota people. I asked him to give our warriors patience. When this was done, I stepped outside to prepare myself.

I knew how to defeat *Mila Hanska.*

Many Oglala warriors were mounted, waiting for me. Despite the holy man's prayers, they had no patience, but a Lakota should not go into battle in haste.

"I will ride," I softly told one of the angry ones, "when I am ready."

He did not wait, but rode off toward the Hunkpapas. Most, however, honored me. They did not like it, but they waited.

My right hand grabbed dirt, which I used to dust myself. I found grass stems, and put these into my hair. I saw other Oglala warriors, saw their impatience. A young Itazipacola joined us, and hollered for me to hurry, but Red Feather told him to be quiet.

Long Nose had built a buffalo chip fire, and over this I kneeled, pulling an offering from the medicine bag around my neck. This burned, carrying my prayers to *Wakan Tanka.* Some others swung from their mounts, and approached the small fire to make their own medicine.

Which was good.

On my face, I painted hail spots, put the hawk feather in my hair, then dusted my pony with dirt. Last, I placed the white stone behind my ear.

By this time, Long Nose handed me my war

axe and a fast-shooting *wasicu* long holy iron. These I lifted to the waiting Oglalas.

"*Hokay hey!*" I shouted, and their echoes drowned out the sounds of Long Knives' guns.

An old Oglala woman ran up to us, pointing north. She yelled that she saw other Long Knives, that they would be striking our camp soon. Many warriors wanted to ride that way, but I pointed toward the Hunkpapas. The Hunkpapas were closer, and our *Sahiyela* friends were already preparing to attack any Long Knives who might strike from that direction.

So were our brothers the Sicangus, Minneconjous, Itazipacolas, Sihasapas, and Gros Ventres. Even the five *Mahpiya To*, who many of us had not trusted when they first arrived at our camp, were ready to fight.

There were many, many Lakotas. Many *Sahiyelas*.

Today, Sitting Bull's vision would come true.

"Our Hunkpapa brothers need us. We must help them first."

I am not a shouter, but my throat hurt after I issued my command, the first any Lakota leader will say before going into battle.

"*Hiyupo!*"

My heart was glad when all the Oglalas did, indeed, follow me. We galloped to the Hunkpapa circle, and the voices made my heart even stronger.

"Crazy Horse is coming! Crazy Horse is coming!"

A woman sang:

> Brothers-in-law, now your friends have come.
> Take courage.
> Would you see me taken captive?

Sitting Bull was shouting, his pony dead. Then I saw Lakota women, and children, and some warriors, lying on the ground, not moving, their spirits gone. Dead. Sitting Bull told me that we must fight, that these *wasicus* did not want to make peace, or bring us gifts.

We were strong. Our spirits were good, for we had just whipped many *Mila Hanska* down south just a few suns earlier. And we all knew of Sitting Bull's great vision. He had foretold of our great victory.

Gall rode over to our conference. He yelled at me, but Gall was always yelling, and rode off, saying he must find his family, that they were rounding up the ponies, and rode away. I saw Rain-In-The-Face ride toward the *wasicus*, and a Hunkpapa woman disappearing into the dust. More women began singing strong-heart songs.

I saw the *wasicus* running into the woods. So I rode that way, close to the woods, waving my rifle over my head, feeling their bullets whistle over my head. No *wasicu* bullet can kill me.

That, too, has been foretold. I let them shoot up their bullets in vain, so that we might kill them much easier.

Back I rode, this time waving my war axe. The *wasicus* continued to shoot, but I reached the Hunkpapas unharmed.

When I turned my pony around, I saw many *Mila Hanska* fleeing the woods, where the dust was not so great, running or riding toward the Greasy Grass.

Till then, I had not fired a shot, nor swung my war axe.

"Here are some of the soldiers after us again!" I yelled to my friends. "Do your best, and let us kill them all off today, that they may not trouble us any more."

So we rode. Again, the dust became heavy, thick, mixed with the smoke from all the guns being fired. It was difficult to see, but it was easy to kill.

My club swung. I felt the bones in the head of a *wasicu* break. I swung again. Another Long Knife died.

Mila Hanska crossed the river. Some of our warriors followed, but as I turned, after the dust had settled, I saw more dust toward the north. I remembered the other *Mila Hanska*, heading toward the *Sahiyela* circle.

To Crow King, a good Hunkpapa, I yelled: "Let these cowards run! There is danger." I pointed.

Crow King cried out, and we turned our ponies. Back to the village we galloped, riding through the Hunkpapa circle, through the other circles, still hearing more and more strong-heart songs.

Through the circles we rode, hearing songs, wailing, crying, gunfire. We crossed the river. Yes, *Mila Hanska* were coming. But we were ready for them.

"They will not cross the Greasy Grass!" Flying Hawk yelled behind me. "They will not harm our women and children."

We entered a ravine, followed it. Our *Sahiyela* brothers had already turned back many *wasicus*. The *wasicus* did not fight well.

Some ran toward us, unable to see us at the edge of the ravine. I tucked away my axe, and brought out my *wasicu* holy iron, worked the lever, and fired.

Killing these Long Knives was easy.

They stopped, kneeling in the tall grass, firing at us, but their bullets flew wild.

"Let them shoot for a while," I told our warriors. "Their guns do not shoot good after a while. And these Long Knives are shooting very fast."

Tossing my war axe and *wasicu* gun to Red Feather, I let my pony climb out of the ravine. Many bullets buzzed past me. My pony did not want to run, did not cringe at the bullets. My pony was very brave.

Calmly I brought the eagle bone whistle to my mouth, and let it sing. Loudly it sang. Even above the noise of gunfire, of Indians yelling, of *wasicus* begging, the whistle could be heard.

My Oglala brothers yelled: "Come back down where it is safe!"

Back and forth I rode, letting the *wasicus* shoot. Much time passed before I allowed my pony to jump back into the ravine.

A *Mahpiya To* who had joined us yelled triumphantly: "You are the bravest man I ever saw."

"*Hokay hey!*" came the cries among the warriors I led.

"*Hokay hey!*" I called back. "Today is a good day to die!"

Mila Hanska no longer shot so fast, and I knew their weapons were not working as they should.

"Let us ride out now," I said, taking back my war axe and holy iron from Red Feather. "Let us kill them all and be done with these *Mila Hanska*! *Hiyupo!*"

Out of the ravine we rose, riding, charging. We sang our death songs. We shot.

"Kill the ones holding the horses," I said.

So we shot them. Arrows sliced into flanks and backs of many horses, and they jerked from their holder's grasps. They bolted away.

These *wasicus* were funny with their horses. Gray horses were all together. Red horses were all together. At first. Soon all the horses were mixed. Many lay dead. Others galloped in all directions. Some of our younger warriors raced after the horses, to capture them for their own. That was good. Most of us, however, stayed to kill those who had come to kill us.

When most of their horses had run off, or died, most of the *wasicus* lost their nerve. The hills were covered with Indians. The Long Knives fled, but there was nowhere for them to go. They could not escape.

There was so much choking, blinding dust, again, it became hard to see, but one did not have to see to kill. My long gun spoke often. More *Mila Hanska* died. When my own long gun no longer worked, I grabbed it by the hot barrel, and smashed a screaming *wasicu* who had fallen to his knees, begging.

Cowards deserve no mercy. His brains spilled onto the grass, and I leaped from my pony to slash his right thigh. Let him carry that mark into the other world.

Holding my horse's hackamore, I looked around. Through the dust, the smoke of hundreds of long guns and short guns, this is what I saw.

Red Feather pulled the cartridge belt from a dead *wasicu*. He held the holy iron in his hand, and put a bullet into the back of a Long Knife who was crawling away.

A red-headed *wasicu* tried to grab one of the fleeing horses, but fell down. He came up, tears in his eyes, saw many Lakotas and *Sahiyelas* charging to him, and he stuck the barrel of his short gun in his mouth, and pulled the trigger just before our braves hacked his body to pieces.

One *wasicu* with the yellow markings on his sleeves shot his own horse. Behind this dead animal, he made a fort, and worked his long gun and short gun. He fought well, but we were too many for him. Arrows sliced into his body. When a young *Sahiyela* tried to count coup, Red Feather stopped him, saying: "Leave this dead man alone. He fought bravely." Then they ran into the dust to kill more.

An arrow thudded into the back of a Long Knife, dropping him to his knees. Another arrow entered his stomach, almost to the feathers at the end of the shaft. This *wasicu* did not fall, however, until the third arrow hit his eye. This killed him, and young Oglalas and *Sahiyelas* stood over him, putting more arrows into his body, but soon stopped, staring at the arrow in his eye. Later, young Black Elk told me that it was a strange eye, splintered by the arrow. The eye seemed to be made of glass. What strange medicine for a *wasicu*. The medicine of the Lakota, however, proved much stronger.

For a moment, the wind blew, parting the dust, and I saw the split flag of the *Mila Hanska*. Many Long Knives had gathered around that flag up the hill. Others were running away.

Those could wait. I leaped back on my pony. I rode to the backbone of a ridge to kill more of my enemies.

A handful of Long Knives gathered in this depression, the one with the sleeve markings planting his split flag in the ground near a dead horse. A brave warrior rode his red dun horse around, but a bullet smashed his knee, and downed both him and the big horse. The red dun horse got up, and hobbled away. Many *wasicus* grabbed the one whose knee would no longer work, and leaned him against a dead horse. Then Gall arrived with his followers, and all of those *Mila Hanska* were no more.

Again, I had to wait for the dust to fall away. Gall galloped up to where I was, pointing over toward the nearest hill.

"*Hiyupo*, Crazy Horse!" he said. "Leave those down there to our women. *Hiyupo!*" He rode away, still shouting: "*Hiyupo!* This fight will soon be over."

Indeed, in just a short time, it was.

Chapter Twenty-Three
Lame White Man

Nothing lives long.
Only the earth and mountains.

I push myself off the ground, spit out grass and blood, and rise on my knees. I try to watch, though dust blinds me, as Human Beings kill these warrior white men.

I sing my death song.

Nothing lives long.
Only the earth and mountains.

I think of this morning.

How beautiful it was, the fur from the cotton-woods falling on our circle like snowflakes in the Moon When Freeze Begins on Stream's Edge. I gave my youngest son the bow of ash that was ready, and a quiver of a dozen arrows with turkey feathers on the shafts. He was pleased. It made my heart glad, even though he lacks strength to pull back the sinew string. He will grow stronger, and will master this bow.

For he is a Human Being.

Nothing lives long.
Only the earth and mountains.

The warrior white men's horses are running. Our *Hotóhkeso* allies and we Human Beings have crushed many, killed many. Soon, all these warrior white men will be dead, though they fight well. Soon, I will be dead.

Nothing lives long.
Only the earth and mountains.

I think of not long ago.
Our Suicide Boys, who vowed to die fighting to defend our people, marched through our circle. Those five young men made me so proud. I told my oldest wife: "I must go up there and ride down in the parade with my boys."

I rode my golden mare. I heard our people singing songs of honor to those brave boys. After that, I went to the river, to the sweat lodge, to bathe in the heat, to purify myself, with my friend, Wooden Leg. That was when we heard the warning that the warrior white men were coming. That was when we heard the gunfire at the other end of the village of all free Indians.

Naked, I ran to my family. I sent my wives, my children north. Out of danger. Family must come first. Always. I wrapped a blanket over my waist, pulled on my moccasins, grabbed my rifle, my bow, my quiver, my knife. Then I rode to meet these warrior white men.

Nothing lives long.
Only the earth and mountains.

I can see nothing now but dust, though I still hear the booming of rifles, our warriors crying: "Hi-yi-yi!" I can picture our brave boys counting coup, lifting scalps. It is hard to breathe. Slowly I sink, trying to stay up, trying to stay among the living, just long enough to see our great victory.

Nothing lives long.
Only the earth and mountains.

We crossed the river, saw the warrior white men, their split flag waving, riding very fast, the first bunch on white horses.

Our Suicide Boys wanted to go. So did many other warriors. "They are too many," I said. "Wait. We must wait."

Those following me honored me. When I slid off my pony, they did the same. "Wait until they are closer," I said.

When they drew near, we opened fire. Many were hit, including one with a big gray hat and red scarf who slumped in his saddle. This discouraged these white men. Two rode to the wounded man, grabbed the reins to his horse, rode away, up the hill. Another followed.

The horn of the warrior white men blew, and the remaining men stopped their horses. Some of them held four horses, but did not fight. Our ponies, however, were trained not to run. We did not need to have one warrior hold our ponies. Other warrior white men approached on foot with their long guns.

"Kill them!" I yelled. We fired again. By then, more Hotóhkeso *friends and Human Beings had appeared on all sides of the hills. No more could I see the falling fur of the cottonwoods. All around me was dust. And smoke from the rifles.*

Nothing lives long.
Only the earth and mountains.

Now I push myself back up, feel saliva running down my chin. I reach up, touch it, find it sticky, and stare at my fingers. It is not water from my mouth. It is blood. I sink onto my hindquarters. Still, I sing.

Nothing lives long.
Only the earth and mountains.

We charged out of the ravine. I found a veho *lying in the sweet-smelling grass. I slit his throat, to make sure he was dead, then I scalped him.*

169

I pulled off his belt with the cartridges, and fastened it around my blanket. I stuck his pistol, the barrel still blazing hot, inside the belt. I pulled off his blue coat, and wore this.

I rose, mounting my mare again, yelling for those following me to come on, to kill some more.

Nothing lives long.
Only the earth and mountains.

I fall to my back. There is no dust here. The battle has moved away from me. I stare at the sky, so clear, so blue, so beautiful. I think of my wives, my children. They will live free, though, because after today, and after our victory at the Rosebud just a few suns ago, no warrior white men will come to bother us again.

Nothing lives long.
Only the earth and mountains.

We rode with Hotóhkeso *allies, and other tribes, and chased some warrior white men up a ridge. Then they came down, maybe forty, dismounting, firing. These* vehos *were brave, accurate with their weapons, so we went down the ridge.*

The fight grew fierce, but slowly we began to inch up the hill, firing arrows, weapons. I emptied all of the bullets from the short gun I had

170

taken. I looked around me, and saw hundreds and hundreds of warriors.

So I stood up, leaping onto my fine mare. I was much older than our Suicide Boys, but I had to be just as brave.

"Come!" I shouted. "We can kill all of them."

Leading the way, I rode, and we crushed those warrior white men. We clubbed them. We shot them. We took many coup, many scalps, and left many dead.

Only a few began running for the hillside, where several more of the warrior white men remained, fighting among dead horses and another split flag.

"Come!" I cried out again, and rode after those fleeing.

I rode hard. Till the bullet hit my breast, and I fell off the horse, stunned. For a moment, my lungs would not work. Finally I breathed, though it burned like hot coals inside me. Weakly I pushed myself off the ground, spit out grass and blood, and rose to my knees, watching, though dust blinded me.

I sang: "Nothing lives long. Only the earth and mountains."

I have closed my eyes, just for a moment, just to rest, just to remember my wives, how beautiful they are, and my children, what great warriors and lovely wives they will grow to be, though I will never see them. Footsteps fall around me, and my eyes flutter open. A shadow crosses my face. At last, my vision clears, and I can see this man.

Holding his rifle, a young *Hotóhkeso* stands over me. He cries out, and more footsteps sound, more Indians gather around me. The first *Hotóhkeso* tosses his rifle to the ground, and draws his knife from its sheath.

"*Palani!*" he shouts.

It is now that I realize I was not shot by a warrior white man, but this *Hotóhkeso*. He has mistaken me for an *Ónone* wolf. I was foolish to have put on this warrior white man's blue coat. All of these Indians, who fought with us Human Beings against the *vehos*, draw their knives.

"Nothing lives long," I sing. "Only the earth and mountains."

The knives come down.

Chapter Twenty-Four

Lieutenant Colonel George A. Custer

I have no strength, no time, to write. Not even paper to record these thoughts. My rifle, empty, lies at my side. My Bulldog revolver rests in my hand, though the muscles in my right arm will not respond. I cannot lift it. I could not even put pen to paper, to tell you how much I love you, how much you have meant to me, how much better my life has been because of you, sweet Libbie.

So I pray that these words, my final thoughts on this earth, will reach you, somehow, carried across the Montana plains all the way to Fort Lincoln.

We've always been so much alike, so much in love. I send my thoughts to your memory.

Oh, dear God, where is Benteen?

To the river we rode, intending to strike across the Little Big Horn and hit the Indian encampment. That would relieve Reno. We would capture the hostile women. We would earn the greatest victory of all the Indian wars, eclipsing the Washita.

Darling Libbie, you know me. When I ordered the charge, I rode at the point. Custer's luck. I thought we had caught the savages napping, but, no, they were ready. More than ready.

A bullet struck my breast, just below the heart. How it missed my heart, I know not. I thought I would fall off of Vic, but Tom and Sergeant Hughes rode to me, grabbed the reins, turned me around, led me up this hill.

I think I told them that we should hold the high ground. Re-form here.

How many Indians are there? Many.

I thought we were flanking the camp, but this village must have stretched along the riverbanks forever. We hit the center. No . . . they hit us.

I wanted to cross the Little Big Horn first. Remember the time during the Rebellion, when General Barnard couldn't make up his mind if we could ford the Chickahominy? Remember what I did? How I spurred my mount, went into the middle of the river? I can still see that look on the general's face. He thought I was either the craziest officer under his command, or the bravest.

This afternoon, we never even got across the river, except for a few young recruits who, unable to control or stop their frightened mounts, kept right on riding after our trumpeter blew the command to halt, to dismount.

Who gave that order?

Remember what I wrote in *My Life on the Plains*?

"If I were an Indian I think that I would greatly prefer to cast my lot with those of my people who adhered to the free life of the plains rather than to the limits of a reservation, there to be the recipient of the blessed benefits of civilization, with the vices thrown in without stint or measure."

I still think that way, for these savages fight like very devils. Even harder, I dare say, than the Rebels during that glorious war that carried me to glory, that carried me to you. I do not think you would have married me, that your father would ever had consented to our nuptials, had it not been for that war.

Custer's luck got me through the butchery of Southern insurrection.

Yet it has failed me here.

More Indians appeared at the top of the ridge. We did not make it.

"Shoot your horses!" Tom called. Tom. God bless him. What a brother to have, what an aide, what a captain. The bravest man I've ever known.

"Use your horses for redoubts. We can hold them off till Reno or Benteen relieves us."

They eased me off Vic. Who soon fell, great animal, shot by one of our troopers or an Indian, I know not. Vic. Short for Victory. Which is why I chose to ride him into battle. The fastest horse in the 7th, never to run again.

They leaned me across another dead horse.

No, now that I look, I see I lean against dead soldiers, God have pity on their souls. They died bravely.

Dr. Lord is dead. Many are falling. Gamely we shall all go to Glory.

I glanced at my right hand, saw the revolver I still held, that I hold now. Tom managed to cock the hammer. He reached somewhere, and produced that damnable, omnipresent flask.

"Drink this, Autie," he said.

At first, I refused. Remember the time I came calling on you, well in my cups? You rebuked me, chastised me, shamed me. Never would I touch ardent spirits again. Till now.

It made me cough. Cough up blood.

"Hang on, Autie!" It was young Bos, grand brother, tears in his eyes.

Oh, now, how I wished we had not picked on Bos so. I remember earlier on the campaign, sleeping out of doors, Tom and Jimmi and Bos and Harry Reed. As soon as Bos was asleep, Tom and I would shower him with clods of dirt.

Or how Jimmi would torment precious young Harry: Jimmi would begin writing, then tap his glass eye with the pencil's point. The look on Harry's face would leave us rolling on the ground.

The guidon was planted.

I tried to give a command, but could not speak.

Through dust, so thick, so horrible, it burned my lungs with every breath, I looked around. Keogh's men. Jimmi's command.

Where's Benteen? Where's Reno? I should have sent Benteen into that camp, should not have rebuked him, back-stabber that he is, denied him of a chance at glory. Benteen is a fighter, a soldier. Reno . . . ?

Too late now. This hand has been dealt.

A trumpet sounds. Or is it Gabriel's? No. One of our troopers has been killed. An Indian blows it. Private Martin? Did Indians waylay him before he brought Benteen my orders? I hear the whistles of Indians. The gunfire. More troopers have joined us. They run from Jimmi's position, what is left of it.

What has happened to Colonel Keogh?

Didn't I tell that newspaper reporter that the 7th Cavalry could defeat the entire Sioux nation? Where is Kellogg? I haven't seen him since he was whipping his mule after us, trying to keep up. Defeat the entire Sioux nation? I forgot that Fetterman said something similar before he led his command to ruinous death outside of Fort Phil Kearney, what, a decade ago?

They say Fetterman disobeyed orders. Will history say the same of me?

Thermopylae. Masada. The Alamo. Will this place be remembered in history alongside those great battles? Will you remember me?

Of course, my darling. Death cannot separate us.

Oh, *Mo-nah-se-tah*, your beauty, your grace. God, never had I met a woman like you. You grabbed hold of my heart when I first saw you among the captives at the Washita. Your eyes, so bright, they held me prisoner. And your hair, not greasy and dirty like most Indian wenches, but shining and smooth like a raven's wing. Young-Grass-That-Shoots-In-Spring. That's what your name meant, I was told. But you struck me in the dark of winter. I brought you to my tent on the way back to Fort Hays. You were my interpreter. You warmed me during the chill. . . .

Forgive me. Those thoughts were not for you, Libbie.

Oh, my darling Libbie, you loved me despite all my failings. That Cheyenne woman that I bedded after my victory at the Washita? She was an infatuation, nothing more. I called her "an enchanting, comely squaw," but you saw through me. You always saw through me. Yet even you could see something in *Mo-nah-se-tah*. "The belle among all Indian maidens," you called her at a dinner at Fort Hays. Which brought a terrible silence to the party.

I knew then that you knew about my transgressions. So did Tom, Jimmi, all of the officers, and, likely, many of their brides.

God, I thought you would leave me. Perhaps I was jealous of all the attention so many of my fellow officers heaped upon you. Not that I can blame them.

Why did you stay? You had every right to leave me, to insist on a divorce. But I know. Now I know. I must have always known.

My heart has always belonged to you. It always shall belong to you. And, yours, I pray, will always belong to me.

The Washita. I wonder. Colonel Benteen always blamed me for abandoning Major Elliott, which was an egregious lie. Has he abandoned my command as an act of revenge?

Is this, as they are prone to say, my life flashing before my eyes?

I remember our reunions. April 9, '69, at Fort Leavenworth, after six months apart. July 19, '67, at Fort Riley. That is the one history will recall, for it resulted in my court-martial. Absent without leave. We can forget the other trivial charges. I left my post, of course, to be with you. To the blazes with Captain Weir. He showed you far too much attention, and I would gladly have pleaded guilty to striking a junior officer had he given me the chance.

That brought me closer to you, didn't it? You saw how much I loved you. That I was found guilty, suspended from rank and pay for a year. That I would gladly sacrifice my Army career just to hold you in my arms, so that no other man could lure you away from me.

Yet the one I remember most is Thanksgiving Day, 1862. Conway Noble, bless him, introduced me to this charmingly delightful, if somewhat standoffish, woman named Elizabeth Bacon. I had just been brevetted captain, and you said: "I believe your promotion has been very rapid?" To which I replied: "I have been very fortunate." Fortune shined on me that night. I met you. Although later, you reminded me, with that devilish laugh of yours, how you—and your father!—had seen me before, staggering down the streets, drunker than a skunk!

That night, I dreamed of you. You have been in all of my dreams, all of my nights, since that glorious evening. I made it a point to walk by your house on my leaves. I must have worn holes in my boots walking past your home. I made an utter nuisance of myself. Remember? You told me: "You should forget me." And I told you: "I can never forget you." You said you couldn't forget me, but could never be my wife. Yet I wore you down, darling. I wore you down.

"Come on, you Wolverines! The Rebs out-number us now, but not for long. What can cannon do to us?"

You should see these brave boys. Staring

straight ahead at death. Courage, boys, courage, my Wolverines. Follow me. Follow me. We plunge into the Rebs, crashing together. It sounds like thunder, like all the cannon at Gettysburg going off at once. Saber against saber. Horses fall. Men are crushed, mauled, mangled, brutalized. Glorious war. Glorious battle. My horse is killed. "Give me the stirrup." Again, I ride, and that horse falls dead. I find another. Ride. Yell. "Follow me, you Wolverines!" There, the Rebs retreat, running back to Cress Ridge. I wanted to pursue, but my grand Michiganders were too worn out. A great, glorious charge. Let the journalists, let my critics spread their slander, that I killed more of my own men than I did Confederates. I won that battle. I . . .

Where . . . am I?

Indians. Oh, God, Cooke has fallen. Poor Cookie, poor Cookie.

"Charge, Wolverines!" I yell. The sergeant turns, looks, ignores my command. Fires his revolver, one hand on the guidon's staff.

Libbie, I want to see your face. I want to feel your lips. God, I want to live.

Ah, but, charge, my Wolverines, charge! Watch those Rebels run! We've licked them again.

No. No. Not Cedar Creek.

Where am I? Darling, where are you?

The battle sounds around me. Tom's yelling. I can't see him. I can't see anyone.

Chapter Twenty-Five

Sergeant Robert Hughes

"Come back here, you damned sons-of-bitches! Stand your ground."

Steady. Damn it.
  "Pry out that shell with your knife, damn it."

"Damn it. Hand me your revolver, boy. Your revolver! Mine's empty! *Sons-of-bitchin' Indians!*"

"Stand your ground! I'm in command!"

"Come back here. Stand your ground, men. Die like soldiers, you God da—"
  Oh . . . Christ . . . oh . . .
  "Holy Mary, Mother of God, pray for us sinners, now, and at the hour . . ."

Chapter Twenty-Six

Gall

It was said that the *wasicus* fought bravely. I say this: Like dogs, they died.

We knew *Mila Hanska* approached. Our warriors had seen the dust. But we had driven those *wasicus* away down along the Rosebud. Let them come, we said. We would whip them again.

Now . . . I . . . wish we . . . had not been . . . so brave.

When we heard the gunfire near the Hunkpapa circle, I prepared myself for battle, mounted the first pony I could find, and rode to Sitting Bull. Yet even before I reached the circle, I heard a woman screaming behind me: "*Dacia! Dacia!*" She pointed toward the high ridges on the other side of the Greasy Grass, and I knew more *Mila Hanska* were coming, to attack us from the north!

Seeing Crazy Horse, I yelled at him, and rode beyond our circle and into the woods and pastures, to find my war pony. More importantly to find my family. I had sent two of my wives and most of our children north as soon as the attack began, but my youngest two wives, and three more children, had been sent into the woods to find our ponies. I had sent them to do this task.

I sent them . . . to their . . . deaths.

In the woods, I found their bodies. *Wasicus* had not killed them, scalped them, had not . . . No they lay dead, their beautiful bodies turned into porcupines from all the arrows that pinned them to the ground.

From my youngest wife's body, I pulled an arrow from her back. "*Palani!*" I said, and spit, breaking the arrow in my trembling hands.

The devil *Palanis*, wolves for *Mila Hanska*, had murdered most of my family. I turned to my youngest son, dead, scalped, butchered, but could not see him, for tears blinded me. I raised my head, staring at the treetops, but saw nothing. Nothing.

For the longest while, I just kneeled there, crying.

Slowly, though, the sounds of battle returned. My tears dried. I rose. The *Palanis* had stolen all of our ponies, so I would not be able to ride my favorite war pony. No matter. I tied up the tail of the painted pony near me. I listened.

The battle no longer sounded near our Hunkpapa circle. It came from the north, beyond where the *Sahiyelas* lived.

I looked at the *wasicu* holy iron I held, but left it with the bodies. My heart was bad. I would kill all of my enemies with the hatchet.

Mounting the paint horse, I rode to the north,

185

through the Oglala and other circles, and came to the Greasy Grass, reining in. Our women brought horses in from the west. Our warriors stood by their horses, waiting. On the ridges, beyond the river, the *Sahiyelas* and Oglalas fought the *wasicus*.

"*Hiyupo!*" I shouted, and my pony splashed across the Greasy Grass.

Lakota warriors followed me, as did *Sahiyela* women. Some went after the frightened *wasicu* horses, running away from *Mila Hanska*. Most, however, followed me.

Straight we rode, into the cowardly *wasicus*. Soon, my hatchet dripped red with blood. Our warriors stopped to gather the guns the dead *wasicus* no longer needed. They tore off the clothing of the dead. They lifted scalps. Some of the younger boys took arrowheads, and pressed them into the toenails and fingernails of our enemies just lying on the ground—to make sure they, indeed, were dead. We found one only pretending to be dead.

Him, we left to the *Sahiyela* women.

At the bottom of a ridge, in a buffalo wallow, warriors stripped one dark-haired man who had fought well, but then they stopped, staring and pointing at the strong medicine hanging from his neck on a gold string. The cross the Black Robes try to teach us about. It had given this warrior strong medicine.

His medicine proved not as powerful as that of the Lakotas.

"Leave him alone!" I pointed up the hill, and rode there. "There. Kill them all."

Crazy Horse reined in his pony, his hair dripping with sweat.

To him, I yelled: *"Hiyupo,* Crazy Horse! Leave those down there to our women. *Hiyupo!"* I kicked my pony into a lope, still shouting, *"Hiyupo!* This fight will soon be over."

Many *wasicus* ran toward the last remaining soldiers on the hillside. Most did not make it.

Some stopped, falling to their knees, yelling: "Sioux, have mercy. Have mercy." I did not understand their words. I cared for nothing they had to say.

These we killed.

Some just ran until our horses overtook them.

These we killed.

Some stopped, turned.

These killed themselves.

Near the top of the ridge, the *wasicus* had formed. There was nowhere for them to go. Lakotas and *Sahiyelas* stood on the top of the hill. Onward we came. Onward from all directions were Indians.

All the *wasicus* could do was die.

For a moment, we stopped. Our warriors reloaded the holy irons they had picked up off the ground. A breeze came, just briefly, clearing away the dust. The split flag of *Mila Hanska* waved, but just like that, the wind no longer blew. The flag died.

So did the remaining *Mila Hanska* when we charged.

Some fled. I stopped, watching our warriors run down those trying to reach the Greasy Grass, and slid off my pony. My hand clutched the pole of the split flag. I stared down at the body of one of the last *wasicus* to fall.

His face was part blackened by a long-ago gunshot. His clothes were white from the dust. I dropped my hatchet, and picked up his fast-shooting holy iron.

I looked down at his eyes, which saw no more. He was a white man, but I saw only *Palani*. I saw my dead wives. My dead children.

I lifted the *wasicu* holy iron and brought the stock down on the man's head. I beat. I beat. I beat.

A Minneconjou woman came to me, said something. Blood rushed so violently that I could not make out her words, but she held a mallet in her right hand, and I knew what she meant. After I tossed away the bloody long gun, I accepted her gift, fell to my knees, and continued to hammer the dead *wasicu's* face.

I smashed his head with this mallet until it was flat as my own hand, until his body could not be recognized, perhaps not even by his own god. I dropped the mallet, I picked up my hatchet, and I chopped him up. I swung my hatchet until I could no longer lift it. I ripped out his heart.

Then, as warriors and women ran about the dead *wasicus*, I raised my head to the skies, to *Wakan Tanka*, and cried.

Chapter Twenty-Seven

Mitch Boyer

I scream: "The only chance we got's to run!"

"Stand your ground!" some damned fool yells. "I'm in command!"

What command? We're finished.

I never should have signed on to scout for the general, damn his soul for all eternity!

"Run, damn it!" I yell to some kid. "Head for the river. That way. Run. That's the only chance we got!"

Maybe they won't see us because of all this dust and smoke.

"Run!"

I lead the way. I know I'll never make it off this damned hill.

Chapter Twenty-Eight

Harry Reed

"Run!" Uncle Tom yells at Uncle Boston and me. "Get the hell out of here!" And he turns back, firing his Winchester, to face a million Indians.

God . . . God . . . God have mercy. God have mercy.

Run, Uncle Boston.

Oh, God. Oh, Uncle George. Uncle Tom.

Run, Uncle Boston. Run!

Merciful Jesus, save me. Save us.

I . . .

Jesus, this can't be happening to me. This . . .

Oh, God, please, Indian, no! Not the tomahawk. Please, God. This can't . . . Not the tomahawk! Not . . .

Chapter Twenty-Nine

Red Horse

We chased the fleeing *wasicus*. Many turned, falling to their knees, crying out *wasicu* words before we killed them. Some made it into a steep ravine, but they never reached the Greasy Grass. My Lakota brothers and our *Sahiyela* friends stood on top of the ridge.

A few *wasicus* tried to climb out of the ravine, their hands slipping, digging. They could not get out. They could only die.

It was easy to kill these men.

Then I heard something strange, and I looked up. There was no more shooting. The echoes of guns had died, except for the occasional shot of triumph, or a warrior firing into the head of a *wasicu* who might or might not still be alive. I heard singing. I heard crying. I heard shouts.

And the sounds of horses running.

I looked toward the top of a hill, and saw one last *wasicu*, riding hard on a red horse with white stockings, pursued by four Indians, one of whom I recognized as my Oglala friend, He Dog. The *wasicu* was riding south, toward the hill where the rest of *Mila Hanska* had been driven.

Still, he grew farther and farther away from his

pursuers, and I had lost many, many races to He Dog and his fast spotted horse he had stolen from the Nez Percé.

"He is going to get away!" Groaning, Iron Hawk turned to me. "How did he get past our warriors?"

"The dust," I said. "His medicine was strong."

Then, the fool *wasicu* did a dumb thing. As fleet as his horse was, as great as his medicine, he would live. He would take the story of this battle to other *wasicus*. He would tell them to leave us Lakotas and *Sahiyelas* alone, that our medicine was too great. He would make it back to his companions on the ridge.

Instead, he pulled out his holy iron from his hip, stuck it against his head even as his horse carried him yet farther beyond He Dog and the other Indians.

We saw the smoke from his gun, saw him topple off into the dirt, saw his horse keep galloping.

Three of the Indians chasing him stopped, looked at each other, turned their horses, and rode back to take more scalps, steal more weapons and trophies. My friend He Dog, though, was very smart. He kept riding after that red horse with the white stockings. He would have another fast horse to race.

If, of course, he ever caught it.

Iron Hawk turned to me. He smiled.

Then, we both laughed.

Chapter Thirty

Kate Bighead

We moved about the field of dead warrior white men. Our warriors sang victory songs, but there were also songs of mourning, for the warrior white men had killed many of our *Hotóhkeso* friends, many Human Beings.

The *Hotóhkeso* holy man, Sitting Bull, arrived, yelling that we should not take the clothes, the guns, the other things of the dead.

Our men, our women, we did not listen. There was too much to take, much we could use.

Horses lay dead. *Vehos* lay dead. Some were only wounded, but, soon, they were also dead.

The *Hotóhkeso* warriors had stripped many of the dead of their clothing. One man lay leaning against a dead horse and other dead soldiers. A warrior chopped off one of this man's fingers, to get to a ring this man wore. They marked his right thigh in the way of the *Hotóhkeso* people. They shoved an arrow up his manhood. One was about to take his scalp, when I said: *"Hi-es-tzie!* It is *Hi-es-tzie!"*

They stared, but did not take his scalp.

Two other Human Being women joined me.

194

One yelled: "Do not harm him any more. He is a relative of ours."

The two warriors frowned, but walked away from our dead relative.

"*Hi-es-tzie*," I said, but now my voice was only a whisper. Yes, it was Long Hair, only now his hair no longer grew long. His chest was bloody from a hole, and he had also been shot in the head. He seemed to be smiling.

"Poor Monahsetah," one of the women said as she wiped away the blood from Long Hair's body. "Will she mourn for her husband?"

Many moons ago, during the Deer Rutting Moon, when I lived with the Human Beings in the south, Long Hair had brought his warrior white men to our camp while we slept. He killed many of our people, mostly women and children. It was terribly cold that morning. The river ran red with the blood of our people.

The warrior white men captured many of our women and children, and took them to the soldier fort. Long Hair saw Monahsetah, how young and how pretty she was. Long Hair fell in love with Monahsetah. He bedded her. It was said that she later bore him a child, but he never returned to claim his son.

Now he never would. Which, I thought, was a good thing. For now Monahsetah's son would grow up to be a Human Being, and not a foolish *veho*.

"He smoked the pipe with Human Beings," an old woman said. "He was warned not to make war on us ever again. If he did, he was told, the Everywhere Spirit would cause him to be killed."

"It is so." Nodding at the memory, the second woman produced an awl, and rammed it into Long Hair's eardrum. "Now," she said, with a little laugh, "maybe he can hear better."

At that moment, Wooden Leg rode up. He was angry. He hollered at our warriors, at the *Hotóhkeso* men. "Come on!" he cried. "There are more warrior white men away from here. They hide on a hill. Let us go kill them, too."

So most of the men, and some women, rode south.

I did not. I stared at *Hi-es-tzie*. I thought of Monahsetah. I sang a song of mourning for them both.

Chapter Thirty-One

Left Hand

Unmoving, I stand. The dust settles. All around me come sounds of victory. The hillside is covered with bodies. Every *niátha* lies dead. Women sing. Warriors strip the bodies. They shout. Into the air, they fire some of the weapons that now belong to them. They take scalps. They count coup. I see the Lakota boy, Black Elk is how he is called, running around with his friends. They shoot arrows into the dead pony soldiers. Or they shove the arrows deeper into the bodies.

I hold the lance. I stare at the man I have killed. "*Tenéi'éíhinoo*," I whisper to myself, but I do not feel strong.

I close my eyes. When they open, I still see the body of the man—no, he is no more than a boy, no older than Black Elk—whose life I have taken. He lies in a lake of his own blood. His eyes stare at me, and, for a moment, I think they have blinked. "*Niiteheib-ín!*" I cry, but I am surrounded by other Indians. They do not know my tongue, for I am Arapaho, and they are too busy gathering their plunder to help this boy.

Again, I look. No, his eyes did not blink. Maybe my own tears fooled me into thinking, hoping, that. Maybe it was a fly attracted to the dead, for it grows even hotter, and already the smell of the dead begins to thicken the air.

Slowly I draw my lance from the body. Angrily I pitch it away, and fall to my knees. I retch. I sob. Staring into the blue sky, I scream. Now, I can feel the eyes of curious Indians I do not know staring at me, but I do not care.

I have killed a boy. I came here with my friends hoping to earn honors by fighting some Shoshones, maybe stealing their ponies. Instead, I have wound up in a great camp of many tribes, and we have fought white men, pony soldiers. It will be a fight spoken of for many, many winters. Many songs will be sung. There will be feasts in many Indian camps.

Yet the boy lying before me was not *niátha.* He was not even a wolf for the pony soldiers.

He was Lakota.

I did not mean to kill him. There was so much dust, it was hard to see. I had leaped off my pony, jumping down to finish off a pony soldier, but this fool white man that I chased put the barrel of his pistol in his mouth and blew out the back of his skull. I counted coup on this dead man, then heard a scream. Turning, I thrust the lance I held, and, out of the dust, this Lakota boy appeared, and the point of my lance drove into his chest. Thinking him to be an enemy, I plunged with all my might, blinded by the dust, and drove the boy to the ground, pinned him to the dirt.

Then my eyes cleared, and I saw the boy, saw him gripping the shaft of my lance with both hands. I blinked. I could not believe what I had done. The boy's hands let go of the lance, and fell into the grass. His eyes stared at me, locking on me in death.

Now, I hear other songs. I know not the language of these other Indians. We always speak through signs. Yet I do not need to understand the words to realize these are songs of mourning. Women wail. They grieve for their loved ones who died in this great victory of all Indian peoples.

Again, I stare at the Lakota boy. Soon, someone will mourn for him.

"Left Hand," a voice calls to me, and I feel a hand grip my shoulder. Turning and looking up, I cannot see the face at first for all my tears, but I blink them away, I sniff, I wipe my eyes, and see that it is my friend, Waterman, who came with me, who speaks and understands the Lakota tongue.

"Come," he says. "Others are going to kill those pony soldiers still on the hill to the south. Come. Let us go with them. This battle is not over."

My heart turns bad again. I push myself up, and yell something. I pick up the lance, and run to my pony. Waterman has already mounted his. Many Indians are riding south.

Chapter Thirty-Two

Major Marcus Reno

1876—6/26
Continued

Ross:

Still in this hole on the hill. indians didn't charge

To pick up my story. we had to get out of those wood. that's why I Retreated.

Now, Does that make me a coward? I was trying to save my command. Custer had abandoned us. Benteen wasn't anywhere to be seen. There were 1000s of indians after us. Killing us. I had to find a tenable position. Had to save myself the men.

Someone yelled: "Every man for himself!"

But it wasn't me, Ross. It wasn't me.

I wasn't drunk.

We rode hard. Fought our way through the red devils. Rode harder.

Varnum. I heard him yelling, "Hold on, men. Let's get into shape. We have to fight it out. You can't run away from injuns."

I yelled back at him, the bloody martinet. "I am in command here, sir!"

& he yells back at me: "Well, Christ Almighty, Major, command!"

Command. That's what I was doing. Commanding a retreat. Getting my men away. I spurred my horse harder. Didn't even realize we had hit the Little Big Horn until water splashed my face. Damned horse almost went down. That would have meant the end of me. Behind me, came those savage cries, bullets & arrows striking flesh. Glimpsed a struggling soldier being carried downstream. A bullet blew out one of his eyes, & he struggled no more.

"For God's sake, don't leave me here! I'm shot through both legs!" It was Hodgson's voice. My adjutant. But I couldn't do anything for him. Ride back. & get killed?

We made it across the river. Water was cold. Seemed to revive me. Some of us. Climbed up that bank, & I saw the hill. It was steep, high. There were some trees. Get there, & we might stand a chance. I pointed. I think I yelled at the boys to follow me. My horse couldn't make it. I had to dismount, slip, slide, crawl, beg, cry. I pulled that horse up behind me

Made it up the hill. could breathe again. God, I was still breathing . . . still alive.

"If we've got to die," someone yelled, "let's die like men. I'm a fighting son-of-a-bitch from Texas." That was Luther Hare. He'd made it, too. "Don't run off like a pack of whipped curs!"

I blinked. I could see clearly. I saw Moylan, dismounting, rallying his men. Saw Hare directing some of our boys to lay down a covering fire. I looked behind me. At the river. At the battlefield. I saw the bodies. The bodies of men . . . that . . . I'd led . . . into death.

Where was Custer? Where was Benteen?

"Dismount!" I yelled. "Dismount!" I reached up. Grab the reins to a horse. Fool almost jerked my arms out of their sockets. The horse stopped. The trooper dismounted.

"Form a skirmish line!" I yelled.

More men, some wounded, some not, came over the rise.

Behind me, Capt. French's voice, "You damned fool, where are your colors?"

Colors? What good was a guidon now? A flag? I turned, & what I saw amazed me. The color guard, a dumb private, unbuttoned his shirt. He had torn the guidon from its staff, saved it. Now he handed it to the captain, & French tied that rag onto a carbine. He rammed it in the ground.

"Major." It was Dr. Porter's voice. "The men were pretty well demoralized, weren't they?"

I just saw those colors. Not waving. There was no wind. But I stared at that flag, & I told the surgeon, "That was a charge, sir!" & walked away.

All those indians had to do was charge up this

hill. They could have finished us. But most of them galloped off to the north.

"Major!" It was Moylan. Awaiting orders.

"I thought it was my duty," I told him. Had to explain to him. I wasn't drunk. Wasn't a coward. "To lead the men. Get here. Observe the ford. The hill. Rally the men. Reform." My head bobbed.

"Sir," Moylan said. "What are your orders?"

I was about to answer. Maybe I did. I can't seem to recall. I realized I'd lost my hat. I fished a neckerchief from my tunic, wrapped that over my head. The Sun was blistering. What to do? But the indians were going north. then I saw more dust. More indians. From . . . No. God be praised. It was Benteen.

quickly, I mounted, rode down the hill, galloped like a madman to Benteen. "For God's sake, Benteen," I told him, "halt your command & help me! I've lost half my men."

Good Benteen . . . brought his men up the hill. I told him I had to find Hodgson. They were listening to gunfire to the north when I went down the hill. Hodgson might have been alive. Only wounded. He was a great favorite, a wonderful friend. & . . .

I found him. But he wasn't alive. A bullet had struck him in the head. I removed his West Point ring. I found some keys. His watch was gone. I cried.

I didn't abandon my men.

Had left Benteen in charge. He's a good officer. I came back.

Found a flask, thank the Lord. Pack train arrived. Must have said something to upset Bible Thumper Mathey, damn him and his hypocrisy. He didn't get Blood Knife's . . . no . . . not writing about that ever again. Want to forget it, if I could. Purge it from my memories.

The brandy helps.

dr. porter has come with questions. Must close till later

Chapter Thirty-Three

Hairy Moccasin

Damn' fool white men. Not listen to us Crow scouts. Not listen to Arikarees. Not listen even to white scouts. Go get themselves killed. Before riding to death, Son Of The Morning Star Who Attacks At Dawn tell us Crow scouts, "Go!" Damn' right, we go. Not paid to fight. Paid to find damn' Lakota. Did that.

Find big damn' village.

Big damn'.

Me, White Man Runs Him, and Goes Ahead ride fast. Make way through coulées, ease way to river, come up ridge onto hill to find major. Big damn' excitement on hill. Major act crazy. Then come other bluecoats.

'Bout that time, all us hear big damn' gunfire to north.

I sign to major, that noise be where Son Of The Morning Star Who Attacks At Dawn now fighting big damn' village.

Major run talk to white-haired captain. Other bluecoats point north. Some start to mount horses.

To me, White Man Runs Him say: "Lakotas will wipe out Son Of The Morning Star Who Attacks

At Dawn soon. Then they will come here."

Damn' right. Won't take long. Son Of The Morning Star Who Attacks At Dawn make big damn' mistake. Not attack at dawn. Attack when all Indians awake, all Indians ready for soldiers.

"Let's go," Goes Ahead say.

Damn' right.

We find our ponies. Done with fool white men. Too many Lakotas for us to fight. Too damn' many for anyone to fight.

We ride away. Ride north. To our village on Yellowstone. Keep big damn' distance between us and Lakotas.

Keep riding north.

Damn' hard we ride.

Ride until we come to Crow scout named Little Face. He works for other bluecoats. We tell Little Face what happened on Greasy Grass. He cries. Says we should tell bluecoat chiefs.

White Man Runs Him tell bluecoat chiefs that Son Of The Morning Star Who Attacks At Dawn be dust by now. Maybe all bluecoats. Just few alive when we ride off. Might all be dust now.

Say this through sign.

Bluecoat chiefs not believe us. Say can't be.

Ask us again. Again, we say same thing.

Bluecoats talk. Then ride south again.

Still think Son Of The Morning Star Who Attacks At Dawn not dead. Think we mistaken.

Damn' fool white men.

Chapter Thirty-Four

Captain Thomas Weir

Give Colonel Benteen some credit. Once we got to the hilltop, he managed to get what was left of that son-of-a-bitch Reno's command into some order. Corinth, Iuka, clashin' with Bedford Forrest's boys . . . none of those fights could hold a candle to what I saw on that hill. The boys who had charged that village with Reno acted as if they'd run into Alexander the Great. Soldiers had broken down. Captain Moylan bawled like a baby. Reno was a gutless wonder. He didn't have a clue how to act, what to do. Benteen took command. It wasn't a mutiny. He just did what any officer would have, should have, done.

We fired at the hostiles on the ridge, drove them off, but they didn't put up much of a fight. Something other than our reinforcements, I feared, sent those Indians loping north, away from the hill, away from the survivors on that hilltop. They were riding at a fast lope toward . . . Custer?

Then, Benteen said . . . well, as fine as a soldier as he could be, it was something I'd come to expect from him. A good soldier, but a lousy bastard.

"Custer has abandoned us," the colonel said, loud enough for the men, even those dreadfully wounded, to hear. "Abandoned us to our fate, as he left Major Elliott at the Washita."

Moylan stopped blubbering long enough to say: "Gentlemen, in my opinion General Custer has made the biggest mistake in his life by not taking the whole regiment in at once in the first attack. You wouldn't believe the number of hostiles in that camp, and they weren't scattering. Damnation, they were fighting. Fighting like . . ."

"Save that for your memoirs, Myles," I told the ashen-faced fool, and walked away.

George Custer was a friend of mine. I'd served on his staff in Texas after the Rebellion. He'd endorsed my appointment as first lieutenant with the 7th almost ten years ago. He was a soldier, the finest ever to serve in this man's army. He was a fighter. He would not abandon anyone, and had not left Major Elliott to die on the Washita all those years ago. Benteen was just jealous. Moylan was just a blow-hard. Reno was just a yellow-livered son-of-a-bitch.

Angrily I didn't stop until reaching the edge of the hill.

Then came the sounds of gunfire off to the north.

"Jesus Christ!" Lieutenant Varnum cried out. "Hear that, Wallace?"

More gunfire.

"And that?"

Before Lieutenant Wallace could answer, I hurried to another point, for a better view. I sighed. The dust was thick way off over the hills. I even made out little trails of dust heading in that direction. More Indians. Heading north to join . . .

"That must be General Custer fighting down in the bottom." Turning, I found the private who had spoken those words, Springfield carbine shaking in his hands.

"I believe it is," I told him, maybe even too softly for him to hear, and walked to find Lieutenant Edgerly.

"Win," I said, but couldn't think of anything else to say. My lieutenant, a solid, young officer, had been issuing orders to our sergeants, but now he stopped. Everyone listened as the gunfire became more rapid. I sighed. "Custer is engaged," I said. "We should be down there."

"Yes, sir," Winfield Edgerly said. First Sergeant Michael Martin, kneeling by a dead horse, staring down at the dust, said: "I'm with you, Capt'n."

I looked around. Benteen and Moylan were still in some animated discussion, likely blasting Custer. Troopers helped the pack train up the hill, putting the animals in a circle to surround what would have to serve as a field hospital. Finally I spotted Major Reno, and I started for him, but stopped, turning around to face Win Edgerly and Sergeant Martin.

"Win, would you be willing to ride down to Custer even if the rest of the command won't?"

"Yes, sir."

I hurried to Reno. I was even respectful to him.

"Major," I said, "Custer must be around here somewhere, and we ought to go to him."

Reno looked ridiculous with that bandanna wrapped around his head. He wiped sweat from his brow. His hands shook like a drunkard's. "We are surrounded by Indians," he said. "We ought to remain here."

Some three hundred to three hundred and fifty soldiers huddled on that hilltop by that time, yet I doubt if there were two dozen Indians at the bottom of that hill. It seemed that every buck among them rode north to join the fight over there.

"Well," I said, "if no one else goes to Custer, I will go."

"No!" Terror rang in Reno's bark. "You cannot go. For if you try to do it, you will get killed and your troop with you."

"The major's right," said Benteen, who had walked up with Moylan. "We can entrench here. Wait for Terry or Crook. Custer has left us no choice."

I looked past Reno. Benteen walked away, ordering sergeants to station their men, but even the colonel, despite his hatred of George Custer, kept glancing at that dust where somebody was fighting. The gunfire wasn't as fierce as it had been.

Well, I'd expected Reno to tell me no. Now I had to make a decision, one that could get me cashiered from the Army that I loved, maybe even land me a stretch at the Leavenworth penitentiary. Returning to my troop, I checked my watch.

It was just about 5 o'clock.

"Let's go," I told Win Edgerly.

They didn't ask if I had orders. I didn't tell them I didn't. Let Benteen and Reno court-martial me. I wasn't about to ride back to Fort Lincoln and face Libbie, who I adored almost as much as her husband, and tell her I'd just sat with the rest of those cowardly, conniving sons-of-bitches up on a hilltop while Custer fought the Sioux by himself.

Gladly I would have gone alone.

The snorting of horses, the clopping of hoofs, the jingling of leather, and the cocking of weapons. Those noises caused me to turn to look behind as I rode Jake down the hill. Tears of joy, of pride, blinded me for just a moment.

My men, the black horse troop, following me.

Riding to the unknown.

God bless D Troop. I loved those boys, every damned one of them.

Turning back, I brought my bandanna to my eyes, wiped away the tears, then drew my service revolver, and, upon reaching the bottom of the hill, kicked Jake into a lope.

Almost immediately, I tugged on the reins, letting Edgerly and the rest of D Troop catch up. This was still Indian country, and our battle far from over.

About a half mile later, I glanced behind me and saw another surprise. Benteen was coming, followed, I guess, by every other troop on the hill. Even Reno had found enough nerve to leave his hole in the ground, or, more than likely, he didn't want to be left alone.

We moved to the right, halting at a path of trampled grass. It never struck me until much later that we likely had struck the trail General Custer had taken.

"Win," I said, "stay in this valley. I'm riding up there."

I pointed up the ridge, toward a sugarloaf, where the grass had been trampled recently by a lot of horses. Column of fours, by the looks of the trail.

"Do you think that's wise, Captain?" Win asked, but I was already leaning forward in the saddle, letting Jake lunge up to the top of the ridge. Once I'd reached that point, I halted, cursing at the sound of hoofs behind me.

Jerking the reins, I turned to yell: "I said . . ."

"I heard you, Capt'n." James Flanagan, another fine sergeant under my command, reined up, spitting tobacco juice onto the grass. Flanagan had fought his way from County Clare to America, had served in the Rebellion, and then in the 2nd Cavalry after the war. Since the winter of '71, he had been in the 7th. You couldn't find a better non-commissioned officer in this man's army.

I was proud to have him beside me. A short while later, I was extremely glad of his company.

I signaled Win Edgerly to keep the command moving, using the ridge as a shield. Well behind him came Benteen, and, beyond him, Reno. They would stay low, too.

Sergeant Flanagan and I followed the trail, littered with occasional horse droppings, a few campaign hats, letters, equipment, canteens, even a Springfield rifle. Yes, Custer had brought his command, at least part of his command, this very way.

Soon Indians began firing. The bucks never shot at Sergeant Flanagan or myself—well, we were out of range, and shooting at uphill targets can challenge even the best rifle shots. I didn't have to order Edgerly. Immediately he dismounted his best marksmen, and our boys exchanged some long-range shots with the savages. Eventually Edgerly's boys ran off those bucks with well-placed fusillades. Besides, Benteen had arrived with his troops, and Reno wasn't far behind. We had those Indians outnumbered . . . but what about Custer, if that were him, fighting in that swirl of dust?

Roughly a mile from the hill where we'd found Reno, I reached a couple of peaks. From this high point, I had a clear view.

Dismounting, I wrapped Jake's reins around a rock, and drew my field glasses from the leather case.

The village lay across the Little Big Horn. Reno and Moylan had been right. It was huge. Only now, it seemed practically deserted. From where I stood, the dust—which was practically all I saw—came on this side of the river, maybe three or four miles ahead of my position. That dust rose in enormous clouds, like smoke billowing from a giant forest . . . *er* prairie, fire. Again, I wiped my eyes. Shots slowly died out on the hills below the white clouds of dust.

"If that's Custer, we should join him," I said, and lowered my field glasses to wipe the dirt off lenses once more, and the sweat from my brow.

"Whatever you say, Capt'n," Sergeant Flanagan said. "Should I plant the guidon here? For a beacon? To let Custer know we're here?"

"If it is Custer," I said in a dry-mouthed whisper. "If he could see anything through all that . . ."

Sergeant Flanagan took that for an affirmative, ramming the staff of the guidon into the dirt. Up here, the wind blew hot, and the guidon fluttered in the breeze.

Suddenly a grim thought passed through my mind. Ugly. Un-Christian. *What if George Custer were killed? Would Libbie . . . ? Could she . . . and me . . . ? No,* I thought to myself, *no, Libbie would mourn Custer for a thousand eternities.* Something else struck me. So would I.

"He is not dead." This I said firmly, aloud.

"Sir?" Sergeant Flanagan said.

Peering through my glasses again, I did not reply to Flanagan, for I detected movement. Indians on horseback, riding this way, that way. Every now and then, one of the savages would dismount, but I'd lose him in the grass and scrub. I would see a puff of smoke, hear the faint echo moments later of a rifle's report.

I scanned the hills west to east, east to west, trying to find soldiers.

Nothing. Nothing but damnable dust. And Indians.

"Where is he?" I said out loud.

I wiped my eyes, stinging from sweat, tried again, sweeping the country.

At that moment, something else came into view.

The sergeant's guidon had alerted someone to our presence.

"Signal Mister Edgerly to halt his command," I ordered Sergeant Flanagan.

I looked again. Something caught my eye.

"Guidons!" I said, and relief swept over me. Guidons of the 7th. By that time, I could even detect horses, the riders wearing blue coats. Galloping toward us.

Lowering the glasses, I shouted: "That is Custer!"

My glee, my joy. Never had I felt so happy, relieved, inspired. A million years of dread left my shoulders. A vision of Libbie entered my mind. She was smiling, as happy as I felt at that moment.

I swung onto Jake, and started to touch him with my spurs.

Then Sergeant Flanagan, God bless him and all the Irish, spoke up.

Chapter Thirty-Five

Sergeant James Flanagan

Said I to the Capt'n: "Here, Capt'n, you'd better take a look through them glasses again. I think they're Indians."

Thirty-seven years old I was, a few months older than General Custer hisself, but my eyes could see as sharp as they had when I was in my teens, starin' at the lovely lasses on their way to communion in Innis. And unlike the general, my hair wasn't thinnin'. Fell in brown locks, it did, and I had no desire to lose it that afternoon.

Capt'n, he pulled back on the reins, put those field glasses back to his head. Didn't take long before he uttered a foul oath, and dropped the glasses, which bounced heavily across his chest, caused that fine horse of his to take a couple nervous steps sideways.

"Sergeant Flanagan," said he, "put that black gelding in a high lope, get down to Major . . . no, tell Benteen. Tell him several hundred Indian bucks are galloping this way. Being below the ridge, I don't think he can see them. I'll alert Lieutenant Edgerly." He paused to take a deep breath, then slowly let it out. "God, Libbie. Dearest God in Heaven."

Then, he sent that great horse of his down the ridge at a breakneck pace.

Me? Fast as them Indians was racin' toward us, I skedaddled myself, findin' a trail down the bluff that was nowhere near as tricky as the one the capt'n had picked for hisself. I hit the hollow, gouged the black with my spurs, and gave that geldin' plenty of rein. When a thousand bucks is right behind you, you needs a full head of steam.

Capt'n Benteen had halted his command, and appeared to be palaverin' with Major Reno, who had caught up. My geldin' slid to a stop, wound up standin' in the stirrups, I did, firin' a jackass salute, and sayin', between breaths: "Capt'n Weir's . . . compliments . . . sir." Which was one mighty shameless falsehood. A cold day in Hades it'd be when the capt'n complimented Reno or Benteen.

"Sir," I said. "There's a . . . hell of a lot . . . of Indians lightin' a shuck . . . in this . . . direction."

Said the major: "Good God!"

Benteen displayed more control. "How many, Sergeant?"

He wouldn't believe me, but I said it anyway. "I'd say five hundred." Likely it was more, but I didn't want to scare the boys.

Now, I admire Capt'n Weir. He pulled the cork far too often—and that's comin' from an Irishman—but I never had no desire to serve under any other officer in the 7th. Except . . . in a pinch . . . maybe Capt'n Benteen. That bantam rooster's balls was made of brass. Maybe cast iron.

"Mister Godfrey," Capt'n Benteen said calmly as Major Reno began moppin' his brow with a rag. The lieutenant pulled his horse up even with the capt'n's. "Godfrey," said Benteen. "Take K Troop forward. Position your men on either side of the ridge."

"For God's sake," Major Reno cried out, "we've got scores of wounded. You need to take . . ."

"Major." Benteen cut him off like a schoolteacher snappin' at an unruly student. "We're not abandoning Captain Weir or Lieutenant Edgerly. You can ride back to Captain Moylan, have him withdraw the wounded he is escorting. We can make our stand . . . how about that ridge we passed? We can hold off the Indians, find a position that will be easier for us to defend."

"Fred," Major Reno said, his voice somewhat steadier. "We've already begun some rifle pits, some entrenchments, back where we were. It would offer more cover, and we'd be closer to the river. We'll need water before this is over and done with."

Capt'n Benteen wet his lips. "You're right, Marcus," he said, and that seemed to revive the major's confidence. The capt'n turned back to

Lieutenant Godfrey. "You have your orders, mister," he said.

Thus, we began pullin' back. Retreatin'? Hell, we was runnin', followin' a bunch of damned pack mules. That's hard for a cavalryman to abide, but, well, there was a hell of a lot of Indians bearin' down for our scalps.

Wasn't the most disciplined withdrawal. I saluted the major, but he was already pushin' his horse back toward the pack mules, the doc, and our wounded boys. Capt'n McDougall nudged his horse close to Capt'n Benteen, and I heard McDougall whisper: "Fred, I think you should assume command. Major Reno isn't fit."

I wasn't eavesdroppin', mind you, but, well, just kinda overheard that confab.

Capt'n Benteen smiled. Hell, he was in command. He knew it. Everybody in the regiment knew it.

Capt'n Benteen deployed his troop as a rear guard, too. Me? I rode along with Lieutenant Godfrey. Waitin' on D Troop. Waitin' on Capt'n Weir.

They showed up shortly after the firin' commenced. I'd see a feather above us, and send a chunk of lead in that direction from my Springfield. Weir reined up first, sweatin', revolver still in his right hand.

"Capt'n," I said, "we're fallin' back?"

"To where?"

"Where we was."

He cut loose with a litany of curses, then said: "All right."

But—and this is what sickens me to this day, what breaks my heart—Lieutenant Edgerly galloped up, his face white, but not from fear of all 'em Indians around us.

"Captain," he says, pausin' just long enough to get his breath back. "Trooper Charley's wounded about a hundred yards back, maybe one hundred and fifty. Took a hit through both hips. I told him to hide in the ravine, that I'd come back for him with a skirmish line."

"Lieutenant," the capt'n said, speakin' formally of a sudden, "our orders are to fall back."

"But, Capt'n . . ."

"We have our orders, Mister Edgerly." The capt'n spurred his black, turned around, and rode up the ridge a spell, firin' his revolver at Indian heads till the hammer fell on an empty cylinder. Now the capt'n wasn't afraid. Yet I never could understand why we didn't go back for poor old Charley. Vincent Charley. The troop's farrier. Best man to shoe a horse in the entire regiment.

"Fall back!" Lieutenant Edgerly's voice cracked.

So we left Vincent Charley back in that ravine. Never did I see him again.

Oh, when it was all over and done, some of the

boys found him. Found him where he'd been left. And buried him. A son-of-a-bitchin' red devil had shoved a stick down his throat.

Well, like I said, it wasn't the finest execution of military order. Started out all right, I reckon, but 'fore long, we was runnin' for our dear lives.

How far had we come from the hill where Reno had dug in? A mile? Two? Felt like fifty. Horses bolted. Troopers cried, screamed. All around us we heard and saw Indians. Felt bullets buzzin' past our faces. Once we reached the bottom of the bluff, up that hill we skedaddled, dismountin', pullin' our horses behind us. Some of the boys turned their horses loose. Some, I'm shamed to say, overtook the boys haulin' the wounded up the hill. Didn't stop. Damned cowards, runnin' like the doc was passin' out free whiskey.

When I reached the top, that fine black geldin' of mine fell. Barely managed to clear the saddle, I hit the dirt, rolled over, came up tastin' blood. Saw my noble beast raise his head briefly, then drop. Blood already pooled underneath that black horse. How long he'd bled 'fore his heart burst . . . well, if this Army would listen to an Irish sergeant, they'd be givin' plenty of medals to horses and not horse soldiers.

"Throw yourself on the ground!" Major Reno's sand had returned. He marched around, barkin' orders. "Return fire. Damn it, return fire."

"We have no cover!" some fool yelled.

"Lie on your belly. Get behind grease weed. Behind a clump of grass. A dead horse. A dead soldier. Return fire. Damn it, return fire. Do you bastards want to die today?"

I crawled back to my dead mount, picked up my Springfield, blew out the sand. Had to pry out the copper casin' with my knife. Then shoved in another round, aimed, fired.

Ain't sure I can exactly describe all the hell, all the commotion, all the panic.

"Unload the packs!" Sounded like Major Reno's voice, but I couldn't be sure. "Make breastworks out of packs. Out of the dead mules."

"Wallace!" That was Benteen's voice. "Form your company, Wallace. Right over there. If those damned Indians overrun us . . . form your company!"

"What company, Benteen? I've got three men. Three men, damn it!"

"Get your three men and your ass over there, Wallace. I'll support you. H Troop! H Troop! Sergeant McCurry, follow me! Assist G Troop."

More voices.

"That weed won't stop a bullet, Corporal!"

"Maybe not, Lieutenant, but it's all I gots, sir!"

"Thunderation. Two horses just deserted."

"Listen to me. If your mounts are still alive, tie them to a picket line."

"And just where the hell do we secure the picket ropes, Lieutenant?"

"To the legs of the horses and mules already dead!"

I turned. Bullets and arrows zipped through the air. You could make out the arrows, and, strange as it seems, it felt as if you could even see the bullets. Horses screamed. The sickenin' sound of bullets and arrows strikin' flesh echoed all around me.

Below us, a couple Winchesters opened up.

"Hell, where'd damned Indians get repeatin' rifles, Sergeant?" a trooper asked.

Michael Martin bitterly replied: "Where the hell do you think?"

Which saddened me. A lot of our officers carried their personal weapons, not the gov'ment-issued Springfields.

Lookin' at my belt, I realized I'd fired my last cartridge for the Springfield. Merciful Jesus, though, a soldier caught a slug right beside me, and fell dead just a rod from my feet. I crawled, removed the dead lad's ammunition belt—didn't recognize him, thank you, Mary!—and returned to my position. By that time, I had company. Another private had joined me.

"You don't mind, do you, Sergeant?" he said.

"Beats dyin' alone," said me back to him.

I leaned against the dead black, already swellin' from the heat, saw a trooper dive behind a box of hard bread. He'd just landed when a bullet went through the box, bread and all, and blew out his brains. I saw this. Saw this bloody, horrible scene, and . . . I laughed. So did a couple others. 'Cause we was rememberin' what one of the boys had said back at the supply depot on the Powder River. Nearby, a corporal stopped sniggerin' long enough to say: "They told us that bread was hard enough to stop a bullet. Well, A.J. just proved 'em wrong."

We laughed again. Just a moment. Then commenced fightin'.

Slowly the sun started sinkin', but not fast enough. Beside me, some trooper prayed. Another wrote a note. I cussed 'em both. "God's got no time to listen to you now, and your wife'll never get that note if some damned redskin kills you. Fight. Damn it, fight. Fight, you sorry sons-of-bitches. I don't want to die today!"

The air stank of gunpowder, of death, of shit—human and livestock. My eyes burned from all the powder, and then I saw Benteen, his white hair plastered to his head, walkin' calmly while the rest of us yellow bastards hugged tightly to whatever cover we was fortunate enough to have.

"Quit wastin' lead!" the capt'n cried out. He stopped, saw the wet-nosed trooper beside me. "You load for Sergeant Flanagan," the capt'n said. "He turned to a couple troopers next to us. "You two, dig."

"Dig what?" one of the damned fools asked.

"Dig your damned grave. Dig a rifle pit, you idiot." To the next soldier: "You load, too." The capt'n looked at me. "Best shots, Sergeant. Make them count. Don't waste lead."

"Yes, sir," said I, and I rolled over, aimed below, waitin'.

Benteen, he inspired us. Made us think we had a chance, that, by the grace of the Virgin Mary and her Son, maybe we would live.

Steadied my aim I did, focusin' on the Indians below. Every now and then, I'd hear the uproar of gunfire to my right or left, maybe even behind me, but I just kept starin' down below. When I had a clear shot, I'd take it. Don't know if I hit nothin', but the Indians soon lost much of their bravery, though one fool buck stood up, and charged. Just charged up that hill.

I fired. So did a few others around me. Saw that Indian's breastplate shatter, saw a mist of pink explode from the back of his head, saw him crumple, and fall not twenty yards from the top of our hill.

What a brave damned fool. Wish all them Indians had that much foolishness. A couple bucks tried to fetch the dead warrior's body, but we drove 'em back in a hurry.

After a while, the gunfire slowly diminished. None too soon, the sun finally dropped behind the hills, and darkness descended upon our hill.

Still, I waited, till I couldn't see a damned thing in front of me. The breeze picked up. Off in the distance, beyond the river and in the village, came the sound of drums, of whistles, of singin'. On the hilltop, just a thankful silence.

Didn't last long.

But there was no more gunfire.

Major Reno started yellin': "Dig, boys! Dig rifle pits! Dig!"

"With what, Major?" came a query from some trooper.

"Your mess kits. Your knives. Your spurs. Your damned fingers!"

Capt'n Weir was yellin', too. "No tobacco! No one strikes a match! And no one leaves his post! We're waitin' here." His voice dropped, but I could hear him 'cause he was walkin' right past me. "We wait here till Custer relieves us."

I rolled over, eased down the hammer on my Springfield. I said to the trooper beside me: "Thanks for your help, lad. We best get to diggin'." I drew my butcher knife.

He didn't answer.

When I reached over to touch him, my hand came away bloody, sticky, and my heart sank. How long he'd been dead, I had nary a clue.

Chapter Thirty-Six

Lieutenant Charles DeRudio

Fred Gerard came up to me that night, and I almost blew his fool head off.

"Lieutenant," our interpreter whispered, not seeing the shaking Schofield revolver in my hand. "I don't see Herendeen or any of those other boys." Hell, he couldn't see a thing. It was pitch black, no moon, and we were in the woods. Had been hiding there since Reno, the son-of-a-bitching coward, had abandoned us. I'm too harsh on Major Reno. Having seen the size of that village General Custer had sent us up against, I understood then that had Reno not been such a craven coward, we would all be dead now.

"They were there. . . ."

"Must have lit a shuck," Gerard said. "They're probably out yonder." He gestured to the open country. "Dead."

"What's goin' on, Lieutenant?" whispered Trooper Thomas O'Neill.

"Be quiet," I said. Night had brought a chill, yet I kept sweating profusely.

Herendeen had left the timber. That meant I was alone with one trooper, Gerard, and the half- or quarter-breed scout, Billy Jackson, who was lying somewhere underneath leaves and twigs, and smart enough not to say one damned word.

I was here, only a few hundred yards from the savage Indians, hiding, because I had been foolish enough to return to the woods to rescue the flag my color bearer had stupidly dropped. I was an Italian aristocrat, to die for that damned American flag?

The drums beat steadily. We could hear the wails, the songs, the eagle flutes.

"Do you think we could make it to . . . ?" My voice trailed off. To where? Custer? Who knew where he was? Reno? As fast as he had been riding, last I saw him, he could very well be in Dakota Territory by now.

"Lieutenant," Gerard said, "Major Reno could be dead along with everyone who followed him."

We had hidden deep in the woods, in the center, our horses gone, either dead or captured by the hostiles.

"Fred," I said, "I'm going to crawl to the edge of the woods, see if I can see anything. Fires from the troops. Anything."

"If they're alive," Gerard said, "they will likely have no fires. Not tonight."

"I'll be back in a minute," I said, and, Schofield in hand, began crawling through the timbers. I thought, fatalistically: *Or I'll be dead.*

Ten minutes later, I wondered if I would even be able to find my way back to Fred, Billy, and O'Neill. I reached the edge, sucked in a deep breath, recalling all those boys of ours who probably lay on that field in front of me. I thanked God for the moonless night, that I could not see their bodies.

I could see nothing. No signal fire. Not over toward the river. Now, in the Indian camp, dozens, maybe hundreds of bonfires illuminated the Indian village. The sound of those awful drums, those guttural chants, they carved up one's nerves.

Then a new sound came to me. Footfalls. Two voices whispering, but they were not speaking English.

I froze, sank into the ground, indeed tried to press my way through the earth, all the way to the core of this globe, all the way to Hades itself.

Briefly the two voices stopped. One laughed. My revolver trembled in my hands. Conversation resumed. The Indians talked, no more than three feet in front of me. I tried to hold my breath. *They must hear my pounding heart,* I thought.

I, Carlo Camilius "Charles" DeRudio, son of Count and Countess Aquila di Rudio, graduate of the Austrian Military Academy, former member of Garibaldi's staff in Italy, who had come to America in 1858 in time to serve with the 79th New York and 2nd U.S. Colored Infantry to preserve the Union . . . I was to die here, at the edge of a woods in Montana Territory.

I was to die, having just pissed in my pants.

Chapter Thirty-Seven

Standing Bear

I was sixteen years old, and I was crazy.

That day, we were all crazy.

When darkness came, many of us remained crazy.

"Hey, Minneconjou boy," a *Sahiyela* called out to me in the Lakota tongue, "are you hungry?"

I had not eaten since breakfast, but my stomach did not grumble for any food. The air smelled of blood. It sickened many of us.

"No," I answered.

The *Sahiyela* laughed. Then our bravest warriors got together. We would not charge the *wasicus* at night, could not see them, but we had the entire hill surrounded.

"We will kill them tomorrow," I heard a warrior say.

"It is true," said another. "They have no water. They cannot have much food. We will wait. Kill them that way. Slowly." He laughed.

"There is not much honor in that," said a Lakota.

"But they will be dead," said another.

"But what if they slip away, since *Mila Hanska* are all cowards, in the darkness?"

"They have nowhere to go. We will stay here. We will send our younger warriors, our boys, our women, back to our circles. They will eat, and bring food back for us."

That was a good idea, all of the warriors agreed.

So one came to me. It was too dark for me to tell who it was, but he was Lakota, Oglala, and he said: "What is your name?"

"Standing Bear," I answered. "I am Minneconjou."

"Well, you go to your circle. You eat. Eat well. Tomorrow we will finish killing these *wasicus*. You bring back food. You can do this?"

"Yes," I said.

So I left the rocks, went down the hill where we had left all of our ponies, to protect them from *wasicu* bullets. I mounted my bareback pony, and I returned to the Minneconjou circle, the third from the south, but no one was there. It was strange, but then, as I have already told you, we were all crazy. My own lodge was empty, but I went inside.

The big fight had begun that afternoon, and I was not ready for a fight. No one in our circle was ready to fight. I wore only my shirt, plus the red feather from a bird I had killed a few days earlier. No time had I even to saddle my gray mare. All during the fight, I had ridden her bareback. So now I took time to dress. I put on my best moccasins, my leggings. I painted my face. I grabbed a hatchet, since my six-shooting holy iron had no more bullets, and more arrows for my quiver. I saddled my pony. I rode to the sound of drums in the center of all of the villages.

I found my mother, and she gave the tremolo. She honored me, for I had taken many coup on that afternoon. My father came to me, pulled me close. I had not seen him since *Mila Hanska* attacked.

My mother wore a blue coat with the sleeves and brass buttons ripped off. My father wore a black *wasicu* soldier hat, and one of the soldier belts around his waist.

"Did you hear?" my father asked. "It was *Pehin Hanska*. He led the *wasicus*. We defeated *Pehin Hanska* on the ridge across the Greasy Grass." He pointed north.

Pehin Hanska? We had killed Long Hair? We had killed the warrior chief the *wasicus* called Custer, who said his medicine was strong?

Ha! Wasicu *power is not match for the power of the Lakota!*

"*Sahiyela* women recognized him," my father explained. "They say he is a relative of theirs. He married a *Sahiyela* woman many winters ago. Now he is dead. Ha!"

He turned, returning to the dances around the nearest fire. There must have been a hundred fires, and the drumming and the singing and the flutes rang out with joy. Now, I could hear the women around the nearest fire. They sang:

> Long Hair has never returned,
> So his woman is crying, crying.
> Looking over here, she cries.
> Long Hair, holy irons I had none.
> You brought me many. I thank you!
> You make me laugh.
> Long Hair, horses I had none.
> You brought me many. I thank you!
> You make me laugh!
> Long Hair, where he lies nobody knows.
> Crying, they seek him.
> He lies over here.
> Let go your holy irons.
> You are not men enough to do any harm.
> Let go your holy irons!

My mother thrust a buffalo rib, dripping with grease, at me. I told her I was not hungry, but that I should take food to the warriors still surrounding the hill where the rest of the *wasicus* waited to be killed.

"You will stay here," my mother said. "You will dance and sing and eat. Then you must sleep. Your sisters and I will bring those warriors food. You will sleep. You must be strong for when the sun rises and we kill the rest of the *wasicus*." She threw both arms into the air, and let go with another tremolo. "My son has counted coup! He has taken scalps! He is a man!" And she ran to the cook fires to gather food for the *Sahiyelas* and Lakotas and other Indians waiting for food, waiting for morning.

Slowly I left the dancing, mounted the gray, and returned to the Minneconjou circle, leaving the celebrating, the singing, the dancing, the feasting, the sounds of the drums, of the flutes. The night grew darker, much cooler, as I came to my own lodge. I rubbed the gray's neck, whispered in her ear, and entered the teepee. I lay on the buffalo robe, hands beneath my head, and closed my eyes.

I saw this scene from that afternoon: *I ride the gray, with other warriors my age, even younger. We come to another Lakota riding back toward our circle. "It is Long Elk," I say, and give a cry, but the sound dies in my throat as Long Elk raises his head. Blood streams from his mouth, and his chest is all bloody, spilling down the neck of his painted horse. We stop beside him, but Long Elk tells us: "Do not be a woman. Be brave. Ride on. There are more* Mila Hanska *to kill." He coughs, spits out more blood, and leans forward, trying to get his pony to take him back to the circle. Where he can die.*

My eyes opened. It was cold, but I sweated. My eyes shut again.

I ride the gray, holding my revolver in my hand.

236

Already, the holy iron has been shot empty. I spy a bluecoat running, and, leaning over my pony's neck, I swing the holy iron. The barrel smashes against the wasicu's *head, and he stumbles forward, falling under the gray's hoofs. I glance behind me to watch other Lakotas trample the* wasicu. *We do not stop to scalp him.*

Again, I jerked awake. I sat up, and, even though my eyes were open, I remembered, and pictured, another scene from that day.

The bodies of our enemies litter the hillside. As we ride up the ridge, a Lakota points to an Indian in a blue coat lying on the ground. "Scalp that Palani!*" the warrior yells, and I start to dismount the gray, but another man has already leaped from his war pony, knife in his hand, and has turned the dead man over. The scalping knife falls from his hand. He looks up, and tears begin to stream down his sweaty face. "It is not a* Palani!*" he cries out to us. "It is a* Sahiyela. *I knew this man!" Our oldest warrior spits. "He should not have worn a blue coat," he says, and charges his mount into the dust, after more* Mila Hanska.

My head shook, but still I could not forget the images of the day. I saw: *All of the* wasicus *are dead on the ridge. Or so we think. We leap off our ponies, and run to count coup. Men and women are stripping the dead. They slash the right thighs of many* wasicus. *A man beside me looks* at a dead Long Knife. He points to the man's face. "I have never even seen a wasicu with two beards on the sides of his face." The dead man's eyes stare up at me. They do not see me, but I cannot help but feel that he is looking into me. The warrior kneels down, and scalps one of the man's beards. He lifts it to the air, and shouts: "Hokay hey!" Then he leaps onto his pony, and rides away.

Turning, I spot two fat Lakota women. They have stripped another wasicu, who lies naked on the grass. One bends to chop off his finger to get at a gold band. Before she can accomplish this, the wasicu jumps up. The two Lakota women scream. One falls on her hindquarters, thinking this wasicu's spirit has come back. He is naked, bleeding from his shoulder and head. Nearby, a Sahiyela warrior laughs at the two women. Another tells them that this Long Knife was just playing dead. The Lakota woman on the ground jumps up. The wasicu screams something and fights one of the Lakota women. Other braves gather around, laughing. The second woman hurries to help her friend fight this wasicu. It is funny, two fat Lakota women fighting a naked wasicu. Then one of the women rams her knife into the naked wasicu's belly. He groans. Blood pours from his mouth. The other woman takes her knife and slits the man's throat. His eyes roll back into his head. His bowels loosen, and the *two women back away from his purging. This causes the warriors to laugh even harder. The* wasicu *falls. This time, he is really dead.*

I tried to stand, but my knees would not work. I fell back against the buffalo robe, and I remembered.

We are at the hill. Shooting at the last of Mila Hanska, *where they have all retreated. The sun bakes down upon us. The air stinks of death. My eyes burn from all the shooting. On the hillside, we hear the sounds of shouting, of ponies screaming as our bullets and arrows tear into them. The* wasicus *fire back. Near me, I hear someone cry out: "Hey! Hey!"*

I crawl past the bush separating me and another Lakota boy. He is even younger than I am, but never will he see another sunrise. A bullet has struck him above his right eye, and he is dead. His eyes are open, but these I close with trembling fingertips.

Right beside me, an Oglala boy stands. He looks down at me and the dead boy, and says: "See how brave I am. I am not afraid to die." He stands up, yells: "Hokay hey!" Up the hill, he runs where the wasicus, *hiding without honor, open fire. The young brave—I do not know this brave boy—staggers, but keeps running until a bullet smashes through his head, and he falls hard, face down, not far from the top of the ridge.*

"We must rescue his body!" an old Sicangu

shouts. Immediately he leads others up the hill. I try to crawl up, but a bullet kicks sand into my eyes. I am not as brave as these other warriors. I slide back down. "Do not let him lie there!" the Sicangu yells.

But we cannot get him. He has fallen where the wasicus *will kill anyone who tries to retrieve this brave boy's body. The old Sicangu, and the other warriors, slide back behind the rocks.*

The sun sinks.

The craziness stops.

Outside of the teepee, I could hear the stamping of the gray mare's hoofs. The noise of singing and drumming had not lessened. I placed my hands beneath my head again, and stared at nothing but the blackness of the inside of my lodge. There was no moon that night. There was nothing.

I did not sleep that night. I could not sleep. All night I remembered all that I had seen, all that I had done. It had not been a pretty day. It had been crazy.

When the sun rose, my father called my name. I stepped out of the lodge, and my father said: "The remainder of the *wasicus* shall die today."

Thus, the craziness returned.

Chapter Thirty-Eight

Major Marcus Reno

1876—6/26
Continued . . .

There is no moon. As if the world ended. Maybe it has.

Capt. Weir has joined me in my rifle pit. I share my brandy with him, but we do not talk.

earlier today, Weir asked to move his company on a scout. Off the hill? No way in hell. I told him as much. I found McDougall. No, he found me. Asking me something. I disremember what. I told him I'd lost Hodgson. Hodgson was his lieutenant. told him to put his men along a skirmish line.

The pack mules arrived. We had ammunition. At last. I think I mentioned Mathey before, the Bible Thumper, but it's too dark. Still can't read what I writ.

Weir rode off, disobeyed . . . no, i told Capt. Weir we had to move. Benteen agreed. Benteen's a good man. Hated Custer. Where the hell is Custer? I told him we must ride out. Scout. Ordered the command into column of 2s. We made it to a point north, but couldn't see Custer, or anyone else. Benteen Weir I planted a guidon.

A beacon for Custer. At the top of the point. And then, God, more damned indians. Riding from the north.

"Major," Benteen said. "We can halt here. Make a stand. Turn back the hostiles."

"No." No, you see, the first hill. That's where we should be. It was better. Water was closer. & Hodgson was there. So we retreated back. I told Benteen where to place the troops. Ordered the men to dig rifle pits. then I walked around. I found the pack mules. Found a bottle of brandy. Found my own rifle pit. I rested.

others might take credit for what happened. Benteen or Weir. they will say they took it upon themselves to ride off the hill. I did it. I was not drunk. I am in charge. Till Custer comes for us. If he ever does—

Night fell, and no longer did the indians fire upon us. I convened with the officers. Not Hodgson. Poor Hodgson. He's dead. God.

"We're facing a great force of indians," I told my officers. "I am not certain how long we can hold out this." I cleared my throat. "If it gets down to this, I hate it, but, well, perhaps we should abandon the wounded. Make a break for Custer. For Terry & Gibbon."

"No!" Benteen spat. The martinet bastard. He STILL doesn't know how many damned indians are in that village. "By God, sir, we will never do that!"

of course not. I told Benteen that we'd never abandon our wounded. I'd never do such a cowardly thing. Custer could find us here. We'd hold out. We had to hold out.

The night is cold. hope you can read this. hope you will find it if I am killed.

Trumpeter Martin blows reveille. It is 2 a.m. Dawn will soon break & indians have returned. We remain surrounded. I have done my best. Will do my best. I am not a coward.

likely we all die today

be a good Boy. Remember you lovely mother, god rest her soul. Please, remember ME in your Prayers

Your father,
M.A. Reno
Major, 7th Cav., US Army

Chapter Thirty-Nine
Dr. Henry R. Porter

I could not save Corporal George Lell's life. When Privates Charles Windolph and Jacob Adams carried him in early on the morning of June 26th, I knew that. There is little anyone can do for a man who has been gutshot. Clean the wound with a solution of carbolic acid. Stop the bleeding, if possible. Maybe, if the patient screams in utter agony, as Private Andrew Moore had been doing when two soldiers brought him in the previous afternoon, slip him some laudanum—not so much for the dying trooper's sake, but to lessen the stress on everyone around him.

Corporal Lell refused laudanum, and he was not screaming. "Save it, Doc," he said grimly, "for someone who ain't a dead man."

When Private Adams handed me the corporal's Springfield carbine and his ammunition belt, I hesitated. Just before the charge into the Indian encampment, Major Reno had offered me his carbine, which, being a doctor, I had declined. By the morning of the 26th, I felt differently. Adams was saying—"Colonel Benteen says you'll likely have need of it this morn, sir."—but I was already grabbing the carbine and belt of cartridges before hurrying to attend the other wounded.

All night I had worked. Almost thirty wounded. More than a dozen dead. Some three hundred others also worked through the night, digging pits with whatever tools they had, even their fingers. Colonel Benteen had given me two assistants, a couple of well-meaning privates named Harry Abbotts and William Robinson. Robinson had carried my bandages and medicine during Major Reno's charge. Abbotts had been assisting Dr. James DeWolf.

Now Jim was dead. Yesterday, I had found his body on a nearby ravine after most of the Indians had raced off to the north, leaving us atop this hill. One bullet through Jim's stomach; another six in his head. For what seemed an eternity, I just sat there and stared at what once had been a young doctor with a promising career ahead of him. Dr. James DeWolf had graduated from Harvard Medical School only a year ago. He had a wife, talked of her all the time. Just a few nights earlier, he had laughed as he read aloud a line he had just penned to Fanny: *I think it is very clear that we shall not see an Indian this summer.* Now, Fanny was a widow, and I . . . I have not the words.

Worse, the Indians had taken Jim's medical bag, which I desperately could have used.

"Doc," Private Robinson had told me, cocking

his carbine and aiming at some rustling bushes several rods below, "we best get back up this hill."

I had found Jim's diary, had packed it inside my own medical bag, had promised myself that I would write Fanny.

If I lived.

The Indians had soon returned, pinning us down, killing more, wounding more, till nightfall brought some relief. For the soldiers. Not me.

George Lord was the 7th Cavalry's other surgeon, but Dr. Lord had ridden off with General Custer. With Dr. Lord suffering from trail colic, I was supposed to have been assigned to Custer's immediate command. The good doctor, however, was not only a surgeon, but an officer, and he refused to let bowel cramps and diarrhea keep him from his duty. He went with Custer. Now I was alone, surrounded by the dying, the dead, and the soon to be dead.

Fortune, I thought, must be smiling down upon Dr. Lord now as he was likely riding along with George Custer and his troops, bound for General Terry or General Crook, leaving us on a hilltop surrounded by thousands of hostile Indians who wanted our hair.

As I ran carrying weapon and medicine on the already hot morning of the 26th, I almost cried.

I do not belong in this Army, I told myself. *I am a contract surgeon, not a soldier. Why in God's name am I here? Why did God let me reach this hilltop alive, and send Jim DeWolf up another ravine to be shot to death by savage Indians?*

I was twenty-eight years old, making $100 a month, but an extra $25 for field duty.

There was no time for tears. I had too much work to do.

Kneeling by another patient, I calmly told my other assistant, who was treating the man's gunshot wound: "Private Abbotts, spitting tobacco juice into a bullet wound does not prevent infection."

"But we always figgered . . ."

"It is all right," I said, and poured the ever so thinly diluted carbolic acid mixture into the shoulder wound.

"How 'bout a sip of whiskey, Doc?" the wounded man said through clenched teeth.

"I would like one myself, Trooper," I said, and moved to the next patient.

I thought of last night, when all around me, I could hear soldiers dragging dead mules and horses to the top of the depression that formed my hospital. It was surrounded by picketed mules and horses. I could not see much. By God, I could not even see my trembling hands, could not see the faces of the men I worked on. I could hear them, though. Hear their cries and moans, their begging for whiskey, for water, for death.

That night turned cold. Men shivered, yet

others sweated profusely from their grievous wounds. Private Moore began screaming again. The laudanum had worn off. I stumbled through the blackness, felt inside the bag, produced what I hoped was the appropriate bottle.

"Someone kill that son-of-a-bitch already!" another wounded man called out.

"Die like a man!" yelled another.

"Shut up!" snapped Benteen, who, like me, like most of us, did not sleep that night. "Save your strength, your voices, for tomorrow."

Private Moore continued to wail, until I found his face, brought the uncorked bottle to his lips, and let him swallow a bit more of the precious fluid.

When he fell silent again, I moved to the next patient.

"Hello, son," I said softly, but he did not answer. My hand fumbled across the blood-soaked bandage across his abdomen, and rested on his hairy chest. It did not move. Slowly I brought my fingers up to his throat, pressed against the artery, and detected no pulse.

He was dead. But it was too dark to see who it was.

My hand slipped to the new corpse's side, and rested on something cold, hard, iron. I realized it was his revolver. Oh, he had not used it to take his own life. There had been hardly any gunfire since the sun sank. Yet it dawned on me that every wounded man in this "hospital" had a weapon by his side. Not necessarily to kill the enemy, but to kill themselves when the Indians charged after dawn.

Through the night I had worked, and then dawn came, ushered in not by the sound of "Reveille," but of gunfire. The Indians were back. Arrows whistled through the air, but mostly the Indians fired carbines and revolvers. The animals pulled at their picket ropes. They screamed. They stamped their hoofs. Some died.

My heart sank as two troopers hurried in with another soldier. They lay him on his overcoat, and I hurried to him.

"He just rolled over to take off his coat," one said.

The bullet had torn through the back of his skull. Likely he never knew what killed him.

"He is dead," I said, and hurried to another patient.

Now, as I explored a trooper's thigh with my silver probe, a horse screamed. I raised my head to see a horse staggering in the makeshift corral, scaring the other horses, throwing his head back, spraying blood all over the place. A soldier ran to the horse, cut the tether, and then the soldier catapulted backward, leaving a trail of bloody mist that the wind carried away. A sergeant ran to the fallen soldier. The horse fell over dead. The sergeant picked up the trooper's carbine, and left the soldier where he had fallen.

I knew not to waste my time checking on him.

The air smelled of death again, of gunsmoke. Dust blew across the hillside. It was maybe 4:00 a.m., and the sun was barely up. Already, the hill felt like a furnace.

"Try to keep the wounds clean," I instructed my orderlies. "That seems about all we can do. For now."

"With . . ."—Robinson had to clear his throat—". . . what?"

He brought around the canteen draped over his shoulder. For the first time, I realized how parched my own throat was, how swollen my tongue felt. I fell onto my buttocks, ran a dry tongue across chapped lips.

"Here, Doc," said Abbotts, spraying the dust between his boots with a river of brown juice. He placed two pebbles in my hand. "Put 'em in your mouth, Doc. They'll stir up a little moisture in your mouth."

Doing this, I felt some, though not much, relief. Private Abbotts grinned. Here was an uncouth New Yorker who I had rebuked for following that old soldier's superstition that tobacco juice could stave off infection. Yet I had just learned something from him that no one ever thought to teach me at Georgetown Medical School. Even my own father, a physician from New York Mills, had never told me about this.

250

Then I heard the moans, the piteous cries for water. "Give the patients some pebbles, boys," I said.

No longer did I carry Corporal Lell's rifle and ammunition. I moved away, thinking of the river, not far from our hill, but, with the Indians guarding it, it might as well have been at Niagara Falls.

More wounds were probed, sometimes with that silver probe, more often with just my fingers, picking out the bits of cloth, cleaning the bullet holes as best I could, then covering the hole with water-saturated lint, topped with oiled silk, and covered with a bandage. Until I was out of bandages. Then I used handkerchiefs. Sometimes all I had was a rag.

I made my way back to Corporal Lell.

Still he declined laudanum, but, as I changed his bandage, I pulled out a tincture, and sprinkled a bit of opium onto the lint, which I then placed on the bloody hole in his abdomen.

I had no chloroform, no ether, and other than digging out a bullet that had not penetrated too deeply, or securing an arrowhead with a wire loop and carefully withdrawing it, I could not, dared not, perform any surgeries. Yet.

The heat became even more oppressive. Yesterday, I had estimated that the mercury had risen to ninety degrees. As the sun rose this day, the heat intensified, perhaps coupled by the cannonade of rifle fire coming in all directions. Many of the wounded no longer sweated, for they had no water inside them to sweat out.

Another volley came from the Indians. Bullets struck the dead horses and mules, followed by the hissing of foul gas from the bloating animals. The stink would never leave my nostrils.

I kneeled by another wounded soldier, brought my canteen to his thigh wound, tried to wet down the lint, but . . . I sighed. The canteen was dry. The soldier tried to speak, but his lips were so cracked and bloody, his tongue so swollen, I shook my head.

"Do not talk," I told him. My own voice sounded foreign.

"*Herr* Doctor," whispered a sergeant lying next to him, his face masked in pain, his right elbow bloody and swollen. "*Herr* Doctor . . . reach into my saddlebag . . . there." His head tilted to the leather pouches next to his unfired Colt revolver.

My aching fingers struggled with the buckles, but finally managed to work the metal, and pull open the leather pouch. Inside, my hand reached, found a jar wrapped in paper and a bandanna. As I pulled away the protective covering, the sergeant smiled.

"It is jelly," the sergeant said in a thick Saxony accent. "Bought it at Bismarck before we rode out."

"What is your name, Sergeant?"

"Weihe. Charles Weihe. M Troop."

"Thank you, Sergeant Charles Weihe. I will never forget your name or your generosity." After unscrewing the lid, I found a spoon in my bag, and returned to the wounded soldier at Sergeant Weihe's left. The soldier's cracked lips opened just a hair—even that took tremendous effort—and I eased the spoonful of jelly into his mouth.

He grinned as he slowly rolled the jelly over his tongue, as if I had served him ice cream.

Turning to Sergeant Weihe, I dipped the spoon inside the jar, and brought it toward the sergeant's dry lips. His head shook, and his lips tightened. After I returned the spoon to the jar, he whispered: "For the boys, *Herr* Doctor. For the boys."

When you are desperate, you will try anything, and not just jelly.

We fed grass roots to some of the men, trying to excite the glands, to get some moisture in their mouths, their throats. Others chewed prickly pear cactus, abundant on the hill, the sharp spines removed, of course. Instead of pebbles, some stuck bullets in their mouths. Anything.

A few even dared try the tasteless, disgusting, and rock-hard bread this man's army seems to think is nourishing. Soldiers chewed on the bread a while, then spit, or more accurately, coughed it out. Out of their mouths, it flew like clumps of flour.

Which proved, I guess, to be my breaking point.

I rose.

"*Herr* Doctor!" Sergeant Weihe called out. "Get down."

Ignoring him, I strode out of the depression, between two foul-smelling horses, and looked around the perimeter. A bullet slammed into the nearest dead mule, and escaping gas almost made me vomit.

"Get down, Doc!" yelled the scout, Herendeen, but I ignored him, making a beeline for Colonel Benteen.

Benteen, too, walked calmly about the field, unprotected, uncaring about the arrows and bullets that flew across the hilltop. Benteen, of course, was a hero, a soldier, trying his best to inspire his men. I doubt if he cared a whit for his own life. I was a contract surgeon, a doctor, trying to keep my patients alive.

The colonel stopped when he saw me approaching. Major Reno appeared from a shallow hole in the ground, and rose to stand beside Benteen.

"Doctor," Benteen said coolly, "how can I assist you?"

"How are the men faring?" Reno asked.

A bullet clipped the branch off a piece of scrub.

"That was close, Fred," Reno said.

"The savages need not fire another shot," I said. "We will all be dead of thirst before long."

The two officers knew this. They were as thirsty as everyone else up here.

"The wounded need water," I said. "We must have water. It is that simple, Colonel. It is that simple, Major. We get water. Else, we die."

The two officers glanced at each other. "Some troopers tried that yesterday evening, before the sun set," Major Reno said. "Indians drove them back. It was a forlorn hope."

Benteen sighed. Another bullet hissed well over our heads.

"I can't order men to that river, Doctor Porter," Benteen said, "but will ask for volunteers."

"Thank you, gentlemen." I coughed. My own voice sounded horrible, like the rasping of a dying man. Quickly I returned to the stinking, miserable hole that served as my hospital.

Picking up my bag, I made my way to another soldier, then heard Corporal George Lell call out to troopers Abbotts and Robinson, who were treating another wounded soldier nearby.

"Lift me up," he said. "I want to see the boys again before I go."

I had to stop whatever treatment I was trying on another wounded lad to watch. They lifted Lell up ever so gently, into a sitting position, and, lips tight against the pain, Lell looked right to left, then left to right. His head nodded slowly, and my two assistants lowered the corporal down.

He was still smiling weakly when I reached him five minutes later, but now his eyes were closed.

They never opened again.

Chapter Forty

Long Road

My brother is dead. Killed when we fought *Mila Hanska* on the Rosebud. Soon, I must join him. My brother, more than anything, I loved. Now he is gone. On this earth, nothing is left for me. I have nothing to live for, so soon, really soon, I shall die.

Hokay hey. It is a good day to die.

We are coming up the ravine. As an Itazipacola, I lead my friends—Hunkpapas, Oglalas, *Sahiyelas*, and other Itazipacolas. This I do to honor my brother. This I do so that the Lakotas and *Sahiyelas* will remember me. They will know how brave I was when I died.

Along the ravines we climb. This country is good. It hides us well from the *wasicus* above. I can stop, lift my head, and fire one of the two holy irons I have taken from dead *wasicus* at the fools on the top of the hill, and duck. This I do many times, as bullets whip over my head, but miss. Soon, I know, the bullets will not miss.

I wait for the other Indians to catch up, but, before another can move on, I am already crouching and running, leading the way. I stop, shove a holy iron into my breechclout. *"Hiyupo!"*

257

I yell, unsheathe my knife, put it in my mouth, biting down hard on the blade. Again, I draw the holy iron, and run, harder this time, a *wasicu* soldier belt draped over my shoulders, carrying more bullets for the holy irons.

We are close now. Close to *Mila Hanska.* Close to my death.

My comrades below, they cry out to me. They tell me not to do this. Not to be so brave. Not to be so foolish.

I do not listen.

I can see the flag of my enemies. It hangs dead, for there is no wind. Soon, all of these bad men will be dead. Like my brother. Like me.

I am running, firing. I can see the white puffs from the *wasicu* long guns. I can hear the bullets striking, whining off rocks. My friends shoot back at the *wasicus*.

One hundred and twenty feet, and I will be at the top of this hill.

One hundred ten.

One hundred.

Ninety.

Eighty.

"Arghhhh!" The *wasicu* bullet has slammed through my chest. The knife, I spit into the dirt. I pull the triggers of the holy irons as I fall. Bullets dig up the earth that rushes to greet me. I land hard.

My lungs will not work.

I hear the *wasicus* shouting.

I hear my friends shouting.

My mother, my father, soon they will mourn again, but not for long. Because they know that this is what I desired. And I died bravely, as a Lakota.

I push myself up.

If I can just crawl the rest of the way. If I can count coup on some *wasicu* before I die.

But I cannot even breathe. I can feel nothing but the blood flowing down my stomach, across my back where the bullet has gone through. I can taste the blood in my mouth.

No longer can I hear the *wasicus* shouting.

No longer do I hear my friends calling out my name.

I hear my brother, and I smile as I sink back onto the ground.

My brother calls my name. He is proud of me.

Now I can see him, beckoning me.

"*Hokay hey*," he says. "It is a good day to die."

Chapter Forty-One

Captain Frederick Benteen

Parched as I was, as precarious as our position, I could not send even volunteers down to the Little Big Horn. Not right now. The Indians were up to something.

I left Reno to return to H Troop.

"I got that red bastard!" Private Pigford lifted his right hand, pumped it in the air, then dropped it to ram a fresh cartridge into his Springfield.

I spit out a piece of potato I had popped in my mouth to stimulate the glands, and continued to walk up and down the lines.

"Colonel!" Lieutenant Hare called out. "Get down, sir. Please. Stop trying to draw the hostiles' fire."

"When the bullet is cast to kill me, it will kill me," I said. "That's all."

Reaching Private Pigford's position, I kneeled, much to the relief of my troops, and peered over the edge at the Indian Pigford had just killed. He lay maybe seventy-five feet from the top, with a hole in his back the size of a baseball.

"Colonel, those red devils are up to something." Trooper Pigford echoed my own thoughts.

Pigford was right. So was Porter, our contract

surgeon. The Indians were mounting some sort of attack, but if we did not get water soon, we were all done for. I rose, walking again, daring the Indians to waste their shots on me.

"Men," I said, though my voice sounded harsh and haggard. "This is a groundhog case. It is live or die with us, so we must fight it out with them."

Some of my men still worked on their trenches, had been digging since this morning. H Troop guarded the hill's weakest point, and one damned savage had made it within seventy-five feet of us. We had reinforcements—that morning, Captain French and M Troop had relieved my troop, so we could dig trenches and rifle pits to protect ourselves (although that had taken some arm-twisting of Marcus Reno).

Now I found myself hurrying back to Major Reno's hole in the ground.

Though I would never admit this to anyone other than my wife and in an anonymous newspaper report, it galled me, having to walk to an idiot, a damned coward, to ask permission, but Reno had rank over me. I tried to figure out who was worse, Reno or Custer. Who was the bigger fool?

I laughed. *Hell, maybe I'm the biggest fool.*

Reno was where I expected to find him, in his hole. Last night, he had been bunking with Captain Weir, another idiot, but at least Weir showed backbone. Now, Weir had gone, which meant the flask beside Reno must have been empty.

I looked down the hill.

By God, things were just as bad here as they were on the south side.

"Marcus," I said, trying to sound pleasant enough, "if we don't do something soon, we're all dead."

No reply.

"Major?" Showing him all military courtesy.

To hell with courtesy. "You have to do something here pretty quick. This won't do. You must drive them back!"

"Can you see the Indians from there?" Reno managed to ask.

I had to choke back the most vile curse. Hell, all I could see were Indians.

"Yes," I snapped, forgetting to add *sir.*

"If you can see them, give the command to charge."

Well, give Marcus Reno some credit. As soon as he said that, he began reloading his revolver.

So I turned, yelling: "All ready now, men! Now's the time. Give them hell! Hip, hip, here we go! The devil take the hindmost!"

To my amazement, Reno crawled out of his hole, managed to stand, even led the charge, firing. Sweat stung my eyes, but I could see clearly. The 7th acted like soldiers. That's all they really needed, a leader, not a braggart like

Custer, the self-proclaimed Indian fighter, author of his self-serving book *My Life on the Plains*, which more appropriately should have been titled *My Lie on the Plains*.

The soldiers acted like soldiers, except for one bastard who remained sobbing in his hole. Like cowards, the Indians retreated down the hill, and Reno led the command back. No one had been killed. We had lost not even one man, except for the crying soldier who had never left his hole. He raised his head as our men came plunging back over to the top. He raised his head just long enough to catch a bullet through the temple.

I wonder . . . if perhaps . . . one of our boys fired that shot.

No matter. I complimented Reno, who could be a decent enough officer, which seemed to revive his spirits a mite. Some of the lads, however, skedaddled straight to the hospital, and I followed them there.

"Out of here, damn you. This is for the wounded, and if you aren't dead, aren't about to die, back to the lines with you. Back to your trenches, your positions. Those Indians will be coming back. Damn it, I say. 'Move!' " This time, I cocked my own revolver.

They, the frightened but unharmed, and maybe even a few soldiers who had been bloodied, scrambled out of that depression, while I made my way back to the southern end.

"Listen to me!" I yelled. A bullet almost shaved the stubble off my left cheek. "I don't know where Custer is, and I don't give a damn. He's abandoned us, and I am tired, I am damned thirsty, and I really want to take a nap. So we're going over the edge, boys, and we're giving these red vermin utter hell. Because right now, I'm getting mad."

Cocking my .45, I yelled something—what, I cannot recall—and H Troop and I ran down the southern ravine, firing, shouting, screaming louder than the lousy Sioux.

I doubt if we made it farther than two hundred yards, probably nowhere near that distance, but the Indians pulled back quickly, scarcely even bothering to fire back. I slid to a stop, slipped on the gravel, and almost went sliding down that ravine. Wouldn't that have been an inglorious end to my career!

A hand grabbed my shoulder, and my slide ended. I turned, grinning at the soldier who had stopped by fall, saw Sergeant McCurry grimacing, his left shoulder bloody.

"Damn you, McCurry!" I said, pulling myself up, then helping the wounded sergeant to his feet. "You've gotten yourself shot!"

"It's all right, Colonel," that glorious sergeant, the stay and prop of the Benteen Base Ball Club said, "it's only my left shoulder, sir. I'll be able to pitch on Sunday." He winked.

Likely he meant it, too.

"Fall back!" I yelled, waving my pistol, by then empty, over my head. "Fall back!" I stayed behind McCurry, making sure he made it back onto the hill, then directed Trooper Pigford to make sure Sergeant McCurry made it back to Dr. Porter immediately.

The last of the soldiers topped the hill.

Sergeant Geiger was the last one up.

"Any wounded, Sergeant?" I asked.

"No, sir!" he snapped, and found his place in the nearest pit.

I remained standing, staring below, watching all of those Indians running out in the open.

"Good God," I said, then glanced at a shaking trooper at my feet. He was a private, but a damned fine shot, and he'd been right behind me during my charge. He was no coward. Hell, none of the men in H Troop ever showed any yellow.

"Windolph," I told the private, "stand up and see this."

He looked at me as if I were daft. "Do I have to, sir?"

"Stand up," I ordered, and he pushed himself up using his carbine. He leaned on it, butted to the ground. Indeed, I think the Springfield was the only thing that kept Private Charles Windolph upright.

"Look at that," I said, more to myself than to the trooper, before I put my hand on Windolph's shoulder and added: "If you ever get out of here alive, which I sincerely doubt, you will be able to write and tell the old folks back in Germany how many Indians we had to fight today."

I squeezed his shoulder, and walked away.

"Ed!" I called, and Lieutenant Godfrey appeared practically on cue.

Out of breath, throat coated with sand, tongue now swollen, I found myself sinking to the ground. Ed Godfrey sank with me.

"I'm thirsty as hell," I whispered. "If you're as dry as I am, we'll not have a better opportunity than right now to fetch water for Doctor Porter . . . the wounded . . . and us."

Chapter Forty-Two
Saddler Michael Madden

Said Sergeant Geiger: "We're bringing back water, Madden, not whiskey."

To which I replied: "And what in hell would a puny damned Israelite from Cincinnati know about whiskey or water?"

That short little Napoleon bristled, he did, but what with me standing over six-feet-one, a good eight inches taller than his sorry ass, nothing more could he do than just bristle and grind his wooden dentures.

"Besides, I am not about to let all you H Troop buckos get all the glory. K Troop's here!"

"You're the only son-of-a-bitch from K Troop that I see volunteerin'," snapped back a D Troop scoundrel, for D Troop had nothing but scoundrels in its ranks.

"I'm all K Troop needs," I replied with a grin. "All the entire regiment needs. Here, hand me those canteens and buckets. I'll go down there meself. It's just a wee little stroll."

"Shut up!" Lieutenant Godfrey commanded, and you bet your bottom dollar every one of us listened, because Colonel Benteen stood right beside me lieutenant.

Our darlin' officers was finding it a mite hard to keep all the laddies from scrambling down that hill in one mass exodus. That's how thirsty everybody was.

So the colonel had asked for volunteers. Just head down to the river, get plenty of water, and get back up here, without winding up knocking on those pearly gates.

Me? Thirsty I was. Prickly pear be fine in a pinch, but a far cry 'tis from a taste of pot still whiskey from John Power & Son. Right now, I wanted a taste of water, not Irish.

Besides, crawling through that Indian-infested ravine, making it to the river, bringing back precious water for the wounded—criminy, for all of us—now that's how legends be made.

Roughly twenty of us had volunteered for this hazardous duty. Even a Crow scout had joined us soldiers, and I'd heard an Indian could go longer than a damned camel without working up a thirst.

Benteen motioned for us to follow, and, crouching, we quickstepped it to the trenches on the southeastern side of our hillside home. The colonel pointed to the draw where those H Troop laddies had just charged down and scared off some cowardly Indians.

"It's about five hundred yards to the river," the colonel told us. "It's steep, but you'll have good cover. Till you reach the flats below. Then you'll have thirty feet or so of open ground to the river." He wet his cracked lips.

"Sergeant Geiger," he called out, "Trooper Windolph. Private Mechling."

Even before he called out the last name, the fight-loving Hun and saddler Voit, already bristling, I was. Another little frolic for H Troop. Colonel's pets, they be. Denying me a fine chance of glory.

"You four are the best shots we have," Benteen said. "You'll provide a covering fire to the rest."

I almost laughed. Sergeant Geiger would be hiding way up here, while us real lads ran for the river. Any fool could stand hundreds of yards from the enemy and shoot a carbine. But to run down this rugged draw, with Indians all around us, then sprint to a river and fill canteens and whatever while Indians shot at you, now that's what makes a man. What makes a legend.

Why, I could already picture meself at My Lady's Bowery, having those strumpets fawning over me, saying how brave I was, not even charging me for their pleasurable company.

"You'll go in fours," Lieutenant Godfrey was saying. "Then come back up the hill. Fill canteens, kettles, flasks, anything you can."

"Is there a medal in this for us, Lieutenant?" Private Pym from B Troop asked.

Lieutenant Godfrey just smiled. His lips was puffy, cracked, bleeding. Looked a mess, he did, but he be K Troop, like me, and a damned fine fellow considering he be an officer. "There's water," be all he said.

"That's all I want," some D Troop horse thief said.

"Let's go," Sergeant Stanislaus Roy of A Troop said, and we followed him and Sergeant Rufus D. Hutchinson of B Troop into the ravine.

Hot, blazing hot, it was. Not a breath of wind, and those empty kettles and canteens rattled like a score of drummers tapping out commands, letting every Indian buck within two hundred yards know we be coming. Down that thick incline we ran, kicking up dust, trying to keep our feet.

Indians fired, but those four sharpshooters up on that slope, well, I'll sing their praises till Judgment Day. They stood, shooting back. Not hiding at all. Hell, when I glanced back, I saw 'em just standing, exposing 'emselves. Most of the Indians was shooting at 'em brave lads, not us.

Down we moved, till we reached the end of the ravine. Not a one of us had even been scratched by anything sharper than brambles or cactus spines.

"Callan, Pym, Goldin, Deitline," Sergeant Hutchinson said. "You're first."

Prayed I did, prayed hard that those fine lads made it across that long, long, flat thirty feet to the river's edge. Bullets and arrows flew from every direction, but the four lads made it to that mighty Little Big Horn. Then, it took seven and a half eternities for 'em to fill their canteens. From the top of the hill, Sergeant Geiger and his marksmen kept firing down upon the Indians, and I made meself a vow never to chastise even a Jesus-hating Israelite like Geiger if those brave souls made it back safely.

Blessed Mary, mother of Jesus, they made it.

"Up!" Sergeant Roy waved 'em on. "Stay low. Keep up the ravine. Stay on this side."

Tormentful, that was. Hearing those canteens sloshing full of water, seeing precious liquid spilling out of one of the kettles. Me mouth and throat ached dreadfully, but all I could do, all any of us could do, was watch those lads head up the draw.

"Bancroft," Sergeant Roy said. "Harris. You. And you." Ah, the fool sergeant didn't point at me.

Again I watched the laddies dodge bullets, hit the banks of the river. Your mind plays tricks, it does, and I swear I heard the water gurgling as it filled those canteens.

Ah, blessed be thy Lord, those four made it back, too.

Finally Sergeant Rufus D. Hutchinson of B Troop, give me the look. "Thompson," the sarge spoke to the puny little private from C Troop. "Welch. Madden."

He only ordered three of us, but that's because Sergeant Hutchinson run with us, too.

A bullet tugged at me collar, another split a rock just in front of me left boot, and then I was diving to that wet bank, and never a more beautiful sight appeared before me eyes. Didn't take us four heroes long to learn what had taken the other folks all that time. Cupped our hands, we did. And drank greedily, hungrily. Water never tasted so fine.

"Not too much," the sarge ordered, and he brought up one of his canteens.

As we filled our containers, Private Peter Thompson let out a cry, for all this while, bullets kept digging near us. Thompson shook his bloody hand. A chunk of lead had blown right through it. He cussed something fierce, but Thompson was not one to shirk his duty. Went right ahead, he did, grabbing one of those canteens, plunging it deep beneath the water's surface. Bubbles splashed. Bullets sprayed us with beautiful, cold, gloriously wet water. I filled one canteen, then another, then took one end of a kettle, as Sergeant Hutchinson grabbed the other.

Now . . . here be something for the legends. We lay on that bank, Indians shooting at us, our sharpshooters blazing away at 'em savages, and from the other side of the Little Big Horn, we heard a voice. 'Twas an Indian, but he spoke perfect English.

"Come on over to this side, you sons-of-bitches, and we will give it to you! Come on over!"

I looked up, staring at the high banks, me mouth dropped open.

Private Thompson swore again, screaming that they's white renegades with the Indians.

"Shut up," the sarge snapped.

On the far side of the river, we heard something else. Those red devils . . . laughing.

"Go!" the sarge yelled at Thompson and Welch, and up they was, and running like hell. I could hear Sergeant Geiger and those marksmen firing away.

"Ready." The sarge never was one for asking. He was telling, but he needed not tell me. I was past ready to light a shuck me ownself.

Damn, that was one big kettle, heavier than a ton of rocks. The sarge and me, we lugged it across the flats, canteens draped over our shoulders. Precious water dropped. On we came, closer to that draw, closer to cover. Thirty feet? Criminy, it seemed like thirty miles. Sergeant Roy and Trooper Pym fired their revolvers. And, then, damnation and piss on those savages, me right leg screamed out in the most mind-numbing pain ever I've felt, ever I'd hope to feel. Knowed I had been shot, I did, knowed me leg was busted below the knee, and felt meself falling, but damned it all to blazes if I was gonna drop this water.

Sergeant Roy rushed out of his hiding places, God bless him and his mothers, but not for me. No, the sergeant had better sense than that. He helped Sergeant Hutchinson with that kettle, get that water to safety.

Flat on me face I fell. Then, felt meself being lifted like I was light as a feather. I cussed. Said: "Leave me. Don't get killed, you damned . . ." And saw I was being carried by . . . that damned Crow Indian.

We made it. He dumped me on the ground. Picked up his canteen. Didn't even look at me again.

Still alive. All of us.

For the time being.

Now, I be cussing like a sailor, cussing those savages for ruining me leg, cussing that damned Crow for risking his life for mine, cussing meself for being so big. Hell's fire, even Sergeant Geiger couldn't have missed a target the size of Michael Madden, I said.

"Brant," Sergeant Roy said, "Stivers. Get Madden up the ridge. Get him to the hospital."

"The hell you say, Sergeant," I fired back. "No lad is riskin' his life for mine. Leave me. Leave me, damn you all."

Sergeant Hutchinson kept wrapping a tourniquet around me leg. Stopped the bleeding, but not the pain.

"Up to the hill. Up to the hill," Sergeant Roy

directed Peter Thompson, his hand bloody, and some other fine young lads up the hill with the water we'd retrieved.

"Put a high price on that water, Peter me boy!" I cried out to Thompson. "God knows, I've upped the ante."

Far from being done, we was, though, because as soon as those laddies started heading up that draw, Sergeant Roy was saying: "Who's coming with me?"

After me bad injury, the sarge wasn't about to order us volunteers into harm's way.

So there I laid, cursing me luck. Watching men hurry to the river and back, water sloshing. By the saints, not long afterward, here came Private Peter Thompson again, bloody bandage around his hand, but game he was, desperate, or maybe he was still just bloody thirsty. Three trips at the least he made it to the river and back.

Me? I'd made it only one, and hadn't made it all the way back.

Me head be lifted, and I tasted water. Blinked away sweat and pain, saw Sergeant Hutchinson letting water spill from a canteen into me lips.

"How long have I been out?" asked I.

He didn't answer. The son-of-a-bitch corked his canteen, then picked me up over his shoulders.

"Put me down!" I cried. "You're not risking your hide for the likes of me."

Like I said, I be not a small man. How Sergeant

Hutchinson managed to carry me, well, he must have been kin to Hercules. Oh, he staggered. He stopped. A few times he almost fell. And for a spell, I cursed him and his mother and his mother's mother—though I reckon what I wanted to do was kiss that big heroic fool. Didn't get a chance. Not to kiss him. Not to thank him. Not even to curse him much more, because that pain, that God-awful pain, sent me into a blinding, deep sleep.

When I return from the dead, I could smell the stink all around me. Knowed where I be. In that hospital, surrounded by mules, surrounded by death. Private Wilber Darcy was right beside me. Reckon he had taken a bullet fetching water, too, and that young sawbones was working on him, putting a splint on his leg. Nope. Darcy hadn't caught a bullet, just merely busted his leg. I smacked me lips, but didn't have guts to look down at me legs. But it didn't take long till I knowed I was still a whole man. The pain told me that fine doctor had yet to saw the right leg off.

Doc Porter turned to me, and not a poker player he was.

"Thank you for the water," he told me as he unwrapped the bandage around me leg.

Already I could smell something that wasn't dead horses, wasn't mule shit. 'Twas me leg.

"Do I get some whiskey before you get your saw, Doc?" I asked.

Doc Porter studied me, and damn me soul if there wasn't tears in his eyes.

"As much as you can hold, Mister Madden," he said.

Mister, said he. A fine educated man like that doctor calling me mister. Reckoned that I'd need to get used to that. For once me leg was gone, they wouldn't be calling me trooper or private or saddler or you damned ignorant Irish bastard no more.

"You don't know how much I can hold, Doc," I said with a grin, and the doc, he grinned back.

"Fire!" some fool shouted. "Fire. Colonel Benteen! Major Reno! The Indians . . . they're burnin' us out!"

The doc stood. Curiosity must have gotten the better of him, because he began making his way out of the depression, past the bloating, rotting, fly-covered carcasses of mules and horses. I stared into the sky, looking for smoke. Could smell it, and it smelled like roses compared to what I had been smelling. Couldn't see it. Couldn't see the doc no more.

But he would return. He'd come back and, sometime soon, off me leg he'd saw.

Ah, but here's the way legends are made, thought I.

They'll say Saddler Mike Madden, fond of

grog he was, and that won't be a lie. They'll say that they sawed off his right leg above the knee, then gave him some whiskey. Maybe brandy. They'll say that Mike Madden then smacked his lips, looked that sawbones in his eyes, and—this, they'll swear as pure gospel—Madden, he says: "Doctor, cut off me other leg!"

That's what the legend will be. That's what they'll say, but it won't be true.

The truth be that they did cut off me leg. And I bawled like a baby.

Other laddies, even Sergeant Geiger, they would give them medals. Me? I got a discharge and a crutch. But, blimey, I hadn't done it for the glory. Not really. Hadn't done it for no stinking medal. Hadn't done it to show 'em all that I was a hero.

Criminy, I'd done it 'cause I'd been thirsty.

Chapter Forty-Three

Sergeant John Ryan

Back at Fort Lincoln, they told us Indians can't shoot worth a damn. Oh, they were handy with bows and arrows, but give one a Springfield or Sharps or repeating rifle, and they couldn't hit an officer's ass at two paces.

Bam! The fourth man on my right sat up.

"Get down!" I shouted, and started to curse, but then I saw the hole in that trooper's forehead, and I knew that he couldn't hear. He was dead. His brain just hadn't told the rest of his body yet.

The corporal next to him, reached up, tugged on his comrade's blouse, and that poor dead bastard sank into the grass.

"Lucky shot," the corporal said. Those proved his last words. He had just spoken when that sickening sound of a bullet striking flesh reached my ears, and the corporal gasped. "I am killed," he said, and slumped over.

I slid toward him, grabbed his wrist, felt for a pulse that wasn't there, and crawled back up to my position, staring at the high ridge. Five hundred yards away, it had to be.

My keen eyes detected that faraway puff of white smoke before the bullet kicked up dirt and grass into my face, and I slid down a mite, cursing, rubbing the crud out of my eyes so that I could see again.

Footsteps sounded, followed by a hard *whoosh* as Captain French dropped right beside me.

"Did you see where those shots came from, Sergeant?" the captain asked.

My eyes kept blinking furiously, but I hooked my thumb back toward that peak. "Top of that knoll over yonder, Captain," I answered.

Captain French crawled up a bit, then slid down. "Jesus Christ!" he snapped. "Who the hell is shooting, Buffalo Bill Cody?"

The chuckle in my throat died there, as another soldier cried out in pain, followed by the faint report of the rifle. The trooper rolled down, leaving a trail of blood pumping out of his shoulder. I could see by then. Could hear, too, for that trooper was cutting loose with every foul oath in the soldier's curse book. Two of the boys came down to plug his bullet hole, and slide him farther out of the line of fire.

"Get that man to Doctor Porter," Captain French ordered, and those two volunteers were happy to obey that order. Happy to get away from that sharpshooting son-of-a-bitch of an Indian.

Captain French kept looking at that ridge through his field glasses. I just shook my head. That Indian had killed the fourth man to my right. Then he had killed the third. He had barely missed blowing off my head. He had just wounded the second. The gentleman next to me had been one of the volunteers to assist the wounded trooper to the field hospital.

There was no mirth inside my soul, but I laughed.

"My number's up, Captain," I said. "You might want to move down a few spots, sir."

The captain jacked a shell into his repeating rifle. His was a fancy rifle, not a carbine, but a long rifle of heavy caliber with one of those brass long scopes affixed to the top. Custom made, he had told me back at Fort Lincoln.

He pointed at my rifle. Mine was a Spencer, a .56-46, and not one of those god-awful Springfield carbines the Army saddled upon its cavalrymen. My Spencer didn't have a fancy telescopic sight, but I was already adjusting the tang sight.

"You ready, Sergeant Ryan?" the captain asked.

"I'd rather die fighting than just lying here waiting to get my head shot off, sir."

Captain French leaped up, and I followed him, yelling: "Onward, boys. Let's kill that bastard!"

Six boys came right behind us, while the rest of M Troop provided a covering fire. Those staying behind shot straight ahead, while Captain French, the boys, and me wheeled right. Dust flew up on that hilltop, me firing that Spencer as fast as I could jack another shell into the breech, the captain emptying his Winchester, the other lads firing and reloading their single-shot Springfields.

"Fall back!" the captain shouted, which I echoed, and we ran through the smoke from our shots and the dust we'd stirred up, sliding back behind cover. I reloaded the Spencer, waiting for my lungs to catch up, for my heart to resume beating.

Captain French leaned forward again, peering through his field glasses. Five minutes passed. Then ten. At last he rolled over, sticking his glasses in the case, and winked at me.

"Either we killed him, or scared him off," he said.

"Hope it's the former," I said, "but I'll gladly take the latter."

Ah, but those savages were not done. A few moments later, they opened fire, maybe the most intense enfilade I'd seen since the Rebellion. My three wounds from Ream's Station a dozen years earlier resumed aching. Sweat streamed down my forehead and into my eyes, and I reached for my canteen, to drink, thanking those brave souls who had risked their lives to quench my thirst.

The firing ceased. Resumed less than an hour later, but not as awful, not as consistent.

Then someone shouted: "Fire!" He called out for Reno, for Benteen. He yelled: "The Indians . . . they're burnin' us out!"

Captain French kneeled a few rods over, so I hurried to him, staring at the smoke.

"They're not burning us out, sir," I said. "Too far away."

"Diversion," Captain French said. "At least, that's my guess."

We watched. We waited. Suddenly a bird chirped. I tried to recall the last time I had heard any natural noise. All around us was this calm, this silence.

"Bet they're mountin' an attack," said some trooper, lying prone. "Bet they'll be rushin' us. To wipe us out."

"That's enough talk, Trooper," the captain said.

We waited. Waited, sweated, prayed. Major Reno came by. He seemed, well, sober.

"What do you make of this, Mister French?" he asked, rubbing the stubble on his jaw.

"I don't know, sir."

"There are Indians on the other side of the river," Reno said. "Just sitting on their horses."

"Could be they want to draw us out. Lead us into an ambuscade."

"Captain," I said, and pointed. "Major."

Slowly we stepped closer to the edge of our fortress.

It was shortly past 7 o'clock. Beyond the

burning grass, through the smoke, we saw an amazing, numbing sight.

To the west, the sun, a bright orange ball, sank through the smoke and dust. Other soldiers came out of their positions, standing, watching. For the longest while, no one spoke.

We simply stared. The Indians appeared to be . . . leaving.

I adjusted my sight, kneeled, aimed. The Spencer bucked against my shoulder. Captain French fired his Winchester once, then again. I pulled the trigger one more time. Turned out to be the last shot fired, I later figured, at the Battle of the Little Big Horn.

"They're out of range, Sergeant," Major Reno said.

"Yes, sir, but this makes me feel better."

Rising to my feet, I lowered the Spencer. The Indians looked like a moving carpet of brown, stretching what seemed to be a mile and a half wide, and perhaps three miles long. And, Lord Almighty, the number of horses they had. You couldn't count them all.

"My God," Major Reno said, and he turned to Captain Moylan, who had just walked up to our gathering. "Look what we have been standing off."

Someone shouted three cheers. A few others joined in with their own hip-hip-hurrahs. I didn't know if they were cheering us, thinking we'd driven off those savages, or cheering the Indians, for letting us live.

We watched, till the sun set, till darkness enveloped our hill.

That night, two scouts, a trooper, and Lieutenant Charles DeRudio made their way up the hill. The officers call DeRudio "Count No Account," but he had returned to the woods to pick up a flag. That flies high with me, and I don't believe those who say he went back to the flag merely to hide. Since Major Reno had retreated, Lieutenant DeRudio, Trooper O'Neill, and scouts, Gerard and Jackson, had been hiding in the woods, practically spitting distance to the Indian village. And we thought we'd been through hell.

Gerard said the Indians must be pulling out, but Reno thought it must be a trick.

"You should have stayed put, DeRudio," Captain Moylan said, spoiling our joyous reunion. "Those savages will hit us tomorrow. Wipe us out. For sure."

Chapter Forty-Four

Julia Face

It was said that the Greasy Grass Fight, which is how we Lakotas called the battle, was the greatest Indian victory.

I do not remember it as such.

As the second day of the Greasy Grass Fight ended, new songs were sung in the Oglala circle.

Sad songs.

Many of us had forgotten the previous day, when we had crushed *Mila Hanska*. When we had killed *Pehin Hanska*.

From a ridge with other women, I had watched the first day's fight. I could vaguely remember the strong-heart songs we had sung. I could just recall walking to the hills, after the last of the *wasicus* was dead, to find our husbands, our loved ones.

One thing burned into my memory, however, was me frowning at our warriors, who acted as if they had consumed much *mini wakan*, "the water that makes men crazy." All around them were dead *wasicus*, stripped naked so that their white bodies glistened in the sun. Warriors kept shouting: "Look, I have found coffee!"

"I have a new holy iron!"

"Tobacco! Tobacco! I now have much tobacco!"

"Two horses I have caught. They will make me rich."

I could remember finding my husband, which made my heart glad, and following him to our circle.

I could remember our *Sahiyela* friends saying that we had killed *Pehin Hanska*—Long Hair—*Hi-es-tzie* is how the *Sahiyelas* call him, but it means the same. Long Hair. Dead. I could remember the *Sahiyelas* and, later, many Lakotas singing songs about our great victory, about the death of Long Hair.

But as the second day closed, more of us mourned. More of our children cried.

Bodies of brave Lakotas, of brave *Sahiyelas*, were brought into a teepee, where we housed the dead.

I slashed my arms, for I mourned, too. Thunder Hawk lived, but my brother-in-law was no more.

It was a sad evening. Many sadder ones would soon follow.

Yet that evening our older leaders and our warriors met. They had to decide what to do.

Lakota women do not take part in matters like this, but my husband told me what was said.

"We should grind them into dust," said my husband.

"Mount our ponies when dawn comes," said

Rain-In-The-Face. "Ride up that hill. Kill them all."

"There are many *wasicus* with many holy irons," Sitting Bull cautioned.

"*Hokay hey!*" yelled my husband. "Tomorrow will be a good day to die."

"We have defeated those warrior white men twice," a silver-haired *Sahiyela* said. "They will not trouble us ever again."

Sitting Bull's head slowly shook. "*Mila Hanska* will always trouble us."

Then, an old Minneconjou lowered his pipe. He said: "If we let these *wasicus* go, it will show the Great Father that the Lakotas have compassion, too. These past several days, we have already shown them our strength. It will send a message to the *wasicus*. That is something to consider."

Rain-In-The-Face and Crazy Horse frowned upon this idea. So did my husband.

There was something else to consider, too. Two Hunkpapa scouts rode in. They told us that more *Mila Hanska*, many more, were marching down from the Elk River.

The old Minneconjou shook his head. "They come like locusts."

"They will always trouble us," Sitting Bull repeated.

So it was decided that we would leave the Greasy Grass. We would let live those *Mila Hanska* hiding on the hill. We would leave, to protect our women, our children. Besides, too many sad songs could already be heard in all the circles.

"Good Weasel," Sitting Bull said, "send runners to our warriors. To all the circles."

"What is the message?" Good Weasel asked.

Eyes turned to Crazy Horse, who nodded. Crazy Horse agreed with the elders. There was a time to fight, and a time to stop fighting.

"Tell them," Crazy Horse said, "that the Greasy Grass Fight has ended."

Chapter Forty-Five
Colonel John Gibbon

"Mister Bradley," I said, "that is the most outrageous exaggeration . . . dare I say, outright lie . . . I have ever heard in all my years in this man's army."

Generally I refrain from rebuking a junior officer so stiffly, and I hated chastising Lieutenant James Bradley in front of the men, but he left me no choice.

"Surely, Lieutenant," Major Brisbin sang out, equally appalled at the young officer's report, "this is some grievous error."

Mr. Bradley glanced at the Crow scout beside him, straightened his shoulders, and stared in defiance at me. "I have not known Little Face to exaggerate, lie, or make an error, sir."

"But did he see Custer?" Brisbin railed. "Did he see this . . ."—the major practically laughed—"this . . . *massacre* with his own eyes."

"No, sir," Bradley replied. "As I said, Little Face ran into three Crows who had been with Custer. They said he was killed, his entire command wiped out. They said there were so many Indians on the Little Big Horn that no soldiers could be left alive."

"Then how are those scouts still alive?" I inquired.

Bradley pointed south. "Here they come," he said. "You can ask them yourself, sir."

Of course, the Crows hadn't seen Custer killed, either. They had simply fled. Or so our interpreter said.

It was hot, and my temper grew shorter. I snapped at the cowardly Indians, told them to go home if such was there desire. I turned to Lieutenant Bradley, almost ready to send him back to the supply depot, but General Terry spoke mildly.

"Gentlemen, we waste time bandying about theories. We are late for our rendezvous as it is, so I suggest we hold off on accusations and defenses until we ask General Custer himself what has happened."

General Terry was right, of course. Later, it struck me that he had not chastised Lieutenant Bradley, he had not even scolded the Indian scouts, or questioned our interpreter. I think the general knew what we would find on the Little Big Horn River.

Even after I saw it with my own eyes, I could not believe it.

That night, the 26th of June, we camped. Smoke turned the gloaming into a haze, and the sun turned into a fiery sphere as it sank. Lieutenant Charles Roe had been on a scout, and he returned to our camp, reporting that he had spied a large column of dust. Thinking it to be Custer, he and his men rode into a party of Sioux Indians, who fired upon the soldiers before rushing off.

The Indians, Lieutenant Roe said, wore the blue blouses of cavalry soldiers.

Still, I did not believe.

On the morning of the 27th, we proceeded down the west bank of the Little Big Horn. When we came to the abandoned village, my anger at those Crow scouts, at Lieutenant Bradley, all but evaporated, replaced with a grim hope, a forlorn prayer, that those Indians, and my usually capable junior officer, had been mistaken.

The village had been massive, three miles of empty lodge poles, two standing ones surrounded by dead horses. Inside, we discovered several dead Indians.

"Their horses were killed for their masters to ride into the hereafter," my interpreter told me.

I was more focused on a hill across the river. Several men stood atop that ridge, staring directly at us.

"Custer?" Major Brisbin asked.

My head shook. "Or Sitting Bull?"

A moment later, Lieutenant Bradley rode into the camp. Never had I seen any man so pale.

"I have a very sad report to make." His lips began trembling. "I have counted . . ."—he stopped, stared at the reins in his shaking hands, could not look up at anyone—"one hundred and ninety-seven bodies lying in the hills."

"White men?" Major Brisbin inquired.

"Yes." Bradley sniffed. "White men."

My eyes closed. I cursed.

"Damn you, Lieutenant," I heard a strange voice, my own, whisper. "Damn those Crows. Damn George Armstrong Custer!"

Chapter Forty-Six

Private Jacob Adams

Well, I guaran-damn-tee you I never cried so many tears of joy when General Terry rode up our hill. The injuns was gone, and I was alive. Forty-two wounded, fourteen dead, but I was alive. Nary a scratch. Thank the Lord Almighty, I still breathed, and still had my topknot!

We slapped one another on the back. Didn't matter what troops we belonged to, didn't matter if we hated one another, fought each other at the hog ranches and dram shots back around Fort Lincoln. We let out several hurrahs, and cheered our relief as soldiers come riding up that hill. There was General Terry. The general. By grab, for the past two nights I'd never thought I'd want to kiss any general's boots, but I sure felt different when I saw him riding up with them beautiful boys in blue.

Colonel Benteen, he asked: "General Terry, have you any idea where Custer has gone?"

And the general, he looked up, and that good feeling left me of a sudden. Because the general, General Terry, tears went streaming down his face.

"To the best of my knowledge and belief," the

general said, "he lies on this ridge about four miles below here with all of his command killed."

No one spoke for a moment. Then Benteen, he said: "I can hardly believe it." He took a deep breath, exhaled, and said: "I think he is somewhere down the Big Horn grazing his horses. Why, at the Battle of the Washita, he went off and left part of his command, and I think he would do it again."

Terry wiped his face. He stared down at the colonel, and those eyes of his blazed with a fury. "I think you are mistaken," the general said, and his voice wasn't quaking, wasn't sad, wasn't anything but like a general's supposed to sound like. "You will take your company and go down where the dead are lying and investigate for yourself. Lieutenant Bradley,"—the general turned to one of his officers—"take Colonel Benteen to the site."

That was all the general had for us. He rode up a bit more, slid from his horse, and started shaking hands as he made his way to the hospital.

"Come on," my sergeant said to me. "Let's go."

I didn't get my hand shook by the general. Didn't get to see him walking among our soldiers, sniffing, shaking hands, telling them they'd done a great job, singing their praises, crying like a kid.

Me? I got to see something else. Druthers had gotten my hand shook.

By the time we was mounted, a bunch of troopers was crying, but not tears of joy, of salvation. Old Neutriment, that sorry-ass piker Burkman, Custer's house slave, was sobbing with the general's dogs. Wailing like a crazy man, saying: "What'll become of the hounds now? How can I make Bleuch and Tuck understand?"

Others looked shocked, couldn't believe Custer could be dead. Some couldn't speak. Some was saying it wasn't true, that General Terry was mistaken, that Colonel Benteen was right. Custer was gallivanting across the countryside.

We followed Bradley, up on the ridge, then into a fair-size coulée, all over that rolling country. Damn, it was hot, hotter than the hinges of hell, and then we come to a dead man. A dead white man. Stripped naked.

"By God," someone said, "that's Sergeant Butler!"

Another boy vomited on his saddle.

We moved about, from body to body. Some had been hacked to pieces. Heads chopped off. Limbs chopped off. The damned injuns had even mutilated some horses.

"There's that newspaper reporter!" someone shouted.

I didn't see him. Didn't want to see him.

On we rode, slower now, nobody talking. You kept your mouth shut. You didn't want to breathe because of the stink, the flies. Nobody felt so happy no more. Well, maybe I felt some relief. On account that I'd been assigned to the pack train. That was the reason, the only reason, I wasn't lying here, naked, scalped, dead.

Somebody said: "Damn those lousy Sioux. That's Doctor Lord. I swear to God, that's Doctor Lord. At least . . . I think . . . it . . . was, *er,* used to be . . . him. . . ."

L Troop we found next. Most of them. Some scalped. Some stuck with so many arrows you could hardly tell that they once were human. Lieutenant Calhoun, the general's brother-in-law, was dead. An arrow had smashed his glass eye. Lieutenant Crittenden was dead, too, but the injuns hadn't scalped him. In a swale not far from them, we found that Irish captain, Keogh. The savages had left one of his socks on, and a medal remained on his naked, bloody chest.

About then, Sergeant DeLacey heard something in one of the little ravines. He moved inside. We thought maybe it was a wounded trooper. We prayed it wasn't no damned injun. DeLacey stayed in that ravine the longest time. He come out, leading a bloody claybank horse. "It's Captain Keogh's horse!" yelled some trooper. "It's Comanche."

That horse was bleeding from a half-dozen wounds, covered with grass and dirt, his head hung down, his nose blowing out cakes of dust. Laboring he was. Half dead.

"Put that horse out of its misery, Sergeant," a dumb-ass officer said.

Sergeant DeLacey, he just stared down that shavetail lieutenant. "The hell I will, sir," he said.

Back up the hill, we rode. The smell gagged us even worser than it had on all them other spots where we'd found dead comrades. Took all I could muster to keep anything down in my stomach. Bunch of our horses wouldn't go no further. At that point, I was all for being a horse holder, but my sergeant ordered somebody else.

So I walked up, around the bodies.

Lieutenant Cooke. He was there. Lieutenant Gibson was kneeling over his body, shaking his head, whispering: "Oh, Cookie. Oh, poor Cookie." Those damned red fiends had scalped off one of Cooke's Dundrearies, but left the other one alone. You just can't figger no injun. Some boys was scalped. Some butchered. Others lay peaceful, hair still on their heads, just naked. Just naked. And dead.

But, God, the stink. And the flies. All around me rose the smell of death. I heard my comrades vomiting. Every now and then, I'd hear a gunshot, and I'd cringe, knowing someone was putting a poor animal out of its misery.

Brass casings was strewn everywhere like acorns back home in Stark County. Our boys had put up one hell of a fight.

"Good God, who is that?" a sergeant said, then started gagging.

"His face . . . ," cried another trooper. "Lord have mercy, his face is smashed to . . ." And he started retching.

Later, someone found the tattoo on that officer's arm. That's the only way anyone ever identified Major Tom Custer, the general's devoted brother.

I moved my way through grass stained with blood, covered with flies. Then I stopped, and looked down at the general.

His body was swollen, ugly, nasty, but the savages hadn't scalped him. They had slashed his thigh—why do injuns do that?—cut off one of his fingers, and shot an arrow up his pecker. They was cartridge casings scattered all around his body, too. He'd been shot in the temple, and in his chest, that bullet must have just missed his heart.

But he didn't look bad. I swear, he seemed to be smiling.

Would have been just like the general.

Captain Weir came up to me, and started choking out sobs. Though I don't know who he was talking to, as he stormed off, he yelled: "Libbie doesn't hear about this! Do you hear me? She never knows this. He was not mutilated. He died without pain. He . . . he . . . he . . ." He fell to his knees, head bowed, bawling.

But, hell, most of us was crying, crying from

the stink, crying from the sight, crying for all our dead friends.

I cleared my throat, had to spit out the bile, and turned. The colonel come riding over. I yelled out his name, waved my hat, waited, not wanting to look back at the dead man I'd just found.

Colonel Benteen swung down, handing his reins to another trooper, and stepped beside me. I give him a little nod, toward the body, and the colonel . . . well . . . for the longest while, he just stared. Like he couldn't believe it.

Hell, none of us believed it.

"By God," Colonel Benteen said at last. "That is him."

Chapter Forty-Seven
Rain-In-The-Face

Many of my people act like women.

Twice, we have crushed *Mila Hanska*. Long Hair is dead. I might have killed him. I remember shooting a man in the head with his own pistol, shooting him so that his face was blackened. I remember cutting out a *wasicu*'s heart. I remember killing many, many *Mila Hanska*, counting many coup. Many scalps hang in my lodge. We have crushed the spirit of the *wasicus*. We could have killed them all.

We *should* have!

Instead, we ride toward the Shining Mountains. We ride south. The great village that we had made on the Greasy Grass? It is no more. *Mahpiya To* have gone to their own circles. Our *Sahiyela* friends, they ride in another direction.

Instead of planning war, instead of continuing our great victories, the old leaders, our holy men, even some of our younger warriors, they talk of peace. Many say they want to go back and live near the soldier forts. They fear *Mila Hanska*. Fear retribution from the pale-eyed fools.

Sitting Bull, Crazy Horse, Gall, and me. We warned against this. We told them we should remain together. Strong. That was how we had defeated those *wasicus*. They could have brought twice as many with them, and we would have slain them all.

But no more. Now, we are small.

Crazy Horse has taken his people to Bear Butte.

Even Sitting Bull, he thinks he shall go to the Grandmother's Country. Up there, *Mila Hanska* will not track him down and punish him. Besides, he says, we did not listen to him. We took the *wasicu* items after we killed all the *wasicus* who fell into our camp, like his vision predicted. His vision forbade taking such trophies. We did not listen.

Wakan Tanka, Sitting Bull says, might frown upon The People of the Buffalo Nation for doing such things. *Wakan Tanka* might punish all Lakotas.

Women.

Cowards.

They think the *wasicus* will simply return *Paha Sapa* to us. The *wasicus* will not do this. They do not give. They only take.

But I have no choice. I cannot fight the *wasicus* by myself. I go with Sitting Bull. I leave my country. I wonder if ever I will see it again.

Chapter Forty-Eight
Captain Grant Marsh

For two days, I had known the wounded were coming, and had tried my best to prepare the *Far West*. Yet nothing could prepare me, could prepare anyone, for the sight of those wretched, worn-out men as they came down to the east bank of the Big Horn River.

Pine torches lit up my ship, and the deck smelled of fresh grass, from which the crew had manufactured a bed on our ship's main deck.

My cargo arrived before dawn, sad, mostly silent, ashen-faced men carried on litters. Forty white men, two Indians, and a horse. A claybank horse.

"You gotta get this horse back to Fort Lincoln," a soldier—one whose right leg had been amputated—demanded. "Leave me behind, Capt'n, but make room for this horse."

"He's the sole survivor!" another wounded man shouted. "I can walk. I swear, I can walk. Take the horse instead of me."

"We'll make room for the horse," I assured them.

Which we did.

Between the rudders, we put up something

that might have passed for a stall. I had two crewmen haul aboard more fresh-cut grass, piling it down. Then I watched as a sergeant led in the claybank—Comanche was his name—and my heart ached when that terribly wounded but magnificent animal lay on its grass bed and snorted.

Just after the horse had found its quarters, General Terry personally requested my presence in his stateroom, and, while many duties needed my attention, I followed the general up to his small cabin. He walked like a beaten man, and when he sank into his chair, I noticed the bags under his eyes, the wrinkles in his forehead. He must have aged twenty years since I'd last seen him, marching off to meet up with Custer and Crook.

"Captain," he said, his voice tired, "you are about to start on a trip with forty-two wounded men on your boat. This is a bad river to navigate, and accidents are liable to happen. I wish to ask of you that you use all of the skill you possess, all of the caution you can command, to make the journey safely." Tears welled in his eyes. Indeed, they formed in mine as well. "Captain, you have on board the most precious cargo a boat ever carried. Every soldier here who is suffering with wounds is the victim of . . ." Here he paused, closed his eyes, and finished while shaking his head: "The victim of a terrible blunder."

A tear rolled down his cheek.

"A sad and terrible blunder."

He need not have given me those instructions. I knew my duty, and I had sailed up these treacherous waters many a time. All the rivers in this territory put even the best and most cunning skippers at risk, testing, or sinking, our wits . . . testing, or sinking, our ships.

But, well, I captained the *Far West*.

One hundred ninety feet long, only thirty-three feet wide, two engines, three boilers, and a fine stern wheel. I picked the *Far West* myself. Light, fast, magnificent, she could navigate on a heavy dew.

It had started raining five minutes past noon when we shoved off on the 30th of June. Raining. That seemed fitting. Like all the angels above were crying for what had happened on the Little Big Horn.

So we sailed, fifty-three miles on the Big Horn to the Yellowstone, and eastward toward Bismarck, where the world would learn of a great disaster, a horrible blow to our Army, to our nation.

First, we had to make it through hard sailing. Sandbars and snags, rapids and islands, spots so shallow I still don't know how we managed to get the *Far West* across.

On July 2nd, the load got lighter.

Standing at attention with my crew along the

starboard, I watched soldiers carry the canvas-wrapped body of another victim of what Terry had called "a sad and terrible blunder." Corporal George H. King, A Troop, had died from a shoulder wound. He was only twenty-eight years old when they buried him on the north bank of the Yellowstone.

At 4:00 a.m. on July 3rd, Private William George died. We would reach the supply depot the next morning, so General Terry decided to bury this soldier there.

As we steamed along the Yellowstone, I thought of poor Mrs. Custer, remembered her begging me to take her up the river, just so she could see her husband again. Now, I wished I had obliged that poor, beautiful, wonderful woman. I remembered the soldiers, could see their faces. General Custer, blond hair shorn but eyes so alive. I remembered the scout aboard this ship, his hand swollen and throbbing with pain, and Dr. Porter and me telling him that he should stay aboard the *Far West*, and him, looking like a child told he could not have cake for his birthday, saying: "I've been waiting and getting ready for this expedition for two years, and I would sooner be dead than miss it." Now Charley Reynolds was dead.

So was the newspaper reporter, who had entrusted me with some of his dispatches to Bismarck, to Omaha, to New York City.

Dead.

More than two hundred men. Dead.

Derrick and jack staff draped in black and the flag waving at half mast, the *Far West* would reach Bismarck at 11:00 p.m. on July 5. Newspapers would proclaim that I had set a record, covering the seven hundred and ten miles in just fifty-four hours. The *Far West* accomplished this. Not me.

One moment, above all, stands out in a voyage filled with moments. Nothing to do with creeping past sandbars and snags, or shooting rapids, or watching young men be buried, watching wounded men fawning over a wounded horse, watching my crew, shirts off, sweating, working without complaint.

Approaching the depot, I looked for a mooring spot while Captain Edward W. Smith, General Terry's aide-de-camp, puffed on a cigar at my right.

"There will be much discussion of this massacre," Captain Smith was saying, "but Custer brought it upon himself with his disobedience."

I said nothing. I was a sailor, not a soldier, and certainly not a second-guesser. Custer had died. Young men had died with him. I would not question their integrity. Let them rest in peace. Let them be laid to rest with honors. They had given their lives for our country.

"He was arrogant, Custer, and . . ."

A muffled explosion on the bank stopped him.

Some soldiers, their nerves taut, cried out in terror, thinking we were under attack. Then they watched the ball of fire explode in the evening air, lighting up the sky, showering the blackness with colorful sparks.

"What are they doing?" Captain Smith cried out. "Are they signaling you, Captain Marsh?"

Slowly I removed my cigar, setting it on the ashtray. Another explosion filled the sky.

My heart sank.

"They are celebrating, Captain Smith," I finally answered. "Today is Independence Day. Today is our nation's one hundredth birthday."

1926

Chapter Forty-Nine

Libbie Custer

The 50th anniversary celebration has ended.

Celebration? Do we celebrate the deaths of two hundred and sixty-one brave soldiers?

Alas, the casualties did not end at the Little Big Horn in 1876. Last year, poor John Burkman, Autie's striker and our Old Standby, shot himself to death in Billings, Montana. He wrote me often, and I to him, but I am told he had become a bitter loner, an angry old man who would curse anyone, even children and those of the fairer sex, in sight. Poor John. He never got over Autie's death. It broke his heart, as well as mine.

Those two miserable, vindictive, lying human beings, Reno and Benteen, are dead, too. In my mind, and in the opinions of many others, they were the orchestrators of my husband's death. Benteen did not obey orders, but tarried while Autie was overwhelmed by the savages. Reno proved himself to be a drunkard and a coward, though he escaped court-martial, and a Court of Inquiry absolved him of any blame—but only because far too many officers of the 7th lied about his actions, to protect the honor, as always, of the U.S. Army.

Well, no matter. Reno was drummed out of the service in 1880 for conduct unbecoming an officer and a gentleman. He proved to be not only a drunkard, but a peeping-tom, the louse. He died in 1889 of cancer of the tongue. Needless to say, I did not attend his funeral.

Alcohol, likewise, led to the demise of Captain Benteen. He left the 7th in 1882, to become a major in the Negro-filled 9th Cavalry, and was convicted of being drunk and disorderly at some post in Utah. He should have been drummed out of the Army, too, but President Cleveland merely reduced his sentence to a one-year suspension— the same as Autie was given, and Autie had not been drunk, merely romantic. Benteen resigned in 1888, and died ten years later.

I shall waste no more energy on those two individuals, although I will say this: There is talk of building a monument for Reno, and, if this goes further than just talk, I will fight it till my dying breath.

Back in my apartment, I stare nine floors down at the bustle of this city. Already, the stores and the city begin to prepare for the next celebration, our country's Day of Independence. So I close my eyes, and remember back five decades.

There was a 4th of July ball, of course. Always a ball, always a dance. I attended with a pleasant enough young man, brother of the post sutler, though now I disremember his name. He showed himself a gracious host, and a wonderful dancer, though my heart was not in dancing, not even on Independence Day. The next evening was sweltering. The wives gathered at my home, and we followed our usual routine of song and Bible verses and tears. Later, I wrote Autie. I cried. I went to bed, my heart heavy with dread, my constant routine since Autie led his troops into Montana Territory.

At 2:00 a.m., I awakened. Something was wrong. I heard voices below, then footfalls. For a moment, my heart sang out: *Autie! My Autie has returned.* Alas, as heavy footfalls came from the back door down the hallway, a man's voice, and not my husband's, said: "Please awaken, Missus Custer."

"Why are you here?" I called out, but no one answered. By the time my servant, Maria Adams, had pushed open the door to my bedroom, I was already up, pulling on my robe.

"Missus Libbie," she said. "They's a capt'n here. Wants to see you."

"At this hour?" I followed dear Maria through the door, around the staircase, in time to watch Captain William S. McCaskey of the 20th Infantry open the door to the verandah, letting in Lieutenant Colonel C. L. Gurley of the 6th Infantry, and J. V. D. Middleton, the post surgeon.

They turned left, and entered the parlor. Numbly I followed them. The lamps were turned up. I clutched my robe till my fingers whitened. Maggie Calhoun and Emma Reed promptly joined us.

"Ladies," Captain McCaskey said. "I have a telegram from General Terry." His fingers shook as he retrieved the piece of yellow paper from his coat pocket. He moved closer to a lamp, unfolded the telegram, and read.

"General Custer and five companies, totaling two hundred and sixty-one officers and men, were killed June 25 at the Little Big Horn River in a battle with Sioux and Cheyenne Indians."

Maggie and Emma fell into each other's arms, sobbing. Tears cascaded down my own cheeks, but I remained the general's wife. Autie would demand that I be brave. "Captain," I said, though my voice cracked from pain, "I would desire to accompany you as you inform the other . . ."— the word seemed strange on my tongue— "widows."

After Maria draped a wrap over my shoulders, I followed the officers into the parlor, and outside. The skies began lightening in the east, and already it felt warm, a beautiful dawn.

As I moved down the steps, Maggie ran out, hysterical, screaming from the verandah: "Is there no message for me?"

Captain McCaskey's head shook somberly. "No, ma'am," he said. "They all died fighting."

Which, I thought as I walked along officer's

row, was how Autie would have wanted to die. Fighting. Alongside his brothers.

When my darling died, my world ended. Eventually, I would leave Fort Lincoln, moving back home to Monroe, Michigan, drawing my $30 a month pension as a widow, later to New York City, spending winters in Florida. Others would write about my late husband, Walt Whitman's stirring poem "A Death Song for Custer," which ran in the *New York Herald*, and Mr. Whittaker's *The Complete Life of Gen. George A. Custer*, written with my approval and help. There would be paintings and other books and monuments, stories told, songs sung, and soon I determined that my duty, my privilege, lay in working to commemorate my husband. That became my life's purpose. It still is.

So I began to write. Writing about my life with Autie has carried me these past fifty years.

From my apartment window, I do not see the automobiles, velocipedes, and pedestrians going about their business in New York City. I see that hillside, the hillside in Montana that I have never seen in person, where Autie, Tom, and others made such a glorious last stand.

And I remember another casualty of that campaign. I remember poor Thomas Weir, who I loved so dearly, who might have once been capable of wooing me off my feet had not my soul been so chained to Autie's memory. Thomas promised me that one day he would tell me all of what he had witnessed, but he never did. Drink, cursed drink, brought him to ruin.

Shortly after the battle, he was assigned to a cavalry recruiting office in this city. I never saw him again, for he was dead six months after the Little Big Horn massacre. It took him only six months to drink himself to death.

Yet he did tell me one thing. He said that on the morning of the 27th, after the party had been relieved by General Terry's forces, he and gallant Ed Godfrey—then lieutenant, now general—rode off in search of my Autie. On a hillside, Thomas and Ed reined to a stop, and Thomas pointed to another hill. The grass waved, for now the wind blew, and all along this hillside were what appeared to be limestone boulders.

"What are those?" Thomas asked.

Ed pulled his binoculars from the case, focused, and lowered it. That was his first view of what they now call Custer Hill.

"The dead," Ed answered in a whisper.

"Oh," Thomas said, his voice trembling, "how white they look. How white."

1933

Epilogue

Black Elk

The agent tells me that the woman of Long Hair has finally died. Since General Godfrey died last year, he says, there must not be more than one or two survivors of the Battle of the Little Big Horn.

I walk away from this fool *wasicu*. One or two survivors remain? Does he not see that he is surrounded by survivors. I am one.

It was at the Greasy Grass Fight that I took my first scalp. I remember it. My knife was dull, and the *wasicu* was still alive. He cried out in pain, so I cocked my holy iron and shot him in the head, then finished taking the scalp. Later, I showed his scalp to my mother, and she gave the tremolo, honoring me. She was proud.

On that day, all Lakotas and *Sahiyelas* were proud.

Our pride did not last long.

Crazy Horse would surrender to *Mila Hanska* as, eventually, all Lakotas did. Just more than a year after the Greasy Grass Fight, a *wasicu* stabbed him in the back with his long knife. Yes, a Long Knife killed Crazy Horse, but, and this saddens me, Lakotas had a part in his death, too. Red Cloud, who had guided The People of

319

the Buffalo Nation to many great victories, had been jealous of Crazy Horse's power. Red Cloud wanted to be the leader. Many Lakotas grew jealous of Crazy Horse, and that is why Crazy Horse was killed.

Sitting Bull was killed, too, by his own people. The Metal Shirts, those Indian policemen who worked for the *wasicus*, shot him dead.

And Custer's Long Knives, the 7th Cavalry, they got their revenge for the Greasy Grass Fight just after Sitting Bull was killed. On a bitterly cold day, *Mila Hanska* massacred many of our people, including Big Foot, who had surrendered.

All these years later, still we grieve for that awful day at Wounded Knee.

We grieve for something else, too. The loss of our country. I remember something Red Cloud said. He said: "The white man promised us many things, more than I can recall, but he only kept one promise. He promised to take our land, and he took it."

I think back to that great fight on the Greasy Grass. When the *wasicus* came to attack our circles, we were many, and we were united. On that day, I was twelve years old, but nearing manhood. Now, all these years later, I am an old man, and I see twelve-year-old boys on our reservation. They are not as I was when I was that age. They wait around. They do not make the bows and arrows the old ways. They do not work hard. They have no buffalo to eat, and not many horses to ride.

We live as prisoners. We are not free. Many of our young men live only to drink *mini wakan*. They spend all their money on this. They become crazy. They have no honor for our people, and no respect for themselves.

So I am glad, I think, that Crazy Horse and Sitting Bull did not live to see what many of our people have become.

I wonder what would have happened if we had followed Sitting Bull's vision on that day. He warned us not to take the items from the *wasicus* we had killed, but no one listened. It was hard to listen. It was hard to leave coffee and tobacco and holy irons and horses and clothes of *Mila Hanska*.

Perhaps we brought this upon ourselves. After the Greasy Grass Fight, we no longer were strong. The *wasicus* came, and they were angry at us, for we had killed Long Hair. They came like the wind. As Sitting Bull said, they would always trouble us.

Many of our young men do not even want to hear the stories of that much remembered fight. They would rather go to see the moving picture shows in the *wasicu* towns, to drink colas or, if they can get it, *mini wakan*. They think of me as an old man, and they are right. I am old.

I am a sad, old man.

Because many summers ago, I took part in the Greasy Grass Fight. I became a man that day. It was the greatest Lakota victory. Yet, also, it proved to be our downfall.

Yes, we defeated Long Hair. We sang victory songs that evening for we did not know the truth, and the truth was this: Our world ended, too, at the Greasy Grass.

Glossary

Agnus Dei: (Latin) Lamb of God. In the case of Myles Keogh, it was the *Medaglia di Pro Petri Sede*, a cross hanging from a golden chain, awarded him by Pope Pius IX for his Papal Army service.

count coup: Touching an enemy in battle, usually with hand, bow, or coup stick. To most Plains Indians tribes, this act won a warrior much prestige.

Dacia!: (Lakota) "There they are!"

Greasy Grass: The Lakota name for the Little Big Horn River.

Hi-es-tzie: (Northern Cheyenne) "Long Hair," the Cheyenne name for George Custer. The Lakotas also called him Long Hair, *Pehin Hanska*. Ironically Custer had cut his hair short for the 1876 campaign.

Hiyupo!: (Lakota) "Follow me!" The first command a Lakota war leader would give in battle.

Hokay hey: (Lakota) A man's exclamation, loosely meaning, "Let's go," or, "Let's do it," and often followed in battle with, "Today is a good day to die!"

holy iron: Lakota's term for a gun.

Hotóhkeso: (Northern Cheyenne) Lakota.

Human Being: Northern Cheyenne.

Lakota: The Northern Plains tribe often referred to as the Sioux. The Lakotas were divided into seven subgroups, or seven Council Fires:

Oglala, the largest sub-band;

Sicangu, more commonly known by the French word, Brulé;

Hunkpapa;

Minneconjou;

Itazipacola, meaning "Without Bows" and known primarily as Sans Arc;

Oohenunpa, meaning "Two Boilings" or "Two Kettles";

Sihasapa, or "Blackfeet" or "Black Soles."

Mahpiya To: (Lakota) Arapaho.

Mila Hanska: (Lakota) Long Knives, their term—because of the sabers often carried—for Army soldiers.

mini wakan: (Lakota) "the water that makes men crazy"—i.e., whiskey.

niátha: (Arapaho) white man.

Niiteheib-ín!: (Arapaho) Help him!

Notaxé-ve'hó'e: (Northern Cheyenne) warrior white men—i.e., soldiers.

Ónone: (Northern Cheyenne) Arikaree.

Paha Sapa: (Lakota) The Black Hills.

Palani: (Lakota) Arikaree.

Peji Sla Wakpa: (Lakota) "Greasy Grass," the Lakota name for the Little Big Horn River.

Pehin Hanska: (Lakota) "Long Hair," the Lakota

name for George Custer.

pte: (Lakota) buffalo cow.

Ree: Shortened name for Arikaree Indians, many of whom served as scouts for the Army during the 1876 campaign.

Sahiyela: (Lakota) Northern Cheyenne.

Takahokuty: (Lakota) The Place Where They Killed the Deer, Killdeer Mountain, an 1864 battle between Army forces and Indians in present-day North Dakota.

tatanka: (Lakota) buffalo bull.

Tosa'ane-ho-ohtse?: (Northern Cheyenne) Where are you going?

Tenéi'éíhinoo: (Arapaho) I am strong.

tinspila: (Lakota) wild turnips.

veho: (Northern Cheyenne) white man.

Wakan Tanka: (Lakota) The Great Mystery, The Great Spirit, The Sacred, The Divine.

wasicu: (Lakota) white man.

wasicun sapa: (Lakota) black man.

wicasa wakan: (Lakota) holy, or medicine man.

Wipazuke Waste Wi: (Lakota) Moon When Berries Are Good, mid-June to mid-July.

Wiwanyang Wacipi: (Lakota) The Sun Dance.

Author's Note

If you want to be totally confused, read as many books about the Battle of the Little Big Horn as I did researching this novel.

Custer was an idiot. He was a hero. He did everything right (just everything went wrong). He did everything wrong (and nothing went right). There were fifteen hundred warriors waiting. There were twelve thousand.

Custer was killed early in the battle; Custer died late in the battle. Indeed, Custer was the last man standing. He was shot in the head by an Indian after the battle, or by an Indian during the battle. His brother Tom, or another soldier, shot him to keep him from being captured alive. He shot himself. He was killed by Gall . . . by Wooden Leg . . . Rain-In-The-Face . . . Yellow Nose . . . White Cow Bull . . . Brave Bear . . . Old Bear . . . Little Horse . . . Charging Hawk . . . Spotted Calf . . . Lazy White Bull . . . a couple of Cheyenne "Suicide Boys" . . . Moving Robe Woman.

I decided to leave that final gunshot wound to Custer's head to the reader's imagination.

This is a work of fiction, however, though much of the dialogue is as was reported in the 1870s or in the years afterward, and much has been recreated as accurately as possible, with some exceptions for literary license. Besides, no one will ever know what really happened on that hill.

My first introduction to George Custer came as a kid, when my father read aloud to me *Custer's Last Stand* by Quentin Reynolds.

Forty-odd years later, I still recall sitting on Daddy's lap at our South Carolina home, and vividly hearing that first death scene of George Armstrong Custer. I've never even forgotten the line: "Two bullets hit Autie at the same time." Custer reaches out to brother Tom, and they die together.

Custer's Last Stand was supposed to be a biography. It didn't take long before I understood that 1951 juvenile book was more novel than history.

After Reynolds's book came two memorable novels—Will Henry's *No Survivors*, and down the road Thomas Berger's *Little Big Man*—and I've lost count of the biographies and books pertaining to the participants and the battle. Not to mention the movies—*They Died with Their Boots On*, *Little Big Man*, *Tonka*, *The Great Sioux Massacre*, and the dreadful *Custer of the West*—and that episode from TV's *Cheyenne* that I just barely remember, not to mention *The Twilight Zone's* "The 7th Is Made Up of Phantoms," which I've never forgotten.

Anyway, I always wanted to write about the Little Big Horn, but never could figure out how to approach it. Until, that is, I attended a panel discussion in Bismarck, North Dakota, on the anniversary of the battle, and historian Brian W. Dippie, author of *Custer's Last Stand: The Anatomy of an American Myth*, gave me the idea that became Libbie Custer's prologue. Other helpers include Tracy Potter, executive director of the Fort Abraham Lincoln Foundation; historians/Custer scholars/friends Paul Andrew Hutton (editor of *The Custer Reader*) and James Donovan (author of *A Terrible Glory: Custer and the Little Bighorn: The Last Great Battle of the American West*); and collector Forrest Fenn, who showed me photos of the 50th anniversary festivities taken at the battlefield in 1926, as well as the event's program. He even let me hold a letter written by Custer to Captain Yates!

The park rangers at Little Bighorn Battlefield National Monument (it was Custer Battlefield National Monument when I first visited in 1987) have been helpful on numerous excursions to southern Montana. Pulitzer Prize–winning journalist Tom Powers, author of *The Killing of Crazy Horse*, even let me tag along with him and some of his family members when they walked the battlefield on a warm summer morning in 2011; and my Lakota friend Joseph M. Marshall III and his wife Connie West helped provide the Indian perspective on the battle. Joe's books include *The Day the World Ended at Little Bighorn* and *The Journey of Crazy Horse: A Lakota History* (for my money, the definitive biography of the Oglala leader).

In addition to those aforementioned titles, other sources for the overall battle include: *War-Path and Bivouac: The Big Horn and Yellowstone Expedition* by John F. Finerty; *Lakota Recollections of the Custer Fight: New Sources of Indian-Military History*, compiled and edited by Richard G. Hardorff; *The Custer Companion: A Comprehensive Guide to the Life of George Armstrong Custer and the Plains Indian Wars* by Thom Hatch; *The Story of the Little Big Horn* by Colonel W.A. Graham; *The Last Stand: Custer, Sitting Bull, and the Battle of the Little Bighorn* by Nathaniel Philbrick; *Custer on the Little Bighorn* by Thomas B. Marquis; *To Hell with Honor: Custer and the Little Bighorn* by Larry Sklenar; and *Son of the Morning Star: Custer and the Little Bighorn* by Evan S. Connell. One of my biggest thrills came when I met Evan S. Connell at a party at Forrest Fenn's house. I told Mr. Connell not to stand, but he did anyway, and shook my hand.

I love that book, though I found the miniseries based on it about as exciting as watching paint dry.

Other references: *Sioux War Dispatches: Reports from the Field, 1876-1877* by Marc H. Abrams; *Fort Phil Kearny: An American Saga* by Dee Brown; *They Rode with Custer: A Biographical Directory of the Men that Rode with General George A. Custer*, edited by John M. Carroll; *The Fighting Cheyennes* by George Bird Grinnell; *Custer and the Cheyenne: George Armstrong Custer's Winter Campaign on the Southern Plains* by Louis Kraft; *Where the Custer Fight Began: Undermanned and Overwhelmed: The Reno Valley Fight* by Donald W. Moore; *The Little Bighorn Campaign: March–September 1876* by Wayne Michael Sarf; *Frontier Regulars: The United States Army and the Indian, 1866–1891* and *Custer Battlefield National Monument*, both by Robert M. Utley; and *Participants in the Battle of the Little Big Horn* by Frederic C. Wagner III.

Biographies/memoirs include *Brandy Station to Manila Bay: A Biography of General Wesley Merritt* by Don E. Alberts; *Crazy Horse and Custer: The Parallel Lives of Two American Warriors* by Stephen E. Ambrose; *I Go with Custer: The Life and Death of Reporter Mark Kellogg* by Sandy Barnard; *Crazy Horse: A Lakota Life* by Kingsley Bray; *Tom Custer: Ride to Glory* by Carl F. Day; *Red Cloud: Warrior-Statesman of the Lakota Sioux* and *Gall: Lakota War Chief*, both by Robert W. Larson; *Elizabeth*

Bacon Custer and the Making of a Myth by Shirley A. Leckie; *I Buried Custer: The Diary of Pvt. Thomas W. Coleman, 7th U.S. Cavalry*, edited by Bruce R. Liddic; *Custer: The Life of General George Armstrong Custer* by Jay Monaghan; *Harvest of Barren Regrets: The Army Career of Frederick William Benteen, 1834–1898* by Charles K. Mills; *Black Elk Speaks* by John G. Neihardt; *In Custer's Shadow: Major Marcus Reno* by Ronald H. Nichols; *Autobiography of Red Cloud: War Leader of the Oglalas*, edited by R. Eli Paul; *Deliverance from the Little Big Horn: Doctor Henry Porter and Custer's Seventh Cavalry* by Joan Nabseth Stevenson; *Cavalier in Buckskin: George Armstrong Custer and the Western Military Frontier* and *The Lance and the Shield: The Life and Times of Sitting Bull*, both by Robert M. Utley; *Old Neutriment: Memories of the Custers* by Glendolin Damon Wagner; *Custer: The Controversial Life of George Armstrong Custer* by Jeffry D. Wert; and *I Fought with Custer: The Story of Sergeant Windolph, Last Survivor of the Battle of the Little Big Horn as Told to Frazier and Robert Hunt* by Charles Windolph.

And, of course, the books by Elizabeth Bacon Custer—*Boots and Saddles; or, Life in Dakota with General Custer*; *Following the Guidon*; and *Tenting on the Plains; or, General Custer in Kansas and Texas*—and her husband's *My Life on the Plains; or, Personal Experiences with Indians.*

Those sources are worth checking out to understand—if anyone can ever truly understand—what happened at Greasy Grass River in the summer of 1876, and why it happened.

Johnny D. Boggs
Santa Fe, New Mexico

About the Author

Johnny D. Boggs has worked cattle, shot rapids in a canoe, hiked across mountains and deserts, traipsed around ghost towns, and spent hours poring over microfilm in library archives—all in the name of finding a good story. He's also one of the few Western writers to have won six Spur Awards from Western Writers of America (for his novels, *Camp Ford*, in 2006, *Doubtful Cañon*, in 2008, and *Hard Winter* in 2010, *Legacy of a Lawman*, *West Texas Kill*, both in 2012, and his short story, "A Piano at Dead Man's Crossing," in 2002 and the Western Heritage Wrangler Award from the National Cowboy and Western Heritage Museum (for his novel, *Spark on the Prairie: The Trial of the Kiowa Chiefs*, in 2004). A native of South Carolina, Boggs spent almost fifteen years in Texas as a journalist at the *Dallas Times Herald* and *Fort Worth Star-Telegram* before moving to New Mexico in 1998 to concentrate full time on his novels. Author of dozens of published short stories, he has also written for more than fifty newspapers and magazines, and is a frequent contributor to *Boys' Life* and *True West*. His Western novels cover a wide range. *The Lonesome Chisholm Trail* (Five Star Westerns, 2000) is an authentic cattle-drive story, while

Lonely Trumpet (Five Star Westerns, 2002) is an historical novel about the first black graduate of West Point. *The Despoilers* (Five Star Westerns, 2002) and *Ghost Legion* (Five Star Westerns, 2005) are set in the Carolina backcountry during the Revolutionary War. *The Big Fifty* (Five Star Westerns, 2003) chronicles the slaughter of buffalo on the southern plains in the 1870s, while *East of the Border* (Five Star Westerns, 2004) is a comedy about the theatrical offerings of Buffalo Bill Cody, Wild Bill Hickok, and Texas Jack Omohundro, and *Camp Ford* (Five Star Westerns, 2005) tells about a Civil War baseball game between Union prisoners of war and Confederate guards. "Boggs's narrative voice captures the old-fashioned style of the past," *Publishers Weekly* said, and *Booklist* called him "among the best Western writers at work today." Boggs lives with his wife Lisa and son Jack in Santa Fe. His website is www.johnnydboggs.com.

Books are produced in the United States using U.S.-based materials

Books are printed using a revolutionary new process called THINKtech™ that lowers energy usage by 70% and increases overall quality

Books are durable and flexible because of Smyth-sewing

Paper is sourced using environmentally responsible foresting methods and the paper is acid-free

Center Point Large Print
600 Brooks Road / PO Box 1
Thorndike, ME 04986-0001 USA

(207) 568-3717

US & Canada:
1 800 929-9108
www.centerpointlargeprint.com